First published in Great Britain by Icepalms 2010

Distributed in PDF Arial/12pt electronic format from
OpenOffice, layout by Icepalms

Print Version £7.99

I0680217

ISBN 978-0-9564989-0-8

The Author would like to thank all those involved in helping make this book a reality. In particular for their sterling contributions and without whose support and I could not have done it. A special thanks to Ali, Sim, Roger, Ol, Pete, Serena, Teresa and Daren for their gracious efforts and support.

Edited by: Roger Fisk, Ali, Ol, and Sim.

Cover designed by: Simeon Tennant

astrosphere.icepalms.eu

Icepalms Publishing

21 Guildford Rd

Brighton BN1 3LW

Astrosphere

A novel by Lucsan

In which

Our planet is threatened by the approach of a mysterious object from a distant star

'Of all the planets in the solar system

of all the stars in the milky way

perhaps the most troublesome is this one

this cloud covered planet called earth

our planet

the home of the human race'

Oliver Postgate – The Clangers

Chapter 1 - Anomaly

David woke to the shrill alarm of the phone. He opened a bleary eye and took a peek at the bedside clock. It was three thirty in the morning. What could be so important, so urgent it required his attention at this time of night?

He reached out from under the warm duvet and fumbled for the phone.

"Yeah blerg?" Was the best he could manage to say.

"David? David Shawdale? Is that you?" An excited voice asked.

"Yes." David mumbled back. Three thirty in the morning for goodness sake.

"It's Graham, Dr Graham Hockley."

"Graham, a pleasure." David found himself saying despite the fact that he wasn't finding it a pleasure at all.

"I'm calling direct from the Observatory in New Mexico, I thought you should be the first to know." Graham continued. "I've just been looking at the data from our star and something strange has happened."

"Strange? How?" David repeated numbly. His mind was beginning to whir into action throwing off the cloying veil of sleep.

"I'm not entirely sure yet. We've observed something unusual."

"It's not disappeared has it?" David asked. This had always been a possibility with the Shawdale-Hockley star.

"No, no. Some kind of anomaly has formed on its surface. Don't really know much about it yet, but I thought you should know."

"Thanks Graham. Do you know what time it is here?" David asked.

"Midnight, One o'clock?" Graham replied. "I must confess I didn't think about it, I was so excited."

"OK, well thanks Graham." David hung up, rolled over and went back to sleep.

The following morning after breakfast David drove his battered old Jaguar XJS onto Durham University campus, where he worked in the Astrophysics Department.

He was struck by the amount of activity on campus and was that a BBC camera crew setting up their equipment? he asked himself as he drove towards the Department of Astrophysics. Turning into the car-park, under the yellow painted scaffold pole that read 'max height two meters', he caught sight of Penelope Jameson, his research assistant, hurrying towards him.

She'd spotted him pulling in, and as he manoeuvred his Jaguar into a parking space she trotted across the damp autumn tarmac. There was something awkward and fragile about Penelope, David thought. Her long thin frame always clad in the derigere denim jeans and thick black roll neck sweater. Today her dark brown bob cut hair was thrust into one of those strange Norwegian looking woolly hats. The ones with ear flaps and dangly bits of yarn hanging from the ends. As she approached him the autumn wind played with the loose hairs around her face.

David got out of the car and took his battered brown leather attaché case and grey mackintosh from the back seat.

"Morning Pen." David said.

"David I'm so glad I caught you before you got to your office." Penelope said pulling a wisp of hair from her pale lips as she spoke.

"Really?" David replied, wondering if this was to be another of her worries about her final paper. He folded his coat over his arm and turned towards the car park exit.

"Your office is under siege, the corridor's full of people from the news wanting to talk to you about H1Z15B." She looked at him questioningly as if he should know the answer and a little surprised that he didn't.

"We shouldn't stand around here David, you might get spotted. We can go to The Montesquieu just over there." Penelope said looking round the car park in such a suspicious fashion that, had anyone been watching them, they would have surely been noticed.

"The Montesquieu?" David was puzzled at the choice.

"Yes, the Sociology department café. It's out of the way." Penelope insisted, and began leading the way through parked cars with rain on their window screens and red, brown and yellow autumn leaves dotting their shiny metal carapaces.

In The Montesquieu they settled down with a drink each. "it's not the best coffee on campus," Penelope said as she brought the mugs over from the counter, "but it's warm in here, and less conspicuous."

David laughed. "You make this sound like a spy thriller and we're the hunted fugitives." He looked round the room they were in. Typical student-run campus café with cheap seating. Someone had made an effort with a soft sagging sofa and a comfy chair in one corner, while an old Soviet propaganda poster glared angrily across the room at a cheap print of Warhol's

Marilyn Monroe. One grim and imposing, the other light and playful.

David sipped his coffee and waited. Glancing at Penelope over the rim of his coffee mug, it became clear she was lost in a world of her own making.

"Penelope, what are we doing here?" he asked her eventually.

"Oh yes, right." She returned to the world around her. Taking a gulp of coffee she said. "The Dean asked me to get you out of the way until you're ready to face the media."

"I take it this is about the Shawdale-Hockley anomaly?" He asked. Up until then it hadn't occurred to him that the anomaly would attract any attention from the media.

"They're camped outside your office and its all "Is Dr. Shawdale here yet?" and "Can we have an interview.?" What's this all about?" Penelope asked.

"I'm not too clear myself." David confessed. "I got a call late last night, well early this morning, from Dr. Hockley telling me he's observed an anomaly."

"An anomaly?"

"Something has formed on the surface of the star. Dr. Hockley hasn't identified it yet, but thinks it might be a giant solar flare. Whatever it is, it's highly unusual, this could be a really exciting development in Astronomy. We might have had a hundred thousand year wait to observe something like this. The light it could shed on star activity, well who knows." David exclaimed.

"OK I guess I need to find out what the media already knows." David said. "There isn't a TV in here is there?"

"Perhaps we can find out on this" Penelope said, producing a neat little glossy pink laptop from her satchel. She placed it on the table and flipped open its lid. "I hope it hooks to the network, I think I've used it in here before. Probably."

They waited patiently for the laptop to do what computers do when they make you wait for them, then Penelope poked at the finger pad and clicked a few keys and scratched her head and clicked some more. Eventually she swung the screen round towards David.

"There you are." she said.

David stared at the web browser on the screen which showed a BBC news page. It was headlined Shawdale-Hockley Anomaly, and went on to say, "Last night from the San Messa Alto Observatory in New Mexico Dr. Graham Hockley reported an apparent anomaly in the Shawdale-Hockley star after noting changes in data made from standard scheduled observations. A previously unseen spot has now been discovered on the Shawdale-Hockley star which was first observed twenty two years ago by David Shawdale now an associate lecturer in Astronomy at Durham University. This star is no stranger to controversy however as its origins remain a topic of hot debate amongst astronomers even today. The recent appearance of a small spot or mark, thought to be on the surface of the star, is just another example of this star's continuing determination to startle us all."

David searched a couple more news sites all of which said pretty much the same thing.

"What do you think? What are you going to do?" Penelope asked, excitement showing in her eyes.

"I'm thinking that there's little I can add to the story right now, a quote perhaps, yep I'll need a quote, and may be I'll get a slot on a daytime chat show, they pay quite nicely. I think we're going to need to get some big scope time as well. No wait, we'll not get that now. I need to make some calls and see if we can get a datafeed from someone." David thought aloud.

"Look I need you to stall the media for a while, tell them I'll be making a statement in say an hour's time? Thanks Penelope."

She scooped up her machine and dashed off in the nervous, energetic way she went about everything. David was left to contemplate the joys of another muddy coffee from The Montesquieu Café. He'd just started sipping through the watery suds that floated in his cup when his mobile phone rang. It was Bob.

"David, I take it you've heard the news by now." Bob's voice rumbled down the phone. "Looks like your lucky star is shining for you again. I don't know, astronomically, if this is going to be something or nothing, but I think we should capitalise on it now. I'm thinking here's a chance to push the biog, perhaps a lecture tour, while things are hot, it's good for you and it sells telescopes."

"Always with one eye on the sales graph eh Bob?" David laughed, "Well I'd thought I might get a chat show out of this."

"Good man, that's the right way of thinking. I'll get someone in the office to call up a couple of TV companies just to see how the land lies so to speak, see what they're thinking. Have you thought of a quote yet? How about 'The potential for space to surprise us is beyond the limits of our imagination'."

"Not bad, not bad I might have to think about stealing that one. I'm giving a press conference shortly and it might come in handy." David said.

"You go ahead and do so Davy boy." Bob laughed.

The call from Bob brought the memories flooding back. Running his fingers through his light brown hair and scratching his clean shaven chin, David remembered vividly how twenty two years earlier he'd discovered a star and been thrust briefly into the limelight.

His father had given him a Harding T41 Stargazer telescope for his twelfth birthday. The T41 was a proper grown up astral telescope and David set up an observatory in the shed at the bottom of the garden at his parent's house in Leeds.

His father had cut a hole in the shed roof and covered it with an ingenious mechanism involving rope and a pulley, which allowed David to open and close the hatch as needed. On clear nights he'd take his leather satchel filled with astronomer's notepad, pencils and a lens cloth, down to the bottom of the garden. After carefully cleaning the lenses he would haul on the hatch rope and tie it off on the cleat, before settling in for an evening of star gazing.

His secret wish was to find a star. He'd known that that was unlikely, but to find a star, to have it named after you, your name remembered in the heavens for eternity. Not likely, but... he remembered the night it had actually happened for him.

Sitting in the shed on a cold November day with clear skies. He made some observations and faithfully noted them in his notepad. He turned on BBC radio four to listen to a light comedy show while he stared into the depths of the universe.

It was about halfway through the show when David first spotted it. He knew the exact time because he'd dutifully noted it in his book, 10:43:35, alongside the coordinates of his observation.

From the beginning David's star had had something strange about it, it was unusual. David had watched it for several nights. At first not sure if it was a new discovery or not. He spent several days checking star charts. Then he wasn't sure it was a star at all, so faint, sometimes not visible at all, he checked and re-checked that it wasn't a fleck of dust on the lens. Still not entirely reassured as it might be a satellite, he watched it for a month before officially filing his observations. Of course it would be a satellite, it was very dim.

It was a few months later when a Professor of Astronomy at the University of New Mexico, called Hockley, got time on a big telescope and was able to confirm David's discovery. Though only to the extent that an object had been observed, that it was persistent, and it wasn't a satellite. It was dully designated UO483752.

David had been disappointed at that. No star, no name. Of course he'd discovered something but what? Even the big scopes couldn't tell and while a small debate raged briefly amongst the international astronomers community they were unable, at the time, to agree on anything about it. However everything changed around a year later.

Despite his disappointment with UO483752 David had remained faithful to it. Naturally he was also looking around for his next big discovery when he noticed UO483752 had got brighter. He wasn't the only one. Over a 36 day period UO483752 continued to increase in intensity to the point where it was clearly a star.

The astronomical community was on fire. This had suddenly become an important event. Firstly had they just witnessed the birth of a star? What else could it be? The debate was to rage for years because the phenomenon failed to conform to predictions. Two schools of thought developed on the matter; one that this was what happened when stars were formed, and therefore the predictive models were wrong; and the second that felt the models were fine, and this was something else, a new phenomenon.

At the time David hadn't cared. He had his star. The Shawdale-Hockley designated star H1Z15B. As a bonus, because of the uproar in astronomical circles and the unusualness of the star, David benefited further. He was invited to become a Fellow of the British Society of Astronomers, and a certain amount of media attention followed which had added benefits for a teenage boy.

There had been several chat show appearances and cameo appearances on shows with science as their themes or where the theme was space or stars. He'd got to blow up a caravan with explosives, drive a racing car, and have a free holiday, but the highlight had been his appearance on Sound Live, a Saturday teen music and cartoon show, where he'd got to introduce the programs, along with the regular hosts, pour gunge on a school teacher, meet the members of a cool band, and best of all, where he acquired the nickname Starman.

After that the Shawdale-Hockley had set him on his path. He wasn't a dedicated student, but he was able to concentrate and finished school with good enough results to guarantee him a place at university. His fame in astronomical circles brought him fortune through a spate of TV advertisements, mainly for chocolate bars and scientific toys, as well as a sponsorship agreement with a local telescope manufacturer, none other than Graham Harding of Hardings Telescopes.

These little pieces of luck had been enough to give David a degree of financial freedom and academic credit. So while he didn't actually need to hold the post at the university, it was a nice addition to the coffers, and welcome academic recognition. It also gave him access to otherwise expensive or unobtainable resources, like scope time with big telescopes. Then there was the biography. Selling nicely in it's second year. Of course that had been Bob Harding's idea. When he'd first suggested it David laughed, who would find his life interesting?

Having taken over the business from his father Graham, and having a keen eye for good marketing, Bob had paid a ghost writer who soon produced what was unarguably a good read that made astronomy exciting, even if there seemed to be things in it about David's life that he'd never heard before.

The book sold moderately well and telescope sales went up.

"It gives young people an insight into astronomy." Bob had said. "What can be achieved if you really put your mind to it. It brings it to life for them and the youth market is exactly the market that the T41 and T38 models are targeted at." he explained to David one evening as they sat around the real log fire in the back room of the Dog and Duck Pub. "This star of yours, man you have a star, a star to follow, it must be luck, do you know just how lucky you are?"

David laughed. "Not just luck, I've spent many nights sat at a telescope," David reminded him.

His lucky star, and now it was changing his life again. Perhaps Bill had been right that night in the Dog and Duck, but was this to be good luck or bad luck? He was brought back from his thoughts by Penelope waving at him from across the table.

"David. David, the news people are getting very insistent and the Dean's demanding you talk to them so they'll go away." Penelope said breathlessly.

"OK well I should try to keep the Dean happy, after all he pays the bills." David got up from the table and they began walking over to the Astrophysics Building.

"What do you think of 'The distant stars shine new light on the cradle of the universe' as a quote?" he asked.

"A bit ponderous perhaps." Penelope answered.

Chapter 2 – Under observation

The air under the camouflage netting was hot and dry. Colonel Betty 'Bing' Saunders could taste it at the back of her throat as she lay in the sniper's foxhole. Next to her lay a Marine sniper so still and silent that she'd begun to wonder if he was sleeping or dead. Small grains of sand blew around in front of her face, on a hot desert wind, and the silence of the sands pressed in heavily on her.

"Alpha squad move in." The big black radio beside her crackled into life and the Marine sniper shifted in his position.

Through her field glasses she had a good view of the valley below. A single pale mud enclosure with a few buildings, the typical single story flat roofed buildings of the region, standing on dusty ground scattered with boulders and rocks. A lone acacia tree stood near the compound wall. The distant bleating of a goat broke the silence briefly.

It was a puff of dust from a boot step that alerted her to their presence, Alpha squad were approaching the pound. The single man she'd seen moving around the enclosure had disappeared into one of the low clay buildings and now nothing moved. What happened next happened very quickly. Alpha squad reached the wall and in a moment were over it. She heard shouting and banging, but no gunfire. Three men were brought out of the buildings and made to sit on the ground in the centre of the compound. Alpha squad members moved in and out of the buildings for a couple of minutes before the radio crackled again.

"Area secure. We have three, I repeat three hostiles."

Bing climbed out of the foxhole and stretched her legs for the first time in a couple of hours. Dusting down her camouflage fatigues she walked back down the hill side to the command post.

"Colonel," Captain Jessop of the marine platoon greeted her arrival. "I hope you enjoyed the show."

"I'm eager to see what your guys have found down there." She said adjusting her dusty blond hair into a bun on her head.

"It's looking good, they've found equipment, computers and what looks like the aerial," the Captain reported.

"Do you mind if I take a look?" she asked.

"No Problem Ma'am. I'll have Hank here escort you over if you don't mind. We may not be the only ones in the valley." Jessop said studying the large map laid out on the field table. A breeze blew through the ops tent, flapping a loose corner of canvas and teasing the edges of the map.

"Ma'am." Hank the Marine saluted her and they walked back up the rough dusty scree, passed the sniper post and down towards the compound. It smelt of goat and dust and male sweat. One of the buildings had three goats in it, in another a table with silver coloured cases, a laptop and a diesel generator. Behind the building she was shown the aerial.

"Can we get this thing running?" she pointed to the generator. One of Alpha team began shouting at the hostiles in a guttural language, Arabic she thought, but didn't really know. A second soldier went over to the generator, looked it over and a moment later it roared into life.

Bing traced the power cabling across the floor with her eye and saw several pieces of equipment powered up. She fingered the laptop and after a moments hesitation turned it on and began to examine the other equipment. Yes, as she'd expected the piece was a transmitter, not a model she was familiar with but judging by the size one capable of satellite transmission.

"Five minutes Colonel" one of the Marines told her, "transport is arriving, and we're gonna haul ass out of here."

"We're going to need the password for the computer," she told the Marine. A back and forth argument began between the translator and one of the hostiles. At one point the Marine hit the man across the face with his gloved hand, then turned and shrugged at her. "They ain't giving anything away Ma'am."

No great concern, she folded up the laptop and tucked it under her arm. As she made one final investigation of the remaining equipment she heard the clatter of helicopter roters in the distance. There was nothing else here for her now, she'd seen all she needed to see. Dust flew up around her and the air filled with sand as the helicopter picked her up. They rose up into the air and Bing cast one last look back at the quickly receding scene. As she watched, several explosions came from the compound that could be heard, though not felt, in the helicopter and a black oily pall rose up into the azure blue sky.

"Thank you Captain, it was good of you to let me sit in on your operation," she shouted at Jessop over the noise of the helicopter.

"No problem Ma'am, it's always a pleasure to show you air force types just how the real work is done." The real work, maybe, but her work saved the lives of his men. Keeping one step ahead of enemy intelligence, just how did the Captain think that his men could end up in the middle of nowhere and be right on top of their objective? They hadn't spent weeks and weeks perusing a small but significant security breach in a U.S Naval system, traced it through satellites and servers around the world to a phone exchange in downtown Nairobi.

She hadn't been able to get in on the Nairobi operation, some black ops team had gone in, "a politically sensitive area", she'd been told, but they came back with what she wanted, a lead out the phone exchange, a simple, single wire, soldered across two connection blocks that created a link to the home of a Government official. From there it had been a breeze to trace the satellite transmitter in the desert.

She ached all over and the hard seats and bumpy ride in the helicopter hadn't helped, but she was feeling satisfied and would soon be in her hotel room in a hot bath before packing ready for the flight back to operational headquarters in Germany. With the desert dust out of her hair and access to the code-busting killo tetra computing system in Halvstad she'd have the laptops secrets in no time. She didn't think it would hold any great revelations, but it would hold the transmission times and frequencies and possibly message partials. Potentially there could be a lot of intel in there.

The nice thing about being in Military Intelligence was that she never had any delays at the airport. Whisked discreetly across the tarmac to the waiting plane she was accorded diplomatic immunity due to being magically attached to the local consulate. She was the last one aboard a civilian flight straight into Berlin where she would take a pool car to Halvstad. In the meantime she could catch up on some sleep.

The drive to the Air Force listening post at

Halvstad was damp and grey after the desert, but uneventful and it allowed her to shake off the aeroplane hangover and think through the tasks ahead. She'd need some crunching time on the big machine and then there would be the data to sift over, an activity which appealed to her methodical, analytical mind.

The following morning after an early morning run she was sat at the desk in her small grey office in the concrete building that was Halvstad listening post. A considerable stack of email had built up over the few days she had been away. She was working her way through the list when her boss General Solomon came in.

"Good to have you back Colonel. Desert not too hot for you I hope?" he asked sitting his large frame in the only other chair in the room.

"The mission went as planned Sir. I'm about to start retrieving data from the hostiles laptop but there's no doubt these are the guys who were accessing our satellite," she reported.

"And the assets?" the General asked in his efficient and orderly manner.

"Hostile assets were handled by the Marines, Sir. They destroyed the transmitter and the generator and of course we have the laptop."

"I expect a full de-brief Colonel, but that's not why I'm here." General Solomon said. "I'm giving you a heads-up on duty changes. I'm sorry to drop it on you like this but it's come out of nowhere. Unfortunately, it's very highly classified and I can't get it to go away, so I'm afraid you're stuck with it." the General said in his soft southern drawl.

Bing waited for him to continue. Solomon held her with a steely eye. He expected his officers to perform their duties to the highest standards.

"I've emailed you the relevant resources and you're now cleared to view the files. What I can tell you about it now is, this comes from one of those sixties think tanks."

"Think tanks?" Bing asked.

"Yes Colonel. In the sixties and early seventies the military used think tanks to develop scenarios and strategies. Some of these ideas were pretty wild, but that hasn't stopped us from pursuing them. We spend billions of dollars on remote viewing or so called 'goat staring' for example. These guys were off the wall thinkers, that's what we employed them for. They were asked to look into the future, to guess it, and come up with possible scenarios, like a Chinese invasion or the fall of the Berlin wall. These scenarios tie into response plans, strategies for what to do next.

Some of these scenarios are First Contact Alien invasion of us. The idea was that if an invading alien army wanted to get here it would require a marker or waypoint to guide them."

"This is beginning to sound very X-files Sir." Bing remarked.

"Don't you know it. So this Shawshank star," the General said.

"Shawdale Sir."

"Whatever star, was seen as such a possibility and we placed several assets in key positions against such an eventuality. Now, this anomaly has been reported and we can't overlook the possibility that it's some sort of space craft alien invasion thing. Of course we're waiting on the astronomy boys to tell us its all hooha, just some dust on someone's lens, meanwhile I need you to check on our assets, see what we've still got. Find out what they know.

You have a contact at NASA, find out from him what we can requisition at short notice, what we can strap a bomb on, how quickly can we get a team of Marines on the moon, that sort of thing."

"It's a stock-taking mission Sir. I'm an analyst not a quartermaster," Bing objected.

"I know Colonel, but security clearance level means we can't push it any further down the chain of command, you're stuck with it I'm afraid. So lets get it over and done with as quickly as possible and we can get on. I'll have someone take the laptop analysis from you and I expect a mission de-briefing in my office at o ten hundred hours sharp tomorrow morning. You're booked on a commercial flight straight into Miami at fourteen hundred hours."

Clear blue sky and a warm breeze greeted Bing as she was driven by Jeep towards Cape Kennedy Space Centre. Across the flat expanse she could see the tall buildings and huge hangars of the Space Centre through the chain link fence that ran along side the road. They drove up to the gate and for a moment or two her driver showed their papers to the guard they continued their drive around the vast lake of tarmac apron towards the main buildings. Though perfectly normal in size the buildings appeared dwarfed by the gigantic equipment necessary to launch a spacecraft. Vast hangers for constructing and maintaining the shuttles, tall launch gantries pointing into the sky. They drove passed an unbelievably large machine used for manoeuvreing shuttle craft and gantry out to the launching pad.

The driver swung the Jeep into the half empty car park adjacent to the main building and pulled up outside the main entrance. Bing got out. She'd decided that a charcoal grey business suit was the appropriate dress for this visit, military uniform might be too high profile, after all this was a highly classified mission even if it was ridiculous.

Her contact was waiting for her. A tall thin man in his early fifties wearing a light grey suit, thinning black hair and wire rim glasses that sat propped on the end of a long nose. "Colonel Saunders," he said with an easy east coast accent, offering his hand for her to shake.

"Call me Bing," she said, "Everyone does. You must be Assistant Director Brooks."

"Please call me Danny," he replied. She followed him across the imposing foyer, passing the shuttle model and pieces of genuine space craft that stood on display stands, and the bits of moon rock, each with it's own explanatory note detailing the date, the astronauts and the craft used. "Would you like the tour?" Danny offered.

"Another time perhaps," Bing smiled politely at him.

"You are aware of the reason for my visit?" she asked.

"Certainly. I've prepared some notes for you, inventories and the like. It's quite difficult without really knowing what you intend."

Bing smiled. "Yes we're very grateful for your assistance Danny, I can say that this is of national importance and directly related to national security issues, I'm sure you can understand, that as such, I'm not at liberty to say more."

"No of course not." Danny agreed, disappointment crossing his face.

They reached his office. Sizeable and well lit. A

wall of shelves and filing cabinets ran down one side of the room while the launch facility was framed behind his desk through the big picture window. Two orange trees in pots stood either side of the window like leafy guardians of the view.

"I suppose you'd like to know more about the anomaly?" Danny asked offering her a chair.

"Anything you can tell me really, I'm not an astronomer and this isn't my usual kind of assignment."

"I see. Well ever since we were alerted by your people we've been monitoring observations from around the world. There's no doubt now that something is coming towards us, but we don't know what or how fast."

"Can you give any kind of idea?"

"This is the exciting part, We know quite a lot about it already. It's spherical and about the size of our own moon. It's already inside the orbit of Jupiter and moving in a trajectory suggesting that in four months time it'll pass fairly closely on its way round the sun before heading out into deep space again. We might see it a second time when the Earth passes round the other side of the sun."

"See it again?"

"Oh yes, it should be clearly visible from Earth at

it's closest point. We should get a fantastic view of it's surface with the Hubble telescope."

"Can't we see it's surface now?"

"Well yes, but we're not able to determine what it's composed of yet. So far the indications are it's made of ice, but spectra-graphical analysis hasn't confirmed it. It should be in range of our satellites in the next few days and we should have a much better picture of it then."

For the first time Bing felt a twinge of doubt about the mission, a vague frisson of fear. Up till now she'd simply failed to believe that there was anything in the crazy scenario. But now, talking to Danny, it had brought it home to her that there was undeniably a giant meteorite heading in the general direction of Earth. The vaguest of possibilities that this meteorite might pose an actual threat formed at the back of the mind, though it still seemed entirely impossible to her that this could be an alien space craft.

Danny had assigned her some office space on the third floor, not as big as his office and without the breath taking view of the NASA campus and launch pad, but sufficient enough for her needs. She setup the basic tools of her trade, the computer and satellite uplink. The phone that came with the office would also prove useful. It was clear she'd be based here for a few days at least, going over the asset list Danny had provided and following up contacts at various astronomical facilities around the World.

Danny came by her office as she was drafting her report.

"They've established a monitoring suite for the anomaly," he told her. "Someone at head office must think it worth keeping a close eye on our friend."

He led her through the uniform corridors and over to another building. The monitoring suite contained several rows of stations in front of which a bank of monitors were available to display information. At that moment there were just a couple of technicians worrying over a computer terminal at one of the stations and only the big screen that dominated the room had anything of interest.

"The display shows a graphical analysis of where the anomaly is." Danny explained. "Basically we can see the sun there in the centre, and the planets with their orbits in yellow. The red dot indicates the location of the anomaly and the two red dotted lines curving away from it are the bounds for it's trajectory."

It was clear to Bing from the display that the Earth was outside the two red dotted lines.

"No chance of it hitting the Earth then?" She added smiling.

"No, no as you can see that's not going to happen, he replied. "The display is being updated in real time though, you see the little red numbers at the side of the anomaly? That's its current position, velocity and estimated time at which it will be at it's closest point to Earth. As we get more information on it the two red dotted lines should come together and show it's actual trajectory." While they watched, Bing thought she saw the two lines move a little closer toward each other.

Chapter 3 – Costume convention

Dai Wakami was excited. The night before his mother had helped him put the finishing touches to his Char Aznable Manga character costume. He was very pleased with it. The bright red uniform jacket and trousers with gold trim and white gloves, white belt and white boots looked just like the one his comic book hero wore in his adventures.

Today was the long awaited Cosplay Convention in Chiba just outside the city of Tokyo. Dai and a few friends were going to the convention to talk comics and show off their attire. The main thing being to exhibit their outfits, literally, to costume play.

These conventions could be very competitive, as he'd found to his cost. For his first convention he'd thought his outfit was great. He and his mother had spent a long time on it, but when it came to the day his costume just didn't have the detail. It wasn't faithful enough to the comic book version. It wasn't considered good enough to enter in a competition.

Since then his ensemble had got better and better. At the last three conventions he'd made it into the competition and last time he'd made it to the finals. So he had high hopes for his Char Aznable outfit. He hoped it would also impress Saiko from his class.

He'd fancied her from afar all year. She'd be going in one of her Sailor Moon costumes no doubt. She only did Sailor Moon, a popular choice, and while it was a good costume it was unlikely to get her into the main contest due to it's over popularity. She did look hot in it though, Dai thought. Last night he'd dreamt about kissing her in her Sailor Moon outfit, or possibly it had been Sailor Moon herself, he wasn't entirely sure.

About ten o'clock his mother called up the stairs to say she was ready to take him over to Chiba. He took one last critical look at himself in his bedroom mirror, in the red jacket and trousers, grabbed his bag, and ran downstairs.

"Don't forget we're picking up Kanji and Tenkou on the way," he reminded his mother as they got into the car.

The traffic in town was particularly heavy that day and the ten minute drive across Shibua Ward to Kanji's house took twice as long as usual. Kanji was waiting on the street for them because Dai had called ahead on his mobile phone to make sure he was ready.

"Good morning Mrs Wakimi," Kanji greeted Dai's mother formally and bowed before getting into the car. "It is very good of you to give me a lift."

"You're very welcome," Hayato replied, she was always impressed with Kanji's politeness. Dai of course knew it was all an act, she should see him at school he thought.

"Wow, your Char Aznable costume looks great," Kanji told Dai. "Your Gunn Ki costume is good too," Dai replied.

"I hope Tenkou's outfit isn't as complex as last time," Hayato said.

The boys laughed. Last time Tenkou had come as ZGMF-X20A Strike Freedom, a complex robot character, whose costume had included several large cardboard arms shaped like long thin pyramids. They'd filled up the back of Hayato's car and there'd still been some pieces the boys had had to carry on their laps.

The heavy traffic continued to slow their journey. "There must be a parade or something going on," Hayato told the boys.

"Can we listen to the radio mum?" Dai asked. She turned the car radio on and they listened to some recent popular songs while they waited for the traffic to move. Eventually they reached the district where Tenkou lived and were relieved to see that his costume was considerably more restrained than last time.

"It will be faster once we get onto the motorway," Hayato said.

"Nice Char Aznable," Tenkou told Dai. "That will definitely get you into the competition."

"I hope so," Dai grinned at his friends.

As they drove through the Edogawa District on their way to the Chiba Highway the traffic came to a complete standstill as a parade came up the road towards Chiyoda Park. The car was held up waiting to turn onto Kenyo Road. They were right at the front of the traffic queue and so got a front seat view.

The parade was not a parade, it was a kind of rally, though with the costumes it could have been mistaken for a parade. It was well attended. Several thousand people, Dai guessed, as the parade passed slowly in front of the car. There were the usual marshals in their bright yellow flash tabards and white gloves. Some people were in ordinary street clothes and some people were dressed in colourful costumes with big strange heads. They carried banners and slogans on poles. There was a drum and symbol band banging and crashing a beat for the group to march too and several people with megaphones berated people to join in the big meeting in Chiyoda Park.

"What's this about then?" Hayato remarked, as banging and crashing, the rally passed by.

"They're protesting about the Saint Petersburg Summit," Kanji, who was up on this sort of thing, said. "Isn't your father at that meeting Dai?" he asked.

"He is. He's in Russia right now. Apparently there

was a bit of a mix up with the hotels and half the Korean delegation ended up with half the French Delegation, though they've sorted that out now."

"What's the summit got to do with this parade?" Hayato asked. "And why are they all dressed like that?"

"Oh, this lot," Kanji said in an off-hand way. "They're protesting at the Governments attitude towards aliens."

"Aliens?" Hayato asked.

"Yep," Kanji replied brushing imaginary fluff from his trouser leg. "They think the Government shouldn't be taking such a hostile approach to the aliens."

"What aliens?" Hayato asked with disbelief.

"The ones that are arriving on the meteorite."

"There aren't any aliens on the meteorite." Dai said to his friend.

"We know that," Kanji replied. "But these silly asses believe otherwise. That's why some of them are dressed up, like aliens. They think that rather than planning to blow them up we should be planning to welcome them."

"Right," Dai said. "And the meeting dad's at is about the international response to the meteorite. They're going to decide whether to blow it up or not."

"Kind of." Kanji agreed. "Also to see if they can persuade the Americans and Chinese not to blow it up anyway. Of course we need them if were going to blow it up, they're the only ones with the rocket power to do it."

"Not everyone wants to blow it up though." Tenkou said.

"No no, not all," Kanji agreed. "The Indians and the Swedish have already made it clear that they want other possibilities considered, but at the moment the Americans and the Chinese are viewing it as threat."

"It would be great if they blew it up though," Dai said. "If we could see it from Earth."

"Yes they could do it so some of the debris becomes falling stars." Kanji said.

"Can they do that?" Tenkou asked.

"It wouldn't be easy," Kanji said thoughtfully. "But I don't see why not, it's just a matter of getting the right charges in the right places so just the right sized pieces of meteorite burn up entering the atmosphere, it happens everyday."

The boys considered the possibilities of this idea for a moment and watched the tail end of the parade pass by. Eventually the policeman who had been holding up the traffic in Dai's road gave them the signal to continue and they pulled out on to Kenyo Road.

Dai was getting more excited and more anxious about his costume the closer they got to the Chiba Exhibition Centre. More and more of the cars travelling their way had young people dressed in brightly coloured costumes eagerly looking out of the windows. Already they are judging the costumes they can see walking down the street.

"Are you sure this isn't an alien protest?" Hayato asked.

"Aw Mum, no this is Manga cosplay, from the comic books." Dai said as if speaking to a rather slow, ancient relative, who was never likely to understand the finer points anyway. "It's completely different, as anyone can tell."

"I'm sure your right dear." Hayato replied in that annoying tone mothers use when they don't agree but are being agreeable anyway. The line of traffic for the Exhibition centre came to a standstill.

"Do you boys mind if I drop you here?" Hayato asked. "It's not far to the centre, I can see the entrance from here."

"Sure mum." Dai said. "Seems as how Tenkou hasn't brought his Strike Freedom costume this time." he laughed.

The boys got out of the car, each taking a backpack containing the things they needed for the day and with space for comics, comic hero figurines and any bits and pieces they might buy to add to their costumes. Joining the steadily thickening throng of people walking along the pavement they made their way towards the exhibition centre.

There were characters from all manner of Manga comics, all brightly coloured, painted faces and masks and enough spandex to clothe the entire Chinese army, and a mountain of pvc and shiny painted cardboard. Already the first dramas of the day were occurring as the odd, badly applied, yet central part of a costume was brushed off, knocked off or simply fell off of it's own accord, and here and there were little clusters of costume emergency repair teams as friends dug deep into their bags to see what tape, thread, pin or other fixatives they had brought with them that could be used in an emergency repair. Despite these early knock outs there were still streams of people whose costumes had made it safely across the wide paved entrance area to the exhibition centre and were entering the arena itself.

Inside, the exhibition centre was spread over the area of 35 football pitches, split into fifteen massive halls and containing it's own transport system including a monorail that ran through all the halls, a fully equipped hospital, an information bureaux, cafés, restaurants and bars.

The boys agreed that if they got split up they would meet by the Saishi Icecream stall near the entrance where they'd come in.

While many of the halls were occupied by sellers of all things Manga, other comic book genre, and cosplay, several of the main halls were reserved for the numerous competitions that covered the many aspects of costume. Dai was hoping to enter himself into several categories.

They started to make their way across hall eleven in the general direction of hall two where the best costume in the Characters' Category Competition was to be held. It was a journey interrupted on several occations as they looked at figurines or robots, comic collections, customised MP3 players and professionally made character props, as well as resupplying themselves with drinks and snacks.

After an hour or so they arrived at hall two. Stages ran all around the walls of the halls. While contestants stood on the stages, other competitors, friends and relatives took advantage of the sea of seats provided. Dai began reading down the lists of competitions and after a while arrived at a short list of those he would attempt to enter. The boys began to move around the room in the direction of the first competition Dai had on his list, when he saw Saiko, but horror of horrors she was with Gaku and Waku.

Gaku and Waku were the thorn in Dai's school life. They were two years ahead of him, two years older. They'd made themselves his own personal bullies and took every opportunity to humiliate him. Was it because he wore glasses Dai wondered, or because his dad was a high ranking civil servant? Gaku and Waku called themselves Yakuza like the criminals and said their dads were in the Yakuza, but Dai knew that Gaku's dad worked in a bakery so if he was Yakuza he must be retired or taking a rest from breaking peoples legs.

Why were they here anyway? They'd never seemed interested in cosplay. They would often tease Dai calling him gay and girlie. They certainly hadn't made much of an effort, Waku's sole effort seemed to be a monster mask which he wasn't even wearing properly, just pushed back on his hateful short spiky hair, and Gaku was wearing jeans with a jacket that might have been a costume piece, or it might have been a bad choice in jackets in a moment of madness at the clothes store. And now they were here standing between him and any chance with Saiku. His heart sank. Perhaps they were with her just to get at him? But he couldn't believe that. Why would she hang out with them? They were too old for her.

But it didn't really matter, there was no way he could approach her now, they'd humiliate him terribly, on sight, so his only option was to avoid them for the rest of the day. This would mean he couldn't enter the competitions, at least not until they'd left the hall, and he'd have to be looking over his shoulder the rest of the day. So that was it, his day ruined, and he was left with the choice of either spying on them from afar to make sure they weren't sneaking up on him, or trying to ignore it all but constantly aware that they might spot him at any moment.

"Guys, guys." He signalled frantically to Kanji and Tenkou. "Over here."

"What's what's going on?" Kanji asked.

"It's Gaku and Waku, they're here, and with Saiko," he told them desperately.

"No, it can't be." Kanji said.

"Look, look over there." Dai pleaded.

The other two boys looked and confirmed the sighting. While Gaku and Waku didn't have any interest in Kanji and Tenkou they knew they were Dai's friends and more than once they'd been given the treatment because of it. There was no real standing up to them, Gaku and Waku were strong and large even for their age. If they saw any of the boys, they'd know Dai was around.

"What are you going to do?" Tenkou asked.

"I don't know." Dai confessed.

"Oh this is a real bummer," Kanji exclaimed. "You wont be able to enter the competitions either."

"Not while they're in here, but perhaps if they go, I might be able to."

"It's still risky." Tenkou said.

"You could watch out for me." Dai suggested to his friends. They thought about this while waiting to see what the two bullies would do next.

For the moment the bullies seemed relaxed where they were, laughing with each other as they ate and drank. Dai thought Saiko was enjoying their company. After almost forty minutes of lurking behind a stage the three boys were beginning to get funny looks from the people around them. Fortunately at that moment the bullies and Saiko decided to move off. They sauntered past several stages mocking the activities on them, while Dai fervently hoped they'd not stay to watch any of them. They didn't and soon Tenkou was able to follow off after them some way to ensure they'd gone.

Somewhat relieved that at least his antagonists were out of the way, he approached the competition entry desk and soon after that he was enrolled in three competitions. The afternoon wore on with Dai doing well in his competitions and in one in particular it looked like he was certainly up for a prize in the authenticity of interpretation category.

He finished a competition in sixth place, not a shoddy performance at all, but now his eye was on the big one. He was in the final five from which the the winner and two runners up would be picked. He gave his uniform one final check over and joined the other finalists on the stage. The compère began her run through of the finalists outfits and gave some of the judges' opinions on them before moving to the sealed envelopes that contained the winners.

That was when he saw them. Gaku and Waku were back. They seemed to have lost Saiku for the moment but even as he spotted them he saw Waku looking around and seeing him. Waku grinned menacingly at Dai from across the room and, nudging Gaku, drew his attention to an increasingly uncomfortable Dai.

They sauntered nonchalantly across the room directly towards the stage in a way that set Dai's heart racing. They pushed themselves to the front of the crowd that gathered round the stage. That was when Kanji and Tenkou spotted the bullies. Tenkou went white and looked horrified, glancing from Dai to the bullies and back.

Gaku was sucking a Jufi fruit drink and watching the stage with his head cocked to one side as the compère opened the envelope for third prize. That went to the costume on the far left of the stage. She opened the envelope for second place and announced Dai Wakimi and at that moment the remains of a Jufi fruit drink flew through the air in a graceful curve and hit Dai squarely on the forehead bursting sticky green fluid over his face and costume.

Laughter came from the audience, and the chant of "second, second, second." Then the bullies moved off quickly, before they could be taken to task by the other onlookers for their behaviour. Dai accepted his prize while plastered in goo which he hoped hid the tears welling in his eyes. As he looked up in the direction his attackers had gone, he saw Saiku looking at him.

He got quickly down from the stage and took the packet of promotional tissues that Tenkou offered him and began wiping down his costume and then his face. He was furious and embarrassed.

"We should get out of here as quickly as possible." Kanji advised. "Those two could be back after us any time."

The others agreed and the three boys hurried off towards the convention exit and the train ride home.

Chapter 4 – Second moon

David was greeted at the entrance to the television studio by the assistant producer, Janice. She led him through studio security and into the bowels of the entertainment hub, down a long corridor with coils of cabling lying loosely along it's length, and finally into a room marked Studio One Green.

"The toilets are just up the corridor to the left, the studio canteen on the right just after the toilets, but if you need anything use this phone, just pick it up and start talking, whatever it is, we'll bring it to you," she said with a smile. "Is there anything I can get you right now David?"

He assured her he was fine. "Well, anything you need just ask. Make-up will be along just before the show starts," she said before leaving him alone.

Looking around the room David saw the usual offerings, a fresh vase of flowers, a couple off pretentiously decorated bowls containing crisps and nuts, a bottle of water and glasses sat on a low casual table surrounded by easy chairs. He sat down in a bright orange chair and took a handful of nuts from the bowl. In the corner of the room a television played the channel's current programme at low volume. A drinks trolley had been parked against a wall under a picture of the studio logo and several shots of the studio's exterior, but David didn't want a drink. He glanced at the magazines arranged on the table but none appealed. He felt the tension before public appearances both delightful and frightening and drummed his fingers nervously on the arms of the chair.

"Hi David." A small, slender woman in her late forties entered the room. Her long glittering dress flowing airily around her as she moved. "I'm Jilly Shoe, host of the Jilly Shoe Show," she said smiling at David. He got up to greet her. "I'm so glad you could make it tonight," she offered him a continental kiss on each cheek. "Everything good for you? Do you have everything you need?" she asked.

"Everything is fine thanks," he replied.

"Tell me have we been looking after you? The hotel? The limousine? Were they just perfect?"

Jilly perched herself on the arm of a bright green chair and threw him one of her award winning smiles. "Have you seen the show before?" she asked.

David assured her he had, which was true. He'd insisted that Larry Findall, his agent, let him see a tape of the show before agreeing to do it. So he knew this wasn't one of those shows that delighted in embarrassing its guests. Jilly's show was mid-evening light entertainment with just a whiff of risqué, a format highly in vogue.

"That's super darling." Jilly said. "So you'll know I

give each guest about five minutes 'me' time before bringing the next one on. By the commercial break I'll have you all on my couch. You'll be second tonight my lovely. I've got Billy Grant the Hollywood actor, he's first on, and coming any moment now, last on is Micky Slapper the dry witted comedian, he's very in right now, he'll coming any moment too." She laughed naughtily at her double-entrendre, one of her trade mark gestures.

David realised she was warming him up for the show, getting him into a light chatty mood. They talked about the hotel for a moment before being interrupted by the assistant producer. "Miss Shoe, Billy Grant has arrived." she said. "And the comedian?" Jilly asked. "His limo's stuck in traffic and he'll be a few minutes late. It's a good thing he's last on," Jilly remarked.

A tall handsome man in his early thirties, with a square jaw, wide shoulders, and a light tan, entered the room. Billy Grant the Hollywood actor had arrived. Jilly went through her gushing guest-welcoming routine again.

"I just loved your latest film Billy, 'Starlord last defender of Earth'. I though you were perfectly cast in the role of Ben Starlord."

"I just loved your latest film Billy. I though you were perfectly cast in the leading role," Jilly told him. Billy was playing Ben Starlord in the new film 'Starlord last defender of Earth'.

"Well thank you ma'am," Billy said, his deep pleasant Californian accent giving warm confirmation that the compliment was well made and received.

He certainly had a presence David thought. There was no doubting why he was getting the parts.

"This is David Shawdale." Jilly introduced him to Billy. "He discovered the star that everyone is talking about at the moment.

"Yeah. " Billy smiled at David. "I saw you on a show in the States the other week, you're the Starman."

"I've been over to the States a couple of times in the last few weeks. This star business is quite popular at the moment," David said.

"I hope my film's as popular," Billy joked. "Your star has got the studios all fired up over alien invasion and meteorite disasters, I've not seen a script without one or the other for months now."

"Well I hope it doesn't come to an invasion," David replied.

"Say Starman, are there really aliens?" Billy asked.

"Now Billy dearest," Jilly cooed at the actor while stroking a finger along his arm. "I must insist that it's my job to interview the guests, besides which you're stealing my best questions," she said lightly and Billy laughed with her. "Now boys I've just got to rush off for final checks, can I leave you in the capable hands of Maurice and Charlotte from make-up?"

Jilly left the room as Maurice and Charlotte opened their make-up cases onto the counter which ran along the mirrored wall. "Who would you like to do dear?" Maurice asked Charlotte, flicking back a long lick of hair that fell across his face.

"I'll do Mr Grant," Charlotte said inviting the actor over to a chair in front of the mirror.

"I bet you will," Maurice said saucily. "It looks like you're with me then Mr Shawdale," Maurice said to David, giving him a long look up and down. "If you would be so good." He indicated a chair for David.

Maurice flitted about, dusting David's face and all the while telling Billy how great he'd been in Starlord. An assistant producer poked her head round the door. "If you could come with me please Mr Grant," she said, and Billy was led away.

Maurice fussed a little then said to Charlotte. "This one's done. Look I don't want to wait around for Mr Jonny-come-lately, would you be a dear?"

"Sure Maurice, I'll do the comedian," Charlotte

said, and in a puff of face powder Maurice was gone.

"That was Billy Grant," Charlotte said excitedly. "Isn't he wonderful?"

"He has quite a presence," David replied.

"He's so gorgeous and hunky," Charlotte insisted.

"I'm sure he'll be pleased to hear that," David said.

"Oh, you wouldn't tell him I said that, would you?" Charlotte replied, now embarrassed.

"Well I might be persuaded to keep quiet," he teased her.

"Oh you, you wont tell. Have you met him before?" Charlotte asked.

"No, no we've just met," David said.

"Mr Shawdale." The assistant producer had returned. "They want you on set now."

Butterflies fluttered in David's stomach and he felt, as he always did before an appearance, slightly queezy, like travel sickness, and also a rush of excitement and energy which he tried to keep under control. They flew up the corridor to the set. Bright lights, some sort of theme music, the applause of the audience, all whipped up and tumbled around in front of David's eyes. Before he knew it he was sat on Jilly's couch next to his new friend the Hollywood actor Billy Grant while Jilly Shoe herself beamed down at him from her trademark, high winged, swivelling chair.

"Starman David Shawdale," she said, much to the audiences approval, and they doubled their applause.

"Thanks Jilly, it's great to be here." He began to fall into the rhythm of the chat show patter that he'd become so familiar with over the last few months.

"Now you were quite young when you discovered the star weren't you David?" asked.

"I was, Jilly."

"Only twelve is that right? And how did it change your life?" she asked.

"Well I probably wouldn't be here in the studio today if I hadn't discovered a star," David said.

"Do you think you were was too young?" Jilly asked.

David laughed. "It's not like show business, generally the world of astronomy is quite slow and dull in comparison, so I wasn't washed away on a sea of fame and fortune. Though I am reminded of a funny story." David launched into the anecdote that Larry Findall had coached him in, the cute one where a dog steals a hamburger.

It made the audience go ahhh in the middle and laugh at the end.

"You've got to have a good anecdote." Larry had said. "You're remembered by your anecdote, people know who you are by your anecdote, it's how they can tell what kind of person you are."

"What people want to know is, what's this thing that's come out of your star?" Jilly asked.

This was the big one, this was what they always wanted to know. David couldn't really tell them anything more than they might have discovered by watching the news, but people liked hearing it from someone authoritative and he appeared to be an authority on it. He'd been so good at appearing to be an authority that he was now the world's leading television expert on all things star-related.

"That's a question I get asked a lot." David replied. "The meteorite is an unusual cosmic phenomenon so we know relatively little about it. It's most likely a large ball of ice which is, I know, disappointingly dull, but we should soon be able to see it in the northern hemisphere with the naked eye and you should get a good view of it with binoculars. It will be visible for several weeks before it travels on past our sun and out of the other side of the solar system."

"Won't the sun melt it if it's ice?" Billy Grant asked.

"That is possible but we don't think it will. It should pass outside the Sun's orbit and things get very cold in space that far out. It might melt a bit on one side, only to freeze again on the other."

"And you have a new book out." Jilly said. "That's A Journey Through Our Solar System by David Shawdale, available at all good book shops I believe, David?"

"It takes a look at the changes in our understanding of the solar system since the introduction of the modern telescope, and examines the nature of the planets around us, it says here on the flyleaf," David joked, repeating the wording he'd memorised from the book's flyleaf. The audience laughed.

"Thank you David. Now for my final guest tonight," Jilly said. "Top comedian and football's favourite funny man Micky Slapper."

The comedian came skipping on wearing his hallmark Arsenal shirt. "Hi Jilly, hi everyone," addressing the audience before sitting on the end of the couch and immediately remarking, "Hey Jilly, you've got a Starlord, a Starman and a Slapper on your sofa tonight." He slapped his head as he said his own name, another hallmark gesture that the audience appreciated uproariously.

"You have a new show going on tour don't you Micky?" Jilly asked.

"Yes, yes I do Jilly, it's called Star Slapper and it's all about what we'd really do if aliens came to Earth. I mean, wouldn't work would it? Unless they can do things no one on Earth can, like get the buses running on time, or dogs that clear up after themselves." Micky went into a prepared spontaneous skit about dogs which involved him running around miming doggy antics like sniffing each others bums. "What if aliens want to sniff our bums? We'll I mean, they might, mightn't they?"

After the commercial break Jilly asked Billy his views on the meteorite and then made her guests act out the solar system with Billy as the sun, herself as the Earth, David as the meteorite and Micky as the moon. To do this they were each given a planet hat and Billy and David were sent through the audience to the back of the studio to perform the meteorite's path. While this was going on Micky ran about clambering over the audience making a joke about the moon misbehaving and running around the solar system sticking it's bum in their faces and sitting on fat girls laps.

Later on the couch her guests once more under control and still wearing their hats Jilly introduced the guest band and after that wrapped up with a further plug for the film, the book, the tour and the album. The studio light dimmed, Jilly's theme tune began to play and then for viewers at home the credits began rolling up the screen.

"Some of us are going for a few drinks after this," Jilly said. "You're welcome to come along."

David agreed and allowed himself to be led down the corridor to the party. There was the usual mix of television people there, cameramen and other technicians, producers, assistants, actors and talent, like David, though he felt he was cheating a little as his talent was 'finding a strange star'. It didn't seem to David to stand up to the likes of 'can tell jokes' or even 'spins plates on sticks'.

He was on his second gin and tonic having just finished a conversation with a producer about their latest project when he spotted someone, which he took by her outfit to be an assistant producer, approaching him from across the room.

She looked to be in her late thirties, with long curls of thick chestnut hair and a boyish figure poured into skin tight snake skin leggings. She wore a simple blue silk blouse and flat heeled over-the-knee boots. She smiled at him with lipstick red lips and white teeth. "David Shawdale," she said excitedly, taking his hand.

"You don't know me but I've been dying to meet you, I'm assistant producer on the Panoramic show, we're thinking of doing a documentary on the Shawdale-Hockley star. I'm Trudy by the way, but my friends call me Tweedie, I'd be delighted if you did too." Her laughter had a note of nervousness in it.

"I'm not sure we know each other well enough for me to call you Tweedie." David said flattered by her attention. "Perhaps we can change that?" he added smoothly.

"I'm sure we can. I'll give it a go if you will." She smiled coyly at him. "I think it would be super if we could exchange our ideas."

"We could get out of here, go somewhere for dinner if you like," David offered.

"Ooooh, dinner with Starman David Shawdale," Tweedie said, "I'd love to. A dream come true," she teased him.

In the taxi she told him how she'd already read both his books and how she was a keen amateur astronomer herself. As they passed Lancaster Gate station she suggested, as it was still a little early to eat, they might like to walk through Hyde Park to a small bistro she knew on the Kensington Road and she asked the driver to stop.

It was a dry evening, with no wind and still light enough for people to be walking their dogs, jogging along, or go horse riding up through Rotten Row.

"It must cost a fortune to keep a horse near Hyde Park," David mused. As they strolled along the gravel path which wound down to the Serpentine, Tweedie slipped her arm through his. Although David was very much enjoying her company, the smell of her perfumed scent, the sound of her ever so slightly plummy English accent, he also felt a sense of unease. Nothing to do with Tweedie. The dogs trotting passed seemed cowed, with heads hung and tails between their legs, as if it were raining heavily.

He heard the sound of a horse snorting nervously as it cantered passed. He noticed a vast flock of birds gathering over the grey waters of the Serpentine. The flock dipped and swooped, the birds cawing and crying as they flew together. He felt static in the air, as in the minutes before a storm. The street lights in the park began to flicker on, even though it was still light. At that moment a light wind blew through the silhouetted trees and the thin covering of cloud cleared to reveal a crystal clear evening sky.

David looked up and saw the almost full moon, it's surface like a large silver coin shining in the deep dark blue sky, and there next to it, a tiny second moon.

"My god, you can see it already!" David exclaimed.

They both looked upwards at the sky. Big moon and little moon. A shiver ran through them.

"We'd better get moving," she clutched his arm tighter and they continued across the park.

It took two cocktails and a starter before David and Tweedie were able to kick the feeling from the park. The sense of disquiet led them to drink more than they should. David found the girl highly entertaining as she kept him amused with stories of television people's antics.

Swaying slightly as he paid the bill David said "We can get a drink at the bar in my hotel." By the time they arrived at the hotel they'd decided a bottle in David's room was more their style. They stumbled into the lift and found themselves in each others arms. David fumbled the key to his room and they fell in laughing and giggling and flopped drunkenly onto the bed together.

They had wild sex. The wildest David had ever had. Tweedie was willing and keen.

Later they lay tangled up together in the ruffled bedding, drifting in and out of dream fevered sleep in that confused way which happens when dawn breaks before falling asleep. David felt Tweedie moving beside him, going to the bathroom then moving around the room. He felt her sitting on his side of the bed and stroking his hair. He opened an eye.

"I have to go now. I've stayed out far too long and my husband will be wondering whatever can have happened to me," she laughed lightly at this confession. "So this is our little secret, all right my Starman? I'll call you about the documentary." She bent and kissed him on the lips. He had one last look at her tight body, her thighs clasped in shiny leggings, a curve of breast and a nipple pressed against the silk of her blouse, then all he was left with was the smell of her body on the pillow and an uncomfortable twist of sheet in the small of his back.

David stared at the celling, he didn't believe she'd call about the documentary, he didn't think he'd see her again. A husband, just his luck. Against the background buzz of his impending hangover he felt the same sense of disquiet he'd felt in the park the night before and he couldn't quite shake it off.

Chapter 5 – Approaching danger

Sitting in the sun on a Californian beach, Bing sipped an ice soda and wiggled her toes in the sand. Two weeks rest and recuperation was just what she needed. Having been thrown onto the Starman project straight after Africa, it had put a great deal of strain on her, which had begun to affect her work performance.

Now she had had almost two whole weeks of lying in the sun, working on her tan, with nothing more important to decode than the safe in her hotel room. As on the first day of her vacation, she'd spent this one lounging on the beach and taking cooling swims in the sea, and like the previous days the sun was dipping over the horizon before she gathered up her beach things and headed back to her hotel.

The hotel wasn't fancy, not on army pay, but she'd booked into a clean pleasant room with a balcony and a view of the sea where she could sit and watch the locals go by as she ate breakfast. She approached the check-in desk and asked for her room key.

"Colonel Betty Saunders?" The girl at reception asked.

Bing nodded."There's a message for you here." She handed Bing an envelope along with the key.

In her room Bing left the message on the small

writing table and took a long hot shower to wash the sand and salt from her hair. As she towelled herself dry she flicked her eyes over the message. She didn't know anyone in the California area so it had to be from work. She pulled on a bra and panties and reluctantly opened the envelope.

Well that's my vacation out the window, she thought as she read the terse message recalling her immediately to Patrick Air Force Base. She picked up the phone and called HQ. They were able to get her on a military transporter out of Edwards Air Force Base near Los Angeles at twenty two hundred hours. A car would pick her up from the hotel in half an hour. She looked over at the floral dress she'd laid on the bed for evening wear, well that could go straight back in the suitcase and her charcoal grey suit could come back out.

Half an hour later she was in the back of an unmarked car being driven along the coast road towards Los Angeles. A hot sultry feeling rose from the streets as they drove into the city.

In the grey light of dusk a feeling of menace and oppression stalked the city streets. Groups of youths formed on street corners. Men in low slung jeans and sports shirts glowered, arms folded, at passing cars, some shouted, at each other or at the traffic, Bing couldn't tell. She heard a clank on the trunk of the car, had someone thrown a rock at them? The traffic began to slow down and up ahead Bing could see the white and red stripes of a road block. The blue and red light of police vehicles blinked across the cars. A group ran back down the street from the road block, banging their fists on both parked and occupied cars. Car alarms began to shrill. In their cars, people locked the doors and hooted their horns. Every face she saw in every car wore a look of worry or concern. In the distance she heard a series of loud bangs.

The car radio crackled into life and she strained to hear what was being said. She heard her driver reply, "Will do, Control."

"Ma'am." He glanced over his shoulder at her. "We're going to have to change route apparently there's trouble up ahead, the police have closed some of the roads."

"Thanks Sergeant. Any idea what's happening?" she asked.

"Couldn't say Ma'am." The Sergeant replied. "To my way of thinking things have been looking to blow up for sometime. People ain't easy about this Star thing Ma'am," the Sergeant added, pulling out of the main traffic stream and down an apparently dead-end street. Things looked like they were going to turn nasty at any moment. As they neared the city limits the streets became silent and empty. As they passed a shopping precinct with a burning car in the almost empty parking lot Bing saw looters making off with goods from an electrical store. The car continued to weave in and out of side streets as it threaded it's way out of the city and eventually onto Freeway Fourteen. As they came up over the hills surrounding Los Angeles Bing saw the moon in the sky and next to it it's new friend, little moon. The sight was still so novel and new it sent a shiver down her spine.

The car raced towards Edwards Air Force Base at Rosamund. Bing could see the base was in a state of alert as she was driven across the black tarmac to her plane. Squads of personnel double timed between buildings, everyone moved quickly and purposefully.

They landed in the early morning at Patrick Air Force Base. Bing noticed the heightened activity here too. She had time to quickly drop her stuff off and by seven o'clock she was sat in a briefing room with the rest of General Solomon's intelligence team.

"Good morning people." The sandy-haired General greeted them from the briefing podium at the front of the room.

"Apologies to those of you who've had your leave shortened." The General began, "but things have become serious in the last twenty four hours."

"For those of you who may not be aware, we now know what the Anomaly is made of Energy. That is we believe it to be made of energy, but as we've never encountered it in this form, we don't know what kind of energy." He paused a moment to looked at his audience.

"This is information that we, along with our allies, have been keeping from the public, but it's no longer possible, the Anomaly is too close and there are too many people pointing telescopes and other instruments at it. We are expecting the media to leak this information later today.

"The nature of the Anomaly now puts it in a new perspective. This is no longer the threat posed by a large chunk of ice charging across the solar system. At the moment we've no way of knowing what kind of response to take, no way of knowing what would happen if we launched a missile at it.

"What we do know is it doesn't pose an immediate threat of the kind we have anticipated up till now. The energy sphere is about the size of our moon and it glows. Analysis of it's trajectory so far indicates it will pass safely between us and the sun. However we must expect disruption to our satellite networks and possibly all electrical devices.

"Our task over the next few days is to monitor satellite behaviour and prepare to implement the communications plan in the briefing documents you've all been given."

The General left his team to familiarise themselves with their new orders. Bing opened her briefing folder and began reading. So it was back to satellite monitoring, but then she noticed that her posting was to Cape Canaveral at the office she'd set up at NASA, which was geared to monitoring the anomaly directly.

By the time she got out of the briefing the Energy Ball was all over the news. In the canteen she had a coffee and some toast and watched the news on television with everyone else in the room.

The television journalist stood with his back to Cape Canaveral, the huge NASA logo on the building behind clearly visible over his right shoulder. "While NASA continue to deny the rumours that the meteorite is made of anything other than ice, unconfirmed sources continue to claim otherwise." The shot cut to the news studio.

"What can you tell us about the new claims Clive?" the studio anchor asked.

"Well Sabrina, while NASA continues to deny any truth to these claims one thing remains true, they're all saying the same thing, that the meteorite is made out of energy, Sabrina."

"How does that work? A meteorite made out of energy?" asked Sabrina.

"Well as I understand it Sabrina, it's not a meteorite at all, we don't have a name for it yet, it's a completely new thing to us. Normally meteorites are made of matter like rocks but the Anomaly appears to be made of pure energy."

"What kind of energy Clive?"

"I've no idea Sabrina, I don't think anyone does, all I can tell you is that NASA is claiming that the reflective surface of a giant ball of ice in space could give false signature readings. I should also mention that world wide the international space agencies are all saying the same thing as NASA."

"So it could be an ice meteorite then, Clive?"

"That still seems possible Sabrina. This is Clive Worth reporting from NASA for PBC news."

"Next our headline news. Following riots in the Los Angeles area last night authorities are concerned the unrest will spread to other cities, more on that straight after the weather report with Simon Trench." Sabrina smiled into camera.

Bing took the short helicopter ride from Patrick Air Force Base to Cape Canaveral and was soon back in the familiar monitoring room. Personnel had increased since she was last here and more of the stations were occupied than previously. The monitor showed the same trajectory graphics it had been showing for weeks now, however a new line had been added to the main screen, one showing the point of passing. The red diamond crept infinitely slowly along it's own red line, towards the point of intersection.

Bing began creating the reports she would be filing and checking the figures she would be using in them. She'd been at it about an hour when a lieutenant interrupted her.

"Ma'am, I think you should take a look at this." He pointed to the main monitor.

As she watched, a second red line appeared next to the first one. It slowly swung away from the original red line forming a triangle of which the Anomaly was the apex. The new line swung on towards Earth. The new red line swung across Earth and almost immediately the original red line began to swing towards earth as well.

"Shit, that's it then," she heard the lieutenant sigh. The whole room stopped and everyone watched the screen.

"Trajectory change confirmed." A technician reported from their station. "New course and speed confirmed. Direct impact in T minus one thousand and eight hours."

Six weeks. They had just six weeks left. The thought hung in the air, everyone in the room knew. For an instant there was a collective shared knowing, a shared fearing.

From the morning's briefing she knew it would be a matter of minutes before the news was all over the television, radio, internet, everywhere. There was no denying this. As General Solomon had said, too many people pointing too many telescopes at the anomaly.

"General Solomon on line for you Colonel." The

lieutenant handed Bing a phone.

"Get your ass over here right now Saunders, I want you to be able to give a full briefing in one hour." The General sounded highly excited. The helicopter taking her back to Patrick Air Base was waiting, rotors running and took off as soon as she was inside. She was the only passenger. She went over her report a final time during the short hop.

Bing realised she was in a top level meeting when she recognised the Vice President who sat at one end of the conference room under the presidential seal. Various generals and other senior air-force personnel sat around the large polished table in leather chairs. Being only a lowly colonel, Bing didn't get a seat but had to stand behind General Solomon.

"As you will be aware," The Vice President began," this is a time of national crisis. There was rioting in Los Angles last night and today it's spread to other major cities including Chicago, New York, Washington, Atlanta and New Orleans. I expect the President to announce a state of emergency in the next few hours. We will be imposing martial law in all 52 States.

In the light of recent developments, namely the change in direction of the Energy Sphere towards Earth, we must seriously consider the idea that this sphere is some kind of craft carrying an invasion force.

I want to know what it is we're dealing with and what we're going to do about it?"

The Vice President's words sparked an idea in Bing's head and she began to do some rough calculations on her notepad computer.

"What if it's an energy weapon?" one of the generals asked.

"We don't have anything," another general responded. "All we can do is chuck what we've got at it."

"How long have we got?" the Vice President asked.

Bing passed General Solomon a note. "One thousand hours. Just under six weeks." Solomon told the room. A second note was passed. Solomon studied it for a moment. "We can't launch anything at it for a further three weeks or in the final week, however we do have some possibilities." He turned to Bing, "Colonel?"

"Sir." She nodded and smiled thinly round the room. "We could fire a satellite at it. This would collide with the Anomaly in sixteen days time," Bing reported.

"Let's do that then," the Vice President said. The generals briefly discussed it amongst themselves then nodded their agreement.

"What else have we got?" the Vice President

asked.

"What if we throw a nuke at it?"

"We have no idea, but as General Solomon pointed out we have a two week window to launch things at the Anomaly."

"If this is an invasion what kind of force can we expect to face?" the Vice President asked.

"I've got some rough figures on that Sir," Bing said into Solomon's ear. The general nodded at her to go ahead.

"As we can't see inside we can't really know what it contains, but based on it's size and assuming human-sized troops, it could be carrying up to a hundred million., Bing reported.

"Homeland Security has a plan, Vice President," General Bedingford of Homeland Security said. "To create guerilla militia from Citizen groups that could allow us to fight a protracted defence on American soil over a long period of time. Because of our great constitution's second amendment, there is a huge amount of weaponry already distributed amongst the civilian population."

"Weapons that are being using against our riot troops," another general remarked.

"I know that in the dark days to come," the Vice President said encouragingly, "your country can count on you to protect our way of life, whatever the cost."

"Good work there Colonel," Solomon told Bing as the briefing broke up. "It's not going to be easy is it Sir? " Bing asked. "We have to prepare for both a massive energy impact and an invasion. It would help us a lot if we knew which if any it's going to be."

The General grunted non committally. "I think we're both realists here," he said. "At least we have time to make peace with God and our loved ones."

In the canteen the same news channel was playing. Now the international space agencies were no longer claiming the Anomaly was ice. They were no longer commenting on anything. For the media this was a field day, and the media were possibly the only people on the planet detached enough from themselves to be able to look on and film as the planet boiled over into rioting and civil unrest.

The President announced a state of emergency and martial law would be effective from midnight. All stocks and shares were to be frozen at their current value and no trading would be permitted. In the United States all internal flights were to come under the authority of the military, meanwhile further summits were being arranged to coordinate international plans of emergency.

Many other countries were taking similar action and it was thought likely that international trading prices would be fixed to help the continued flow of goods. Local Militia were organised in some countries, while others put troops on the street and yet others did neither. Some countries closed their borders entirely. European countries on the whole carried on as normal.

A general Tannoy announcement informed base personnel that all leave was cancelled and that Defcon two had been declared.

Bing thought she needed to get back to Cape Canaveral and start working on the satellite details, the main question being what kind of sensors could they strap on the satellite and how soon would they report back. Danny had been talking about several measurements they could take, infra-red, heat, gravity, magnetic, and they could film it up close. Bing would be needing yet another ride to Cape Canaveral before the day was over.

Chapter 6 – Mass hysteria

Caroline Bierhoff sat slumped at her desk holding her pretty blond head in her hands. Outside the window Stuttgart's morning traffic rumbled past in the street below. The sound of keyboards clicking and paper shuffling came from the cubicles around her but so far Caroline's hangover had defeated all her attempts to work.

Her head ached with a dull ringing and a sensation of tightness and vibration at the base of her skull. That was the result of the Death Moon Rave she'd been to the previous night. She'd not been to a party in the middle of the working week since her student days, a week ago would never have, but everything was different now. The world had changed overnight, the colour of life was different. The world she had lived her twenty two years in, had seemed to have an order, a place for everything and everything in its place. Now everything had come crashing down into a big jumbled pile.

Why had she even bothered to come into work today? She'd done nothing all morning but mope at her desk, not even bothering to pretend that she was working. What was the point? No one had been over to tell her to get on with it. As with everyone else left in the office today, she'd only come out of habit. Left in the office. That thing had only been in the sky one week and already there were those who were left and those who had fallen. What had happened to the others? That Italian girl Carmine, they said she'd committed suicide. She'd always seemed a bit quiet to Caroline, just the type she always suspected might kill herself, but never really expected them to actually do it.

At first it had been quite exciting in a way. The news had broken on a Thursday afternoon. Everyone in the office, except Gunther of course, for whom nothing was important enough to drag away from his work, had gathered around the television in the meeting room to watch the Bundeskanzlerin, the Chancellor's announcement. For the first time since the end of the Second World War martial law had been declared and once again German soldiers marched through Germany's streets.

The Chancellor announced a range of measures for the interim; the expected suspension of the Stock Exchange, price freezing as an anti-inflationary measure and power, water and other infrastructure industries to be temporarily under government control. All measures intended to maintain peace and economic stability during the crisis, the Chancellor assured the public. The Chancellor's speech continued into the details and Caroline grew bored of it and wondered off back to her desk before it ended.

Even though it was only lunch time everyone went to a bar near the office and got drunk. Quiet conversations were held in corners as fellow workers discussed the meaning of it all, their worries about food, money and loved ones. No one returned to work that day, but out of habit, the following day Caroline found herself amongst the select band of those who 'had come in today'.

By the following Tuesday this band of people had become even more select, and Detrikt put everyone's name on a whiteboard and began striking through the names of the missing, Caroline was relieved he hadn't made a column for putting the reasons for absence. Since then, the number of names struck through grew everyday and the remaining list got shorter.

Now on the anniversary of last Thursday, the first Thursday, as it were, a third of the people hadn't turned up to work. Caroline was also beginning to wonder if it was worth while. The insurance company she worked for couldn't have sold a thing in the last week, who would want insurance now? The bookies on the other hand were doing a roaring trade, after all, many of them didn't believe they would be here to pay out, so they took the money now and spent it. Others, now fearing they had nothing to lose, had bet the lot on the first horse race of the afternoon.

The only reason she'd kept coming in was because Louis Niemann, her boyfriend, had said it was important to keep a sense of normality about things. He said it helped put things into perspective. Not that she doubted him, but here in the office with her hangover she was struggling to see the point. The party last night, that had been fun, worth the price she was paying now. The loud music, the ecstasy tablets she and Louis had taken had been good ones and she had floated the night away on a soft warm sea of mutual loving, techo trance beat and flashing lights. She and Louis had made love last night in a public place, she'd never done that before. They'd left the club as dawn broke and in a dark ally, round the corner, Louis has pushed her roughly against the cold damp brickwork, pressing his lips hard against her mouth and using his finger to pull her panties down. She'd been startled, scared and turned-on. She smelt the garbage in the alley and felt cold water on the back of her neck as he entered her. She'd liked it, and not liked it. Being taken in a back alley like a cheap whore. But later, back at their small flat on Forststraus Straus, they lay in each other arms for an hour or so before Louis announced he was going to work. She'd hung around the flat alone for half an hour and then decided she couldn't bear being alone any more. At least there were people in the office.

She realised she'd changed. Louis had changed. Everyone had changed. There was Kirsty for example, she and Kirsty had been office friends for almost five years now. They'd got on really well, worked well together, chatted and gossiped, but now Kirsty had changed.

Caroline and Kirsty's friendship had fallen victim to a most divisive split, the one that lay between those who thought the world was coming to an end and those who didn't. Caroline was in 'the end is nigh' camp, the nihilists, Kirsty wouldn't believe it, couldn't believe it, that was not what was going to happen. Kirsty wouldn't see the inevitable, that the Death Moon would come crashing into the Earth and it would all be over. Perhaps it was punishment from God, perhaps it was a fearsome weapon of alien origin, perhaps it was random chance that the universe had blindly thrown at them, perhaps it was attracted by radio or television or microwaves, perhaps it wanted to consume all the electricity in the world. What ever it was, whatever it was going to do, it was going to be really really bad, anyone could see that, Louis could see that, the Death Moon Ravers could see that, but not Kirsty.

No, Kirsty had to see things differently didn't she, for Kirsty this was going to be a good thing, it would bring great change, yes, but for the better. Perhaps it would consume all energy or destroy machines and computers but that would only force humanity to reassess, to return to rural and ecologically sound values. No more industry, no more conveyor belt landfill and endless lorries. No, Kirsty believed that the ball of energy would harmlessly pass through the Earth. If it's appearance meant an invading army for Caroline, it meant an army of ecological angels for Kirsty. A sign from God? A warning, perhaps, but not Armageddon.

Already the office had split physically in two. The nihilists on one side of the room, the coffee machine in their territory, the survivors on the other side, they got the water cooler. Some people had changed desks, partitions had been rearranged. The ideological battle was fought in the medium of petty actions. Accusations of staplers borrowed without permission, reports slammed grumpily on desks, refusal to talk to certain people, cutting remarks hissed while passing by.

Even within the two main camps there were schisms. On both sides there were Alienists who lined up against the Non-Alienists and amongst the Alienists those who thought they should or could do something and those who thought otherwise.

The previous day Caroline had heard crying in the women's toilets. It had gone on a long time. She and several others had been in and tried to console whoever it was behind the closed door, but the weeping had just gone on and on till everyone had grown weary of it. Caroline thought she knew who it had been, and she was sure the girl wasn't in today. Maybe that was why Caroline had acted the way she had with Louis last night.

She really didn't think she could stand it in the office much longer. She became aware that when she left her desk to go and get a sandwich from the shop next door, she wouldn't be returning. She'd take her sandwich and eat it sitting on a bench in the Rosensteinpark and after throwing the wrapper away and feeding the crusts to the pigeons she'd get up and walk somewhere, anywhere, except back here. She thought she'd probably never be here again, in this dreary room, on this grey backed swivel chair, never ever see these people again.

In the end she didn't buy a sandwich at all. She walked right past the shop as the others went in to make their choices from what was already a dwindling selection of tasty sandwich fillings. There was already a shortage of cheese and a hand written notice in the sandwich shop window apologised for the lack of it.

Caroline went into the park. She didn't stop at the bench to eat the sandwich she didn't have, but kept on walking and soon found herself wondered aimlessly through the streets of the city. Some shops were having sales, others had put all their prices up despite the law and others stood half empty. There had been panic buying whick the Government could do little about except continue to reassure the public that they were doing everything possible to maintain regular supplies of essential goods in the shops.

Soldiers stood on every street corner, guns slung over their shoulders. The people didn't look at the soldiers, they moved quickly past, and for their part, the soldiers ignored the people. A silent, unspoken agreement had sprung up that as long as things were quiet, they'd each pretend the other wasn't there.

Caroline noticed there were two kinds of people on the streets. Those who moved with purpose going about some errand or task, and those without purpose who drifted around the streets and squares. They wondered glaze-eyed into shops and out again, not really seeing the wares, not buying anything, not going anywhere, not doing anything, just milling around aimlessly. Caroline realised she was one of these.

Amongst the dreary shops Caroline noticed a travel agent's window. A bright colourful poster offered the eastern comfort of a holiday in India. Caroline stood and stared. she'd always wanted to go to India. It was on the list of thing to do before they died, the list which Caroline and Louis had made in the coffee shop over breakfast the day they moved in together. Suddenly it seemed to be the thing she wanted to do most, suddenly she didn't want to die before she'd experienced India.

She ducked into the café opposite and ordered a cup of coffee. While she warmed herself with little sips of the hot frothy brew she called Louis on her mobile phone.

"Hello darling," he answered. He didn't sound at his brightest, unsurprisingly.

"I think we should visit India," Caroline said without preamble.

"Eh, uh India?" Louis was momentarily confused.

"It's on our list of things to do before we die, and I've just seen a poster, and I so want to do it now.

Now, before it's too late" she blurted into the phone.

"I, well, yes, er," Louis still struggled to keep up.

"Are you busy? Come and have a coffee with me in Kissingerstrasse, I'm in a little coffee shop there," Caroline said.

"Eh, OK. I'll be ten minutes? Glad to get out of here actually," Louis said.

When he arrived she was on her second coffee. He was wearing a suit but he'd loosened his tie and top buttons and there was a worn crumpled look to the jacket as if he'd been sleeping in it.

"How's work going?" she asked.

"Oh, you know, the Director didn't come in today, someone said he'd killed himself and his family in the night, but I don't see how they could know that," Louis told her. "What's this idea about India then?" he asked.

"I was thinking, well not really thinking, you know what I mean, anyway I saw this poster for India and I remembered how we said it was something we always wanted to do, and now, well, I think we should do it. What have we got to lose?" she added, the words bubbling out of her.

Louis wrinkled his forehead in deep thought and ran a hand through his dark curly hair. "Well what about your mother and stepdad, don't you want to be with them at the end?" he eventually asked.

"We can go and visit them on the way, make our goodbyes and go."

"You make it sound so easy."

"It is easy. We just walk across the road and buy the tickets," Caroline insisted.

Louis opened his mouth to voice another objection.

"And don't say work, Caroline interrupted before Louis could say a thing. You're right we needed the perspective of carrying on normally for a while, but I don't think that's working any more, not after last night, not after what we did, we've changed, things have changed."

Louis scratched his unshaven chin. "Yes, you're right," he said. "I can't continue to rot in that office day after day waiting, that thing hanging over us. Your right, let's do something. Let's do it."

"Oh Louis," Caroline wept and threw her arms around his neck. "I'm so glad you agree," she mumbled into his collar. "I love you."

"I love you too," he told her and stroked her hair.

Hand in hand they went straight across the street to the travel agent. The shop behind the colourful poster was small and scruffy. Two desks which had at some time been painted with a sky blue gloss were surrounded by adverts for far off exotic destination. After a moment a small, well presented woman in her fifties came out of a back room and smiled at them.

"How can I help?" she asked pleasantly.

"We'd like to two tickets to India please," Caroline said looking at Louis.

The woman sat herself at one of the desks, straightened some loose papers, poked at the keyboard then began asking questions like; When do you intend travelling? There were travel limitations and restrictions in place because of the emergency, and many flights were suspended but with a little work the woman was able to book them a flight and they bought two air tickets to Mumbai on the Indian East Coast, they didn't buy returns.

Louis needed to tell his office he was off on holiday but Caroline went straight back to the flat and began packing for them both. Then she rang her mother to say she and Louis would be coming to stay for a few days. She didn't say why, just for a break, though she wondered if her mother would suspect that this was a final goodbye.

Louis returned from work. "Might as well not have bothered," he said. "No one cared."

Caroline took one last look around the flat that had been her home for three years. The cosy chairs she and Louis had rescued from a skip, the art deco coffee table they'd bought at an auction.

"The rent's only paid till the end of the month," Louis remarked.

"I don't think Gustave will be too annoyed if we're a week or two late with next month's instalment. He never has before." Caroline said.

"I guess," Louis shrugged, taking off his suit and putting on jeans and a clean shirt. He picked up his backpack.

"Are we ready? Have you rung your Mum? Shall we begin our ever-so-big adventure?" Louis said.

"Yes, lets," Caroline replied, and without looking back she pulled the door firmly closed behind her and with it closed the door on her old life, now safely locked up in a room in Germany, for her to come back to, if there was any coming back to be done. Somehow she felt calmer and certainly happier than she had all week, she found she was excited about the trip and keen to see her Mum, it was the first real sign of feeling anything after the numbness that had fallen on her a week ago.

As they drove north through the German countryside they played the radio and sang along to the songs as they sped up the black asphalt highway that wound through the dark green forest. They pulled off the main autobahn and onto a side road that lead to the village where Caroline's mother lived.

Her mother greeted her at the door with a big hug. "It's good to see you both, how long it has been," she said. "I've just made a cake, let us have a slice while it's still warm."

They sat in the kitchen for a while and her mother chatted, telling them aimless bits of news from the village, but where before her mother had talked about whose daughter had married whom and what he did for a living, it was now what strange things had happened in the village, and though no one said it, they knew this change was because of the sphere.

"Your stepfather's not been so well lately," her mother said. "He seems to have caught a bad cold and hasn't been to work since the weekend." They all knew what that meant, that he was feeling depressed again.

That evening over a quiet supper, her stepfather said nothing, but spent his time constantly coughing or blowing his nose in a way which reminded Caroline of the girl weeping in the toilets at work. Her mother tried to keep things light. "These are particularly good carrots I get them from a man who grows them in his own garden," hadn't really done the trick and soon the meal fell into a silence punctuated by a cough here and a snivel there. After that Caroline and Louis went out into the garden together.

Holding hands, they looked up at the two moons. The Death Moon now a good quarter the size of the old moon appeared to be getting larger. The usual moon, the lovable normal moon of poetry and fairytale and romance, the moon which had looked down on mankind since they'd evolved from monkeys, the moon which had looked over the earth as life itself began, now joined in the night sky by a sinister, evil, tiny twin, and crossing the sky, they jostled nightly for position.

"I think we should leave tomorrow," Louis said.

"I agree," Caroline replied.

Chapter 7 – Military response

For several weeks now, Bing's life had been one assignment after another. The military is skilled in keeping occupied, the minds of those in mortal peril. The drills, the exercises, endless duties and routines. Everything on the base had been painted, twice. Every plane engine stripped and cleaned, every medal polished, every centimetre of tarmac scrubbed. Recruits marched endlessly up and down the exercise squares.

The deep space probe was launched an hour ahead of schedule and sixteen days later reached the Anomaly and began transmitting data, before all contact with the satellite suddenly ceased. It appeared the probe had been completely destroyed.

There were several more probes on the way and a substantial amount of data had already been gathered from the first one. They now knew the mass of the sphere. It gave off no heat and the probes electronics hadn't failed until the moment of impact. The object was deadly and yet strangely beautiful.

Pictures from the probe showed the object to have a vast, white, pink and grey mother-of-pearl sheen that swirled and curled constantly across its luminous surface. It emitted a gentle glow, not the bright light of a star, but a soft low hum of light.

As the days passed the Sphere drew closer to Earth and more probes reached the Sphere. Some were destined to collide with it, while others passed harmless by. The collisions left the Sphere unmarked but destroyed the probes. The Sphere acted like a solid object but appeared to be composed of energy.

The Chiefs of Staff had another meeting. The window of opportunity to send a warhead was rapidly closing. International pressure began to mount with some nations in favour of attacking it and some against. The deadlock was broken when the Indian and Swedish Governments began broadcasting welcome messages to the Sphere. This sparked the Americans, Europeans and Chinese to respond with a message demanding the sphere stay out of Earth's space and identify themselves, or they would be forced to take action.

The Amero-Euro-Chinese conglomerate continued their broadcasts for three days before their patience wore thin and the launch window began to close. That was the day they used Bing and Danny's home made bomb. The thought of it sent shivers down Bing's spine. She'd been both excited by it and very afraid. Naturally the whole thing was kept out of the news, the whole thing was done in secrecy, the cover story, just another probe.

There had been questions raised afterwards. It had seemed a particularly explosive probe. Again they had valuable information from the exercise. The sphere had remained undamaged. Not a scratch or scorch mark on it, no cracks, not a wobble or spark. It continued unabated as if nothing had happened. Then at 70 hours to impact something did happen.

In the monitoring suite Bing had watched as the velocity indicator on the main board began to fall. Moments later every calculator in the room was being worked overtime as calculations were made and checked and verified. The red line that until now had shot a laser beam of death that pierced the heart of Mother Earth, began to rapidly shrink until its tip rested just slightly beyond the moon's orbit. The Sphere was slowing down.

A cheer went up around the room. Hugging and back slapping occurred. Kissing, tears, laughter, hysterical chatter. Over the tannoy a technician announced, "Houston, we've got Aliens."

That night the Earth celebrated. There were parties everywhere, everywhere was a party, an inescapable mad festival of mass relief to which all were invited, all expected, a distraction that insisted everyone join in and dance the mad dance of today. We survived obliteration, but will we be slaves tomorrow? Right now who cares what tomorrow brings? Today we will live the day.

Bing went into town with half the base personnel. She drank in one bar, sang in another and danced in a third. Late in the night she bumped into the waitress she'd slept with, when had it been? Was it just three nights ago when things had seemed at their darkest, when the Sphere had towered over the world bringing the certainty of death. She wasn't embarrassed about the passionate sharing of fears, the desperate need to cling on to something, someone in the final hours, but that was yesterday and this was today, and they had a drink together and a kiss and each danced off their merry way.

Later, much later, Bing found her way back to Cape Canaveral, following the double moons. Now the second moon was three quarters the size of the old moon. At Canaveral the party was still going. She'd had enough for the day and went to bed sleeping in her clothes.

Several hours later she awoke from a deep sleep, went for a run and took a shower. After that she made her way over to the canteen for lunch and then to the monitoring suite.

The place was a mess, though two orderlies were already beginning to clean up the discarded cups, plates and paper hats, they even found a pair of panties. She was one of only five people at their station, but the big monitor continued to play and she was relieved to see the red line hadn't moved. The sky was not going to fall on them today.

Nor the following day when the Sphere came to

rest 300,000 miles from the Earth, just 50,000 miles further away than the old moon. It established an orbit roughly the same as the moon's and in the night sky old moon was now followed by it's smaller shimmering sister, a quite quite beautiful sight.

Now things were as they had been before, without the panic of imminent danger, but with the constant threat of what might be to come. It now seemed clear that the Joint Chiefs of Staff had been rash in their decision to bomb the Sphere,and if this wasn't an invasion force, it had to be some kind of warning.

The Chinese and Americans continued to broadcast their messages, asking the Aliens to identify themselves, respect interplanetary boundaries, and local customs. Other countries broadcast their messages, some claiming ownership of the moon or Mars and issuing threats if their borders were broken, and some offering the hand of friendship, invitations to join in mutual exchange of ideas, technology, music, anything and everything.

An international Cult of the Sphere quickly grew in honour of the new moon. Shining torches, laser pointers and when they could get them, searchlights, were pointed into the sky at nightly meetings, even though governments asked people not to, and also not to shoot at the moon.

Sister moon hung in the sky for two days when the President of America began to talk about a return to normality, a plan to end martial law and re-start trading. Troops around the world were being returned to their bases. People began to return to their jobs. People began to ask, if this is an invasion, where is the invasion, why wait? Earth had already demonstrated itself to be defenceless against the Sphere.

Bing's satellites continued to chatter happily amongst themselves, were they being listened into? Did it make a difference? On the big monitor the graphic of the solar system and the Sphere's trajectory had been replaced by an image of the Sphere itself, larger than it appeared in the sky.

Bing could have viewed close-up images of the Sphere, if she'd wanted to, but the sphere remained unchanging, in its ever-changing way.

Her thoughts were lost in the constant swirl of the Sphere's surface when General Solomon ordered her to a briefing.

"Bing, your friend Danny here has come up with an interesting idea which I think is worth giving a go," Solomon said.

"I thought it might be worth while trying to put a listening device on the Sphere," Danny said. "I know it's a long shot but we can learn quite a bit more about the Sphere if we send up a space shuttle, you know, kind of knock on the door, see if anyone's home," Danny smiled apologetically for his analagy.

"I think it's worth giving it a shot Bing, don't you?" Solomon said. "And I want you to go on this mission."

"Me Sir? Why me?" Bing asked.

"You know as much about the Sphere as anyone, and more than most. You're one of our top satellite technicians, and you're my eye in the sky on this one," the General told her.

"You need to get over to Medical right away," Danny said, "We've already started preping a shuttle for launch."

Bing reported for her medical and was put through a series of tests. The medics took blood, saliva, urine and faeces samples. She was measured and weighed. Her breathing was tested, her heart rate measured. This was followed by a spin in the centrifuge after which it was pronounced she'd survive Space. Then it was across the hall to a suit fitting and a gruelling hour spent in the plunge pool familiarising herself with how the suit worked under pressure, finally she was ready for the pre-flight briefing.

She sat with twenty other people, two teams of astronauts who were going up in two shuttles. She was introduced to her naval counterpart, Commander Simon Peccutio, a communications specialist.

"I realise that some of you in this room have not been into Space before, and that you have received little or no training for this," the General giving the briefing said. "Let me reassure you, that the people whose hands you are placing your lives in, are the very best, the most experienced, and highly trained on the planet.

This mission is composed of two shuttles, Discovery and Atlantis, these will be Team Mission and Team Support, you have already been assigned to your shuttle. Team Mission will enter orbit and begin to approach the sphere. Team Support will follow. Team Mission will then attempt to dock the listening device with the sphere, during which time Team Support will stand by.

Assistant Director Brooks will now explain how the listening device is to be attached."

Danny stood up and walked over to the podium. "The listening device is a series of sensors mounted in a cup," Danny explained. "To this we've attached a small propulsion jet. The idea is that the jet will keep the cup pressed against the side of the Sphere creating an air-tight seal which we can then fill with air from this cylinder here. We hope that, much like a doctor's stethoscope, we will be able to listen what is going on inside."

"Thank you," the General thanked Danny and continued." Any questions?"

"What if it doesn't stick to the Sphere?" someone asked.

Danny stood up briefly. "We think it will."

"Have the Chinese launched a similar mission?" someone else asked.

"We don't think so, we think that we'll be the first to try and establish contact with the Sphere in this way," the General said. "Now if there are no further questions launch is scheduled for oh five hundred hours people. I suggest you make best use of this time."

The would-be astronauts filed out of the room. Bing thought about calling her mother and father, they had spoken only a day or so ago after the Sphere had stopped speeding into the Earth, but this would be a dangerous mission. She wondered off towards her quarters to make the call. She was about to dial when the phone rang in her hand and she recognised Danny's number.

"Danny?" she asked.

"Bing you've got to come to the monitoring suite right now," Danny insisted, the urgency clear in his voice.

"What is it?" she asked already jogging down the corridor.

"The Sphere is changing," Danny replied.

"I'm on my way," she snapped the phone shut and ran.

She arrived breathlessly at the monitoring station and leant heavily on the desk with one arm, breathing hard, and looked up at the screen.

The same image of the Sphere was there, but something wasn't quite right. She looked more carefully, yes, there was a distinct bulge, not immediately clear because of the ever-swirling surface and because the bulge was facing towards them. As the minutes passed the bulge grew bigger and became more distinct until it became a small flattened sphere, a lensoid, like two contact lenses put together. It remained attached to the big sphere by just a tiny thread.

"Can we get some estimate of size on that thing?" Bing asked.

"Looks to be three kilometres across and a kilometre high at its widest and highest points," a technician replied.

A message came through on the intel monitor from launch control. The Listening device mission launch was put on hold.

Eventually the lensoid detached itself from the mother Sphere and began to move slowly away. Immediately the image of the Sphere was replaced by an orbital graphic showing the relative positions of earth, the moon, the Sphere and the lensoid. Yellow and green lines appeared on the graphic, showing orbits and velocities for each object except the lensoid, which showed a trajectory in red. The lensoid began to accelerate and it's trajectory curved towards the Earth.

"We have point of impact and ETI," a technician announced to the room. "We have twenty four hours before our guests arrive."

Bing left the mission suite, called to a Chiefs of Staff meeting in the conference room, who's primary question was, "how many troops could the Sphere hold?"

"Naturally any estimate is highly speculative. We should consider these figures to be base estimates of enemy fire-power. Based on the premise that invaders would be human sized and equipped as our troops would be then, ten, perhaps as many as twenty million troops. Though twenty million would not leave much room for equipment, vehicles or supplies," Bing reported.

"And the point of impact?" she was asked.

"New York," Bing replied.

"OK people, that puts it right in our backyard," said the General chairing the meeting. The Vice President was at NORAD with the President and half the Senate.

"We have a defcon one situation here and I'm advising the President that we mobilise all our defences to protect New York." There was general agreement to this.

"I think the Generals are being over confident," Bing expressed her concern to General Solomon after the meeting.

"What do you mean?" He asked.

"Look at the Sphere's behaviour so far. It's not been very predictable, and we've seen how manoeuvrable it is in Space, the little one, the lensoid, could change direction at any time and land anywhere," Bing said.

"OK, I want you to make a guess at where that might be," General Solomon said to her. "If you can tell me where to send the troops, I'll send them there," and he walked off.

Bing thought about it, where would she land? What was the meaning of the lensoid? An invasion craft? It seemed less likely, not enough troops, unless it was going to break up and land small groups of invaders in each capital city, would that work? It might contain bombs, thousands of bombs each capable of flattening a city. You can't protect everywhere, but then again it seemed foolish to put everything in one place. Perhaps that was the plan, blow up New York and the surrounding armies and navies.

There was something wrong here. Bing could sense it. She wasn't sure what but something didn't quite fit, some uneasy, slippery, thought at the back of her mind, teasing her by being there and yet not revealing itself.

The following day the lensoid approached Earth. As it came through the satellite field it slowed further and began weaving this way and that to avoid debris. Bing watched this merry dance on the monitor. The point of impact moved around the globe like a teenager teasing a cat with a laser pointer. As it began to enter the Earth's atmosphere the lensoid became visible over Europe and North Africa. The point of impact appeared to be central Africa but as it slowed down it seemed to be heading towards the Mid-Pacific Ocean.

As ground radar began tracking the lensoid it sped off across the Pacific Ocean and the U.S. Pacific fleet was alerted. The Chinese seemed to have launched every military aircraft they had. The Australian fleet which had been off the coast of New Guinea saw it pass overhead and began to give chase, but the lensoid moved relentlessly out towards the middle of the pacific and then floated down to sea level before sinking beneath the waves far from the nearest ship or submarine. Within moments all radar trace of the lensoid had disappeared. Suddenly no one knew where it was.

OK Bing thought to herself, that's were I'd go, the largest most empty piece of sea on the planet. That's where I'd go if I wanted to disappear, but why would I want to disappear? Could they be landing spies? Saboteurs? Was that it, now safely hidden, it could break up into many small craft capable of delivering human looking alien spies across the World, to do their dirty deeds. The problem was that even now, with an alien thing, a craft or energy ball or what ever it was, on the planet, lurking under the sea, they still knew almost nothing about it or its purpose.

Bing supposed she should tell General Solomon her latest thoughts. Well when she saw him, but for now she'd let them rest. Best to wait and see what happens next, she thought.

Chapter 8 – Unusual greetings

India was glorious. At first Caroline and Louis took the tourist trail of elephant rides, snake charmers, rice farmers and photographic hunts, but after two weeks the touristic candy-floss failed to ease Caroline's sense of impending doom and she suggested they try an Ashram. A couple of fellow travellers they'd met in a bar recommended one.

At Ashram Sri Ayurveda, Caroline and Louis tried yoga and meditation, they ate vegetarian food and wore sarongs and beads. In the mornings they gathered by the lakeside with the others and chanted with Swami Ghujaru Assam and in the evenings they sat in the main building, a large open sided space with a tin roof, and listened to the Swami tell tales from Hindu and Buddhist traditions and offer his spiritual advice on almost any matter.

After a few days they felt that perhaps the Swami's brand of spirituality was not quite for them, and hearing a rumour that there was an end of the world party happening on the beaches in Goa, they caught a train south and a day a later were lying on the golden sands of Baga Beach sipping cocktails and swimming in the sea. They rented a hut just down the coast from the beach.

Caroline was pleased with her new home, yes it was just two rooms, the bedroom and the bathroom, and yes the bathroom was primitive by Stuttgart standards, just a cold shower, a small mirror hung from a nail and a hole in the floor for a toilet but that was all they needed. Food was served twice a day at the main building, a low concrete affair built back from the beach itself, with a simple dining area, a kitchen and small office where the formidable Mrs. Hinjuli ran her holiday business. There were always a few idle locals lounging around, the cook, a taxi driver or two, sometimes a local policeman.

Touts constantly walked the sands, some targeting sunbathers, other would approach the accommodation huts directly. They would crouch down near the potential customer and offer their wares which were many and varied, from tourist trinkets to pharmaceutical-grade drugs. Barmen were kept constantly in action, crossing and re-crossing the beach all day and most of the night carrying drinks to the thirsty sunbathers and party-makers.

Here in the warm sun, the surf washing gently on the smooth sands, Caroline felt her troubles from the weeks before were now a thousand miles away, even if the Sphere still hung in the sky. Without any real news she was able to put the whole thing to the back of her mind, but there it sat, the timer slowly ticking down and no amount of alcohol or drugs could quite make that go away.

Caroline and Louis were now rising at lunchtime, getting a plate of curry or beans and then heading to the beach. At night they were attracted by the thumping trance and techno music from the bars and the bright flickering lights of the numerous fires which people lit on the beach. After a cocktail at their hut, brought them by the very polite Asif, and having taken the drug of the evening, Caroline and Louis would make love. They had sex in their hut, and on the beach, a desperate urgent lovemaking that sang of their need for each other in the face of the end they knew was coming.

Later at the beach bar they met other travellers, mostly Europeans and Americans, and they quickly befriended many of them. Everybody knew everybody even if they didn't know them. Everybody laughed and sang and danced and drank and took drugs, but nobody mentioned the Sphere. It was the one taboo subject at the End of the World Party. People talked about their experiences in India, at the Ashrams, the trips into the jungle, the drugs they were doing, who they'd fucked, what they though about god, art, music, and the food they liked, and how great the dolphins and whales were. No one talked about who they'd been before they arrived. At the End of the World Party everyone had someone they used to be.

As the last days approached the party became bigger, the orgies more frequent, the fucking more desperate. Now the End of the World Party continued without end, the music was endless, the drinks, the drugs, the dancing, endless. Everything a colourful, hazy swirl of smells and sweat and flesh for Caroline. The only thing she wore now was her sarong and when it slipped off or was pulled off or she threw it aside, she would find it again and wrap it round her plump waist and carry on dancing. When the tide came in washing the dancers up the beach, fallen comrades were dragged out of the surf by those still dancing and left high above the tide line in the shade of the palms to recover.

High and Drunk Caroline and Louis danced and danced through the night to the deep pounding hypnotic beats that came from the sound systems. Rubbing sweaty body against sweaty body. Caroline danced bare-breasted, with the cool sand pressing between her toes. Dancers pressed against her, pushing their hips into hers and swirling and gyrating and grinding. As the night wore thin people began to collapse in the sand, some just wearied, resting before their next dance, some exhausted, and others in various states of over-indulgence. A young man vomiting his cocktails and curry into the surf. A girl lying comatose at the edged of the dance, dribbling into the sand as she sleeps.

The pile of bodies surrounding the dancers grew. Exhausted herself, Caroline fell to the sand, pulling Louis with her. They lay there, stroking each other staring at the stars. A couple of dancers tripped over Caroline and fell next to her and Louis. They immediately began kissing each other, then kissing Caroline and Louis. All around them a sea of bodies writhed and moaned as some fucked and some slept and all the while a few continued the dance.

Caroline awoke in the early afternoon with the sun trickling through the cooling palm fronds. She pushed herself up on her elbow and looked around. A young man she'd never seen before slept peacefully and happily on the sand next to her. She looked around for Louis. It looked like a battle had been fought on the beach before her.

Sand churned by thousands of feet. Here and there a few survivors danced. Bodies lay everywhere. Picking their way between the bodies the still standing dragged their unconscious friends from the field of honour to the shade offered by the palm trees. Caroline realised she wanted to spend her last few moments with Louis, no one else, just Louis. She began wandering the beach, looking for him in all the bars. At one bar she found Claus, a German they'd met earlier, who thought Louis might be at a bar further down the beach. Caroline continued along the beach. As the affects of the drugs wore off she became dry mouthed, and dragged her feet in the sand as she walked . Finally she thought about going to the main hut and getting something to eat. When had she last eaten? She couldn't remember, but thought it might do her good to lose a little weight.

It took her a while to orientate herself before walking back the way she'd come. She found the concrete building with Mrs. Hinjuli's office and the dining area. She sat down to wait. Someone was talking in the kitchen so she hoped food was being prepared and all she had to do was wait, and worry about Louis.

She didn't know how long she'd waited, maybe an hour, maybe two, she had drifted in and out of drug-induced daydreams, when a girl with blond hair and tanned breasts came into the dinning area. She waved at Caroline.

"Hi," the blond girl said joining Caroline.

"Yeah. Hi," was all Caroline could muster as a reply.

"My name is Anna. You have been here long yah?" the blond girl asked.

"I don't know, an hour or more," Caroline replied.

"I mean on the beach," the girl laughed.

"Yeah, sure, days and days," Caroline said.

"Me too," the girl replied. "Is good time yah? I have slept with many people." the girl confessed putting a hand on Caroline's knee.

"I've lost my boyfriend," Caroline said pathetically.

The girl squeezed Caroline's knee and said "But girls are good too, yah?"

Caroline looked at the girl then kissed her on the

lips, a quick kiss, not a lingering one, but an affectionate one. "Yeah," She replied. "Good too, but now I need to find my boyfriend."

"That is good., the girl said understandingly. "When we have eaten I help you find him OK?" she offered.

They chatted on the merits of the various bars. Anna told Caroline she had come with a group of four girls from her home town in Sweden. More people came into the dinning area and the sounds and smells of food being prepaired came wafting from the kitchen. Each time another hungry soul entered the room Caroline looked to see if it was Louis. As the food was served and the room filled with the sound of people eating. More people drifted in as others finished and began returning to the beach or to their huts.

Caroline began to contemplate a night searching for Louis and was discussing with Anna which bars they should look for him in first, when she felt a hand on her shoulder followed by a warm wet kiss on her lips.

"Louis," she cried in excitement. "I've been looking everywhere for you." She leapt up and hugged him.

He smiled sheepishly and gave a little shrug. "I'm starved," he said, sitting down. "And who's this?"

Caroline introduced Anna to Louis thinking how worn he looked, thinner with black bags under his eyes and a sallow pale look to his tanned skin. He seemed to pick up after eating a massive plate of aubergine curry and rice. Around them the diners were finishing their meals and those left were relaxing, sitting around chatting on the wire frame chairs. A large bearded man slept soundly in the corner.

"We need to talk," Caroline said to Louis. "Sorry Anna, I need to talk to Louis alone," she told the girl.

"That is no problem," Anna said cheerfully. "I must meet my friend Ingrid now at Bhaui Bar." Anna kissed both of them on the mouth, her right hand brushing against Caroline's nipple, before she sashaying off across the sand.

"It's not long to go now. Not long before that Sphere thing comes crashing down on us," Caroline said. "I want to spend these last moments with you."

"Me too," Louis agreed.

Holding onto each other they made their way to their hut, staggering across the grass that ran along the edge of the beach. They lay down on the thin mattress and made love passionately as for the last time. Clutching each other tightly they kissed a final goodbye kiss and fell asleep believing it to be the last time, that eternally long sleep. Outside the hut the twin moons rose and shone their eerie light upon the shimmering sea.

Caroline awoke with a start and looked at her watch which she'd hung on the wall next to the mirror. It was mid-afternoon, but something was wrong, something different, she couldn't quite put her finger on it. She checked the date, they should be dead. Then she realised, the endless beat of the sound systems had stopped. Where before there'd been the thump, thump, thump, thump of base speakers, now there was only the sound of the surf. She woke Louis and hand in hand they went for a walk along the beach.

"It's strange," Caroline said, as they walked. "I thought today would never happen. It's like we shouldn't be here, yet we are. It's like we're being given a second chance, a new beginning, an opportunity to start over afresh."

"You mean today is the first day of the rest of our lives?" Louis remarked glibly.

There were few people about that afternoon. The morning tide had swept the dance floor clean leaving a strip of pristine flat sand between the bars and the surf. Above the tide line, under the palm trees, people were sleeping off the kind of hangovers that follow a week of non-stop partying.

As they approached Bhaui Bar a droopy Asif smiled his best, weary smile, apologised that the bar was closed, and asked would they care to settle their bill? Now that the party had ended, without the world ending, the locals were suddenly keen to see debts settled. It seemed while doom had not descended in the night, it was, instead, to be a day of recompense.

Caroline felt numb. She knew she should be pleased, excited even, about surviving, but it seemed such an anti-climax, it seemed as though something was needed to say it was all over, like a big explosion or something. Through her numbness memories of her old life began to surface, would she still have her job? She supposed she'd be needing it again now.

They stopped by Mrs. Hinjuli's office and paid her, then began the long slow possession up the beach to argue the bill at each bar. Asif was not only smiles but positively energetic at the sight of Louis' wallet and once they'd paid their bill the bar was miraculously open again and they ordered a pineapple juice each. From Asif they learnt the Sphere had come to a halt and something, no one knew what, had fallen from the Sphere into to Pacific Ocean.

More people came up to the bar as dusk began to fall and the first thump, boom, boom, thump of the sound systems floated along the beach.

"We should celebrate," Louis said. "We should celebrate being alive, lets have a drink." They ordered wine and toasted life and not being obliterated. An Italian girl at the bar finished rolling a cannabis cigarette and after inhaling deeply on it, passed the joint around.

The twin moons rose, one a half moon, the other

full. Out on the beach the sound systems played but their were few dancers.

"What's that?" the Italian girl with the good grass asked, pointing out to sea. Caroline turned to look. Offshore the surface of the sea appeared to be glowing and lifting. At first Caroline thought it a trick of the moon light, but a vast dome began to rise up from the sea. The sound systems along the beach fell silent. As the sea rose the dome became a flattened bubble which lifted above the sea and began to slowly drift towards the beach, it's multi-coloured swirling surface weaving and writhing with a myriad of pinks and silvers, white and gold. Then like a mist the colour and the glow gently fell from the bubble's apex right down to its base.

At first it looked as if the bubble was melting, but as the colours evaporated they revealed something inside, an upside down triangle that looked remarkably like an island. Beneath the surface dirt and rocks and trailing tree roots could be seen. On the surface there were features and structures. Buildings and parks, hills, forests and a small lake. It was a floating island.

It hovered with it's lowest tip trailing in the sea until its lip was near the shore line, this was as close as the island could come without rising higher. A large golden globe stood on the island's edge. The globe began to glow rhythmically, getting brighter and dimmer, but never extinguishing. It rose from the surface of the island and began to float down towards the beach. As it drew closer Caroline became aware of a pounding beat coming from it, thump, boom, boom, thump, then she became aware of a haunting melody. The golden globe descended from the sky shining in time to the beat. The rhythm and the music grew louder and louder until the globe came to rest its lowest point on the beach. Suddenly multi-coloured light burst from the globe, sending enormous beams of light streaking across the sky. The lights and music played together, dancing to the same beat. Across the beach Caroline saw people moving slowly towards the golden globe, some dancing, some just entranced.

Louis took her hand." We have to see this," he said and led her from the bar towards the globe as the beach around it began to fill with the curious and the excited. There seemed to be an invisible wall about two hundred meters from the globe beyond which no one yet dared pass. Instead they stood in a loose semi-circle dancing to the music.

The globe glowed for a while longer then slowly opened, lotus like, into seven large golden petals which reached down from a central platform to the beach. In the centre of the platform, a golden pagoda, and around it golden tents. Silhouetted figures stood amongst the tents, human like shapes which began descending the petal ramps to the sand. Caroline saw there were a lot of these figures, possibly several hundred of them. As the first of the alien figures stepped on to the beach the beat and the lights from the pagoda globe fell dead. Darkness leapt in surrounding everyone in its cloak of absence. A loud alien voice sang through the darkness."Everybody lets dance now."

"Boom, Boom, da, da, Boom, Boom," the beat blasted across the beach as spotlights and lasers burst into an extraordinary sky display. Fireworks exploded in arcs above the floating island. A massive cheer went up from the crowd. Caroline was cheering, she didn't know why, just intoxicated by the spectacle.

The tall alien figures began dancing and inviting humans to join in with them. Louis held onto Caroline's hand, and slack jawed simply said. "Fuckin A."

Chapter 9 – Presidential tea party

President Pahal Ghandri of India was working late. She was in one of her favourite places in the whole world, the opulent study in the Presidential Palace in New Delhi, at one of her favourite times of day, the hour of quietness that descends over the palace just before midnight. She was surrounded by the grandeur of the old Raj. The desk which had belonged to Queen Victoria, which Victoria had even used once. The bookshelves with their intricately carved patterns, the velvet covered chairs with gold filigree inlay. The enormous crystal chandelier which hung from the small central dome in the centre of the room. Pahal enjoyed being surrounded by these fine things.

She was finishing her personal diary when her private secretary, Janya Shama, came into the room. Her red, gold and green sari swished quietly with each elegant step she took across the richly woven carpet. The long dark tresses of her hair hung down her back almost to her waist and swung gently as she walked, her small delicate toes encased in golden sandals peeped from under her sari with each light step.

Janya approached the President at her desk. To Janya, President Pahal Ghandri of India looked like everyone's favourite grandma. A naturally cheerful woman with a thick head of curly grey hair and a pleasant round face. Like Janya, the President was dressed in a traditional sari, in a dark royal blue with a thick gold border. At this time of night she also wore a pale blue angora shawl across her shoulders.

"Madam President, I'm so sorry to disturb you at this late hour," Janya said softly.

Pahal liked Jnaya despite her advantage of youth and beauty. She came from a good family. Her father was in the Diplomatic Service, there was no chance of any leaks from that quarter, the Shama's were completely loyal to the Presidency.

Pahal put the Monte Blanc fountain pen down, took off her heavy gold rimmed reading glasses and carefully folded them, placing them on the desk next to her pen. Then looking up at Janya she said. "Janya, you shouldn't be working this late," Pahal admonishing her gently, more or less from a sense of duty. Just because she kept a punishing schedule, didn't mean her staff had to wear themselves out as well, though she appreciated the ones who put in the extra effort.

"I thought you should know about this immediately, Madam President." Janya said. Pahal gave her a questioning look. "Aliens have landed in Goa. They appear to have come from the new moon."

"In Goa? Aliens in Goa?" Pahal couldn't imagine why aliens would be in Goa.

"What are they doing?" she asked.

"It appears Madam President, that they are dancing."

"Dancing?" Pahal was bemused.

"Yes Madam President. It would seem that they are having a party. They've landed some sort of craft on the beach, a giant golden orb, and now they are playing music and dancing with the people on the beach. According to the report we've just received."

"My heaven's, well well," Pahal said, truly amazed at this news. "Whatever next? Well I shouldn't be surprised I suppose, after all, this is India."

"Now what are we going to do about it?" Pahal asked voicing her question out loud. Janya waited patiently for President Pahal to answer herself.

After some moments of reflection Pahal said. "I wonder if we have a protocol for visiting aliens? I'll need to see Gurdeep, if anyone knows, he will." Pahal paused for thought again." Are they demanding anything?" she asked.

"No Madam President," Janya replied.

"I Think I need some tea. Would you like some tea Janya? I'll just call down for some." Pahal picked up the phone on the desk and in a moment had ordered a pot of Darjeeling.

"Well is there anything they need?" Pahal asked as they waited for Gurdeep and the tea. "It would seem we have guests, and if I'm not mistaken, we invited them in our broadcast to the Sphere," she added.

"Yes Madam President. We did," Janya agreed.

Cabinet Secretary Gurdeep came into the Presidential study, his hair a little dishevelled, his jacket creased and the lack of a tie indicated to Pahal that he'd probably been woken from a nap in his chair.

"Ma'am," Secretary Gurdeep performed a curt bow.

"Now Gurdeep, I was hoping for your advice on matters of Presidential Protocol," Pahal said.

"Of course Ma'am. Am I to understand that we're talking about the landing in Goa? They are aliens yes?" His deep voice seemed to boom even when talking quietly.

"I believe so," Pahal replied.

"Then if I may lay out the social landscape, as it were." Gurdeep brushed a loose lock of white hair back onto his head and straightened his jacket. "If I may?" he indicated a chair.

"Of course, of course Gurdeep, please make yourself comfortable."

"Ma'am." He bowed again and sat on a nearby chair. When sitting he was less imposing than when stood. In his late sixties and only two years older than Pahla, Gurdeep still had a large imposing frame which towered over most other people. His hawk-like gaze and small spectacles were a common sight around the palace.

"it occurs to me Ma'am, that we have but two simple choices. We go to them, or they come to us," Gurdeep said. Pahal nodded in agreement. "Now it would be unseemly for us, that is for you Ma'am, to go to them, they should, I think, present themselves here at the palace. It is, however, appropriate that visiting dignitaries of this importance pay us a visit here, no matter which planet they are from." Gurdeep smiled. Pahal nodded her agreement.

"Therefore I suggest we send a welcoming delegation led by a high ranking Minister, perhaps the Chancellor, to invite our guests to a reception here In New Delhi Ma'am." Gurdeep advised.

"As usual old friend I think you have it," Pahal said. "That is indeed what we will do. There is another matter I would like your advice on also."

"I am, as ever, at your service Madam President," Gurdeep replied.

A functionary entered the study with tea and placed it on a low glass topped table with gold lion's paw legs, around which the President and

Gurdeep were sat. There was a momentary pause and a series of subtle gesturing between Gurdeep and Pahal, a conversation held in the flickering of eyebrows, a cock of the head, a turn at the corner of the mouth that said, "Shall I pour or you? No I'll pour. Thank you for asking." Such as passes between those who know each other well.

The delicate bouquet of Darjeeling tea filled the air. Gurdeep reached for milk while Pahal and Janya took a slice of lemon each. Pahal was always amazed at how a nice cup of tea could always put things in perspective, even things as strange and perplexing as alien visitors.

"It occurs to me," Pahal continued once everyone was served, "that the Chinese and Americans, indeed the whole world, will be interested in coming to meet the aliens, but as you know, many countries have taken an aggressive or hostile stance in their broadcasts . Who should we invite to meet the aliens and who should we not?"

"You will forgive me for reminding you Mrs. President that in the first instance we must give full security to both yourself and our guests, therefore the last word on such matters should come, I feel, from your security advisers Ma'am," Gurdeep offered.

"And you are quite right, however, I value your thoughts on this matter and would be agreeable to hearing them none the less," Pahal replied.

Secretary Gurdeep put down his cup and saucer. "Of course Madam President. As I see it, the Americans are a particularly tricky problem. They were the ones who launched a missile at the aliens. The Chinese, North Koreans and Iranians have also been particularly threatening with regard to violation of their airspace."

"Quite so," Pahal agreed.

"The Swedish, Dutch, Bolivians, Zambians, Ethiopians and Kazakhstanis however have all extended invitations similar to our own, and the leaders of these nations, I believe, should certainly be invited. We could also take this as a opportunity to strengthen ties with our allies, the Commonwealth, and those who border us."

"Well we can't not invite the Chinese and Americans, that would certainly strain relationships between us, we should invite those who extended an invitation of their own, it's beginning to look like the whole world will have to be invited," Pahal said.

"Indeed it is Ma'am," Gurdeep agreed gravely.

They were interrupted again, this time by the arrival of Gurdeep's aide, who whispered in his ear and passed him a folder, while Gurdeep signalled his deepest apologies to the President for this whispered interruption.

"I see, I see," he said after a moment. "Keep me

informed of every new development," he ordered his aide, who left swiftly.

"Ma'am, in light of the news I have just received, I feel we should revise the advice I have just given."

Pahal nodded. Sometimes the man was infuriatingly slow at giving his advice. "And what is it you've heard?" she asked.

"It would appear the American and Chinese fleets are heading towards India Ma'am."

"Is that going to be serious, do you think?" Pahal asked.

"I doubt they'll enter our territorial waters, "Gurdeep assured her. "But they pose a threat. The situation demands we consider our response carefully, too much action may look hostile, not enough may encourage them to be liberal with our borders."

"The situation isn't getting any easier,l" Pahal said as yet another aide came into the room and passed Gurdeep a note. He read it and frowned.

"An armada of small boats, sailing yachts, fishing boats and ferries has been reported by the Coast Guard to be crossing the Gulf of Oman in the Arabian sea and heading down our east coast. I'm told the cost of a fishing boat in Doha has risen from two thousand dollars to two million and people have been selling passage on fishing boats for tens of thousands of dollars," Gurdeep said, looking up from the note to the President.

"We don't have time for the Government to debate these things, we must move swiftly and decisively. Of course we can only act in the Country's best interest and to do that we need to get things moving. Prime Minister Pradeshi and Parliament can begin debating the finer points tomorrow morning, tonight I'm declaring a temporary state of emergency," Pahal said.

"Very wise Madam President," Gurdeep agreed. "Where is the Prime Minister? I'm surprised he isn't here."

"He's returning from talks with the Pakistani Government. He should be here soon," Pahal said.

"Something we have not yet discussed is the threat the aliens themselves may pose," Gurdeep mused. "We know so very little about them. The best we can do is try to put ourselves in their shoes. Why would we come all this way to dance on a beach? Is this how we would introduce ourselves to another world? What do they hope to gain by this?"

"As you say my dear Gurdeep, we know so very little about them, at the moment we can only suppose. At present, however, we can trust to the idea they're not threatening us in any obvious way. Perhaps it is like us putting on a display of our dancing and music when the Queen of

England, Head of the Commonwealth, comes to visit us?"

"A cultural display. It is an interesting idea, Ma'am," Gurdeep agreed.

Another of Gurdeeps' aides came in and passed a note. "We have a similar issue with shipping in the Bay of Bengal," Gurdeep informed Pahal. "Boats are crossing from Myanmar, Thailand and Malaysia."

There is also trouble on the roads. Those into the country are becoming blocked with traffic pouring in across the Pakistani and Bangladeshi borders, and both countries are reporting similar movement from their neighbouring territories. Airports in the Goa region are unable to handle the increase in landing requests and it's being reported that light aircraft and even parachutists are landing illegally in fields surrounding the area," Gurdeep said.

"You realise Madam President, we're about to host the biggest event the world has ever seen, bigger than the Olympics or the World Cup, we're to play host to every nation of the world and we need it organised yesterday."

"You are right Gurdeep, we find ourselves unprepared," the President said. "But we are India, we will rise to the challenge."

Pahal turned to Janya and said, "Could you tell Prime Minister Pradeshi I would appreciate a word with him as soon as he arrives." The girl nodded and left the study.

"You have some thoughts Madam President?" Gurdeep asked.

"I have. I'm thinking that we need to get our invitation to the aliens at Goa with the utmost haste. we should also send gifts. You know, the usual, typical Indian craftsmanship, examples of our art, a nice set of chairs perhaps, that sort of thing.

"Your reference to the Olympics has given me an idea. We should arrange for the nations of the world to visit with the aliens in order of those who were welcoming first and the most hostile last. My most pressing concern now is where to accommodate all our guests, we do not have enough accommodation or facilities."

"It occurs to me Madam President, that at this time many nations may look favourably upon a request for aid from India. We could build a tent city outside Gurgaon, to the south of New Delhi. It is perfect for communications with the International Airport already there."

Pahal considered the idea. "We could ask the Saudis for the tents," she said.

"We can ask the world for tents, and pick the winner Ma'am," Gurdeep remarked.

"Indeed we can. Indeed we can," Pahal said

thoughtfully. "And we need someone to print the invitations." She added. "The English have and excellent printing facilities, perhaps the Bank of England would oblige?"

Gurdeep smiled.

There was a fresh interruption as Prime Minister Pradeshi arrived having come straight from the airport. Looking at her watch it was clear to Pahal that she wasn't going to get much sleep that night, but then it didn't look as if anyone would. She began briefing the Prime Minister on what had been discussed and the finer points of his impending mission to Goa. An aide brought a list of possible gifts. A report came from head of security, and preparations were made for the Prime Minister's transport to Goa.

While Pahal briefed the Prime Minister, Gurdeep issued instructions that every available Indian diplomat be engaged in the tent city planing.

All troops were told not to fire on anyone and ammunition was not issued to regular soldiers. The Security Chief ordered all Indian military in the Goan area and around New Delhi to be on full alert and reinforced where possible. The Indian fleet was dispatched to the Gulf of Oman, and into the Bay of Bengal to try and stem the flood of boats, or at least, give help to those in trouble on the sea.

Instructions were sent to the Vice Air Fleet Commander that Indian Air Force services would be used to ensure that adequate food and water supplies reached the Goan area. Pahal did not want an international crisis on her hands.

Several hours later Pahal had a television wheeled into the study, something she'd never done before. An aide turned the television on and tuned it to the Indian National News channel.

The camera shot showed daylight breaking over the sands of Baga Beach and as far the eye could see the sand was covered entirely by brightly clothed people, spinning and whirling to a rhythmic beat. In the middle of it all, presiding over the mass of dancers, stood the golden alien pagoda.

Seven large black cars moved very slowly from the road leading through the trees out on to the sands. Soldiers mounted on jet black chargers wore bright red jackets, long black boots and silvered helmets with fans of feathers. They cleared a path through the dancers for the Prime Ministers' cavalcade behind which foot soldiers in ceremonial uniforms kept the path back to the road clear.

The dancers became dis-coordinated and stopped when Indian music played by a military band began to clash with the alien rhythm as the cavalcade crawled closer to the pagoda. As the alien music fell silent, Indian music took its place. At the same time a black shape was be seen dropping from the floating island towards the beach.

The cavalcade came to a halt in front of the pagoda and the mounted troops cleared a space for the Prime Minister and his retinue.

The pagoda was surrounded by unusually tall human figures. Watching the scene on television, Pahal suddenly realised she was looking at aliens. Tall, definitely human-looking, some wearing long, flowing robes which in some cases looked quite like saris, while others did not look like any style of clothing Pahal recognised.

The dark craft from the island floated down over the beach and came softly to rest next to the pagoda. It was the size of a small two-storey office building and shaped like an egg. The front of the craft opened outwards and onto the sands, forming a ramp. For a moment nothing happened, then there was a movement in the door way and six creatures that looked like dog sized wasps standing about five feet tall and dressed in red uniform jackets came marching out on four hind legs. Each creature wore a ceremonial sword and a more practical looking side arm on a belt around their diminutive waists. The wasp like creatures lined up in a regular formation with the ramp to their backs and drew swords which they held vertically in front of their heads.

There was a momentary pause, then the cavalcade doors opened and the Prime Minister's retinue stepped out of their cars onto the beach. There was a momentary scuffle as they arranged themselves according to their status.

After a few seconds several of the humanoids, dressed in white uniforms with flat peaked hats, emerged from the strange craft. Their uniforms looked remarkably similar to those worn on cruise ships, though instead of trousers they wore long, pleated skirts which came down to their ankles. They lined up on the beach at the end of the ramp. A final humanoid followed them out.

This one was like the others, except, dressed in a deep blue uniform and accompanied by what could be a child. The figure moved to the head of the white uniformed group. As if by some secret signal the Prime Minister's retinue and the alien retinue simultaneously moved towards each other. The sinister looking wasp creatures remained standing where they were.

Prime Minister Pradeshi gave a bow to the alien. The alien smiled and bowed back.

"I'm Prime Minister Pradeshi of the Indian Republic. I offer a gracious welcome to all who come to this country in , seeking knowledge and wisdom." he said in Hindi. He was about to repeat this in English when the alien spoke, in a light melodic voice. Vocal chords not used to the specific air-mix of earth sounded slightly strange, yet pleasing to the ear.

"I am Commander Wayfarer, captain of the floating island you see behind me, which we call Sashoo. We are honoured to be considered welcome guests in your beautiful land. I am sure there's much we can learn from each other," Commander Wayfarer replied in English.

Gurdeep looked away from the television and caught Pahal's eye.

"I was thinking Madam President, this is going to really boost tourism."

Chapter 10 – Tent city

Images of the aliens began appearing on the Internet within minutes of their landing. Dark grainy cell phone photos and films were flashed across the networks. By daybreak TV studios had camera crews on the beach, helicopters, light aircraft and boats loaded with telescopic lenses vied with each other for a better, closer image of the floating island and it's inhabitants.

Just after eleven o'clock in the morning, the defining image of the moment was globally syndicated, an image of a large bird of some kind surrounded by humanoids. These figures could be seen moving around the island's plateau. From the aerial images the plateau appeared to have a central plaza with a large ornate building in the middle. Four wide avenues radiated out from the plaza to the plateau edge, cutting the island into quarters. Occasionally a brightly coloured vehicle raced up one or other of the avenues.

At what appeared to be the rear of the island, furthest from the beach, stood a small mountain, at the foot of which lay a lake fed by a sparking waterfall and surrounded by woodland. Running from the foot of the mountain towards the front of the island a chaotic multitude of random structures. No two buildings were the same shape or colour. The streets ran crooked with twists and turns everywhere. No one knew what these buildings were for, but it was assumed these were aliens' houses.

The front of the island, closest to the beach had structures near the plaza, but these soon ended, and a vast green, grassy looking area ran to the edge of the plateau. This was the area the aliens had launched the golden globe from, and where Commodore Wayfarer's craft had first appeared. The only thing on the grass now, however, was a large flat silver dome, the purpose of which remained unknown.

Sat on his sofa David watch the news while tapping an envelope on his right knee. The envelope contained his invitation to attend the reception at the Presidential Palace in New Delhi. As the discoverer of the alien star David was a special guest and one of the few non-political invitees. He felt honoured to be involved but he had a problem. International air travel was still in chaos despite the easing of national air flight policies and all flights going anywhere near India were fully booked, how was he to get there?

The phone rang, it was Bob Harding, "Hi David, look, Harding Telescopes would like to sponsor your trip to India, you know, cover all your expenses." Bob offered.

"Wow, sure Bob," David replied.

"Just one small condition," Bob added.

"Yes."

"I'm coming too."

"That's great. I could really use the company." David said.

"Great, that's settled then. I'm watching the news here, it looks like getting to India is going to be difficult, seems a very popular destination right now," Bob said. "I can't get us direct flights, not even with your name. We have to take a train to Turkey and should be able to get a flight from there, or if not, perhaps a ferry into the Lebanon."

"Wow Bob, that sounds like a trek," David replied.

"Yeah, I know, sorry David, but we're going to have to fight for our ride as it were. I've got people working on getting us a flight out of Istanbul in four days time and I've organised a helicopter to take us to Calais so we can catch an international train from there, so I need you ready to be picked up in one hour."

"One hour, I can't cancel the milk or the paper and what about my potted plants?" David protested.

"Don't worry about that, leave your house keys with the driver and someone will tend to them. The important thing for you to do now is pack for India."

"How long do you think we'll be away for?" David asked.

"A fortnight," Bob replied.

"Two weeks?" David exclaimed.

"I doubt it will be any easier getting out than it is to get in," Bob predicted.

In a daze David grabbed a suitcase he didn't recognise, when had he bought it? He wondered, it still had the shop tags on the handle. Scooping up clothes from his wardrobe and drawers he piled them into the mysterious case. Passport, money, David told himself, those are the two essentials, with a passport and money you can go anywhere, buying whatever you need on the way.

In a daze David grabbed the first suitcase he could find and frantically stuffed it with clothing scooped from his wardrobe and bedroom draws. "Passport and credit card, passport and credit card," David told himself, with those two little items you could go anywhere. He spent a moment debating which coat to take.

A horn pipped in the street outside. As the driver picked him up at his front door David felt excited, exhilarated and a little nauseous.

The car took him to a field near the telescope factory where Bob and a helicopter were waiting for him. Two hours later after a cramped bumpy noisy ride in the chopper they were boarded the train for Paris to connect with the Orient Express to Istanbul.

On the train David took the opportunity to rest, while Bob continued working, sending emails and making numerous calls. Eventually he said, "We're on a three am flight to Mumbai out of Istanbul International Airport."

Arriving in Istanbul in the middle of the night was confusing for David. He'd been fast asleep when the train pulled into the station. Bob had to shake him awake. After that it had been a race, first dashing across the station to the taxis, then through the busy city to the airport. The airport was packed with thousands of people. The arrivals board showed many originations, but the departures board was almost exclusively destinations to India, mainly New Delhi, Mumbai and Goa. The place was in chaos, touts openly sold tickets for flights to anywhere in India, flights had been over-booked, security was over-run and ground-crew were taking bribes.

Even when David and Bob had boarded, the plane was disorganised and people without tickets had managed to get aboard. Eventually after several people were ejected, the plane was able to taxi out onto the runway and lift-off. Several hours later at New Delhi international the aeroplane was held an hour in the air stack above the airport before they were able to land.

David and Bob walked out of the airport into the maelstrom which was New Delhi. The Indians seemed to be just about coping. For a town like New Delhi, a few thousand, even a few tens of thousands of extra tourists, was something it could absorb. Anyone who owned a car was offering exorbitantly priced taxi rides. Anyone with cooking skills was making food to sell on the streets and in the Tent City. The entire city was motivated and active in supplying the many visitor's who were arriving.

Families slept in the one room and rented out the rest of their home. Restaurants hired extra waiting staff. Hotels hired extra service staff, and anyone with anything to sell was out on the street selling it at twice the normal price. But as the number of visitors crept up into the millions, New Delhi began to feel the strain. Bob quickly found them a ride to Tent City.

Gurgaon was a sea of white, gently flapping, canvas tents, and brown dirt roads. The taxi carrying David and Bob bumped along dust blowing through the vehicle's open windows. Smells assaulted them from all sides, cooking food, incense, pine, and sometimes odours of a less pleasant nature.

The taxi stopped at an apparently random spot and the driver indicated they had arrived at their destination. After paying the driver in dollars, and picking up their luggage from the dust David and Bob walked along the wooden duck-boards that ran between the rows of tents. At the end of the row was an open space and a large tent which served as a reception area. Inside it was hot and sticky and smelt of canvas and diesel oil. A row of fold-up tables stood in the middle of the tent and behind them sat a row of officials. Two Indian Army soldiers stood guard at the entrance.

David and Bob approached a vacant table and introduced themselves to the official sitting there. The official consulted his laptop before asking David and Bob to present their passports. After checking their papers he handed David a map of the Tent City. The official marked the reception tent with a cross and put a circle on the map.

"This is where our tent is?" David asked.

"Yes, yes," the official replied, handing back their passports, and two identity cards which made them official residents of Tent City, for ten days. Outside the reception tent they took a minute or two to orientate the map and after a brief discussion they set off to find their tent.

Half an hour later, having passed the reception tent twice in their search, they found the tent assigned to them, marked with a small card hung on its front pole. The facilities were basic; a ground sheet over the dirt floor, four military folding beds, four folding chairs, a folding table and a canvas screen which cut the tent in half then in half again to make two bedroom areas at the back. Bob dropped his luggage on the floor and collapsed into a folding chair.

"Wow, India," Bob said mopping his brow. "I wonder where the toilet is?"

"Apparently there are facilities available all around the compound in specially marked tents," David replied, reading from a leaflet.

"Ah yes, I think I saw the toilet tent, or rather smelt it," Bob laughed.

"There's not much to do in here," David said, looking around the spartan accommodation.

"We should explore the area, it won't be easy to find the tent in the dark," Bob said.

"Sure," David agreed. They had hours to wait before the Presidential reception.

Having stowed their luggage under a bed David and Bob left their tent and began exploring Tent City. It was clearly a hastily built, but well organised, site. Long trenches had been dug and covered in wooden duck-boarding, some of which carried cabling and water pipes, while others operated as open sewers. The trenches ran from front to back of the site and alongside the dirt roads. A grid work of walkways crossed the main arteries at right angles. Area borders were marked with crudely sprayed orange sticks and every so often a sign denoted the area designation with a simple letter, number and grid reference.

This first layer of organisation was being developed further. They passed a tarmac spreading crew that was quickly and crudely laying a surface over one of the dirt roads. On one side of the site soldiers were erecting more tents. A lorry drove slowly down the lines of orange sticks while at regular intervals a soldier pushed a bundle of white canvas and wooden poles off the back of it. A trenching crew were extending the service trenches and a marking crew was laying and staking out more grid. On the other side of the site a tarmac road had already been laid and construction workers were pumping concrete foundations. Further along brick buildings were rising from the earth.

They came upon an area which had older buildings. Food sellers, beggars and tourists swarmed the streets.

"I could do with getting a shower." Bob remarked. David agreed he could with one himself. A wide avenue led to an area with traffic. Taxis and a multitude of other vehicles were arriving and picking up fares. Rickshaws, tuk tuks, family saloons, even a guy on a moped with the word taxi crudely painted on his windshield.

Suddenly from out of the chaos David heard his name being called. "Mr Shawdale, Mr David Shawdale?" A man of medium build wearing a blue turban, a black beard with wisps of grey and a big beaming smile advanced towards him, hands held out in greeting.

"You are Mr David Shawdale?" the man asked in English, heavily laced with an Indian accent.

"Do you want to see my passport?" David asked.

"No no., the man laughed. "That will most certainly be not being necessary. I recognise you from your picture on televison. Please excuse me I am Gudup Jeep and my son is a big fan of yours. I am having a car myself and it would be an honour to drive you anywhere you like. Yes, yes, just to tell my son who has been in my car today is reward enough, if it is you Sir."

"We need somewhere to wash," David told Gudup,."We've been travelling for two days."

"But of course. I know just the place, come come, my car is this way." He led them off through the throng of people to a small dirty white car parked haphazardly at the side of the road.

As he drove towards New Delhi Gudup continued. "You would be most pleased to be using my own bathroom."

"We really couldn't impose," David said.

"No, no imposition at all, "Gudup assured him. "While you are here my house is your house, I would be greatly honoured for it to be so."

David looked at Bob who shrugged back.

"Well I guess we could if that's OK."

"Oh yes, it is more than being OK, I am deeply honoured," Gudup said.

"That's great Bob," David said.

"Bob!" Gudup exclaimed. "Bob Harding of Harding Telescopes?"

"The same." Bob replied, his Yorkshire accent sounding more pronounced.

"Oh my, this is going to be such a day for my son. He is having one of your very telescopes as well. You must be excusing me for a moment I am having to be calling my family," Gudup told them as he dialled his mobile phone with one hand.

They wove in and out of the mad New Delhi traffic. Between honking and shouting out of the window Gudup conducted a frantic conversation on his phone. David began to wonder just how many arms, and eyes, Gudup had as the near misses became more frequent.

They stopped outside a modest block of flats in south New Delhi. Gudup led them up several flights of stairs and along an external balcony covered in a variety of potted plants. A woman Gudup introduced as Mrs. Jeep was waiting in the doorway for them and ushered David and Bob into the flat with much ceremony. The whole thing was beginning to feel completely bizarre to David, though he was thoroughly enjoying it.

After drinking tea, eating cakes and meeting family members, David and Bob were shown a room, clearly the son's room, as charts of the stars hung on the walls and in one corner stood a T-37 Harding Telescope.

"Bloody hell," Bob said inspecting it. "This is one of my grandfather's telescopes. I'll get the kid one of our latest, and maybe he'll let me have this old one," Bob added.

Gudup left to retrieve their luggage from Tent City and inform the authorities where David and Bob might now be found. They ate more food while they waited for Gudup to return then showered and changed for the reception. Now they felt refreshed and well fed and as the cooler evening air began to breeze over the city, Gudup took them across town to the Presidential Palace.

They walked along a wide tree-lined, marble paved, boulevard and up the wide steps of the white marble Palace. Some guests arrived dressed like David and Bob, in evening wear or dark suites, while others wore national costume, uniforms with grand hats, robes or togas. Sashes and medals, gold and silver buttons were everywhere. At the entrance to the Palace, David was asked by a liveried functionary to identify himself.

"David Shawdale yes, and this is?" he raised an eyebrow at Bob.

"Mr. Shawdale's security, Bob Harding," Bob said.

David looked at him but the functionary merely made a note of this on his palm-sized computer and waved them in. They followed a red carpet to the security check point. Once through security yet another functionary asked David his name.

"Ah yes, Mr.Shawdale, the star discoverer I believe?" the functionary asked.

"President Ghandri herself has requested you join her retinue when she greets the aliens tonight. If you could make your way to the state room for eight o'clock the President would be pleased to meet you. Food and drinks are being served on the Palace terraces if you would care for something to eat while you wait. I can show you the way if you like."

"If you could tell the President, I am honoured to be invited to join her and am happy to do so," David replied.

"Of course." The functionary dashed off and David and Bob made their way with other guests to the terraces where stripped awnings which earlier in the day had provided shade were now festooned with lights. Waiting staff in white jackets and white gloves glided smoothly through the crowd carrying trays of drinks and canapés. Bob lifted a couple of slender glasses from a passing waiter and handed one to David.

"Your health Mr. Shawdale," Bob grinned at him and raised his glass to the toast.

"And your prosperity Mr. Harding," David replied as they chinked their glasses in salute.

They wandered through the crowd hearing every language known to man as people stood chattering excitedly in small groups. Everyone was excited about meeting the aliens, and almost everyone seemed to be a diplomat, envoy or politician. The major powers hadn't sent their leaders, that would have been too much of a risk, what if all this was an alien trick to destroy the world's leaders? So the Americans hadn't sent their President nor the Chinese their Chairman, and not wanting to break with this protocol the Russians, French, Japanese and Germans hadn't sent their leaders either, but Australia had been happy too, and Europe sent it's President. The British sent their Prime Minister, the Iranians sent a Cultural Attaché and the Holy Papacy sent a senior ranking Cardinal.

An area of the terrace seemed to be unofficially marked out by the English-speaking delegates. David was soon recognised by a British diplomat and was forced to endure a flurry of introductions as he was taken around and introduced as the Starman, the great British discoverer of the alien star. Before he knew it, he was acquainted with the ministers and ambassadors of twenty different countries. He was just being circulated around the Europeans when Bob put a hand on David's shoulder and said, "You're expected in the State Room now Mr. Shawdale," and he led David off.

At the State Room door Bob was sidelined and sent to join the other security personnel and body guards. David found himself in the company of some of the most august people on the planet. He was briefly introduced to the Indian President who greeted him warmly before he was moved on to his position in the ranks. David was a peculiar fish from that point of view, having no official status, he had no natural place in the hierarchy. He was put at the back of the front as it were, next to a Nobel Peace prize-winner and an Indian film-maker. In front of them the representatives of the favoured nations, behind them, the neutral nations and at the back, the previously antagonistic nations.

Eventually they were all assembled in some sort of order and a moment of quiet fell over the five hundred dignitaries as the grand doors at the end of the State Room opened and an alien retinue numbering two hundred or so beings, entered the room led by Commodore Wayfarer and the child.

The Commodore and the child approached President Ghandri.

"President Ghandri, it is an honour to meet you." For a moment Pahal was taken aback, the Commodore had spoken without moving his lips, protocol had said nothing about this, but then she realised it was the child who spoke. "I am

Chungfew, Lord of Sashoo and appointed representative of the Lowai Clan owners of the Astrosphere. It is our greatest pleasure to be here," the child said, in a high pitched and melodious voice.

"It is our pleasure to welcome you and extend to you our hospitality. I would like to introduce you to Mr. Guntherson, President of Sweden, whom you may also be aware extended an invitation of welcome to your people," President Ghandri said.

"Indeed I do, and I would be most pleased to visit your beautiful country as soon as we have negotiated passage across your planet for Sashoo," replied Lord Chungfew.

Chapter 11 – Formal reception

The morning after the floating island appeared from the sea, Bing found herself aboard the American aircraft carrier USS Ulysses, currently on manoeuvres in the Gulf of Oman off the Goan coast. The ship's intelligence suite buzzed with information about the alien landing.

Spy planes circled over the alien island all morning, and a wealth of images were gathered. Nothing looked obviously like a weapon, There was also no obvious military activity, except for the wasp like creatures, who seemed to be soldiers, but their movements were restricted to the guarding of certain buildings on the island. As to the purpose of these buildings, there was no way of telling at this stage. The alien species led by Commodore Wayfarer and encountered on the beach, had also been seen on the island.

Around mid-day American spy drones spotted a civilian attempt to parachute onto the island. The parachutist dropped from several thousand meters towards the island plateaux but a thousand meters above it, his parachute appeared to collapse around him and he slid in a graceful arc down to the edge of the island, where he began falling again. Though his parachute clearly entangled him, he did not fall quickly, but rather floated down, and was soon deposited safely into the sea, from where, he swam the short distance to shore.

The Americans immediately dropped a spy plane to sea level and tried to fly it over the island. This too met with resistance, slid down the invisible bubble that seemed to encase the alien base, and it floated down to the sea, to be retrieved several hours later by an underwater recovery team. From this the intelligence team concluded that the alien island had some sort of invisible barrier protecting it.

In the late afternoon an event on the island created a big stir in the Intelligence suite on the Ulysses. A large black cigar-shaped object appeared suddenly on the landing field situated at the front of the island. Bing had been watching a live feed of the area at the time. One moment the landing field was empty, the next moment, as if by magic, a large cigar like object was sitting on the grass.

Bing ran the tape again in slow motion. In a few frames it was possible, with magnification, to make out a small black ball appearing from nowhere, which grew instantaneously into a cigar shape. The original black ball was identical to the cigar in every detail, save size. Bing thought she'd seen something like a flicker of lightening come from the silver dome, at the instant the cigar appeared, but this had not been captured on any footage.

By early evening Bing's orders had changed. She was to join the American delegation at the reception in New Delhi as Alien Adviser to the American Ambassador. The USS Ulysses was ordered up the coast so Bing could be taken off ship by a helicopter.

The chopper ride gave Bing the chance to catch up with reports she'd received. The first report summarised observations made of the alien's behaviour on the beach, which drew the unsurprising conclusion that the aliens liked to party. More informative was a report from inside the Indian delegation which had met with Commodore Wayfarer. According to the report, the aliens called the big sphere the Astrosphere, and the floating island, Sashoo, of which, Commodore Wayfarer was the captain. Three alien species were confirmed, a tall humanoid species that referred to themselves as the Langonai, a short humanoid species capable of flying and calling themselves the Cherubim and an insectoid species called the Vespida.

Bing's helecopter made its approach to New Delhi International Airport. Over the chopper comm she heard air clearance being given to a craft which was arriving from Sashoo and cleared to land at the Presidential Palace.

When Bing arrived at the palace, darkness was falling and many delegates had already arrived to greet the aliens. Bing was taken directly to the American Ambassador who was waiting in the terrace gardens. There She briefed him on the aliens.

Once the American delegation reached the State Room, Bing was taken off to the side, along with other advisers and security staff, while the Ambassador went to line up with the American delegation at the far end of the line of waiting dignitaries. The Chinese Peoples Representative fumed and hissed at the indignity of being so far down the line, but the American Ambassador, a seasoned diplomat, knew when to fight, and when to put on his best smile and claim it had all been a big misunderstanding. With the President's popularity falling like a rock back home, and yet another 'war costs' domestic crisis on the horizon, it was clear the President needed to back peddle any apparent hostility and get the aliens to a ticker tape parade in New York as soon as possible, his success in the next election depended on it.

There were as many attendants as delegates and Bing found herself in a crowded room split into two groups. One one side security staff waited anxiously while their charges were out of sight, and on the other personal assistants were unsure whether to return to the terrace or to wait in the anti-room for the return of their delegate.

Taking an orange juice from a long table of drinks Bing stood watching the groups. Suddenly a voice behind her asked, "You with the Americans then lass?" Bing turned to see a handsome middle aged man looking at her with a warm smile and a glint in his eyes.

"Yes," she replied. "I'm science advisor to the American Ambassador," she wasn't quite sure why she was telling him this.

"Thought so, I saw you with the Ambassador. I'm with David Shawdale, you know, the Starman?" he said. "I'm Bob Harding of Harding's Telescopes, it was a Harding telescope that David discovered the star with."

"But you didn't get invited to meet the aliens," Bing stated.

"Unfortunately, no," Bob confessed, "but I'm hoping to meet an alien anyway. Have you met one yet?"

"No, not yet," Bing replied.

They chatted a moment or two longer before Bob excused himself and Bing was left nursing her glass of orange juice while she waited. As midnight approached delegates began leaving the State Room, and with them, the aliens. Bing now had her chance to get close to one of these creatures. She went over to the American Ambassador who was deep in conversation with a Langonai humanoid.

The alien towered a good head above the humans. "Ah Colonel Saunders, I'd like to introduce you to Diamond. Diamond this is Colonel Saunders, my scientific advisor."

Bing got her first close look at an alien. Diamond, like most of the Langonai, had long hair. Diamond's head was about the same size as

Bing's, but the jaw pushed forward creating a small chin and a slight fox like look. The alien had wide shoulders and a slim waist. The jacket Diamond wore and the shirt underneath were loose fitting and he, or she, might be concealing breasts, it was not possible to tell.

"Colonel Saunders," Diamond leant forward and held out a slender, long fingered hand, to be shaken in the human fashion.

"Diamond, is that really your name?" Bing asked looking up into the eyes of the creature. The iris were oval and of a blue far deeper than any humans, the eyelids decorated, with shimmering blue eye shadow.

Diamond smiled, "Some of us have chosen to take Earth words as our names. These are more familiar to you and less threatening are they not?"

"So you pose no threat then?" Bing asked.

"No no my dear Colonel. Well perhaps biologically, but then it's already far too late to worry about that." Diamond looked at Bing.

"Biological threat?" Bing asked.

"Certainly, if we're genetically close enough, then you may catch some of our diseases, and we may catch some of yours. These may or may not be lethal, we just don't know," the alien said matter of factly.

"You mean we could all get galactic flu and die, like the Aztec's who were wiped out by the common cold?" Bing asked incredulously.

"It's a possibility, yes," Diamond replied. "Unlikely, but possible."

Much as she disliked the idea of potentially lethal alien diseases in Earth's' atmosphere, Bing's primary objective was assessing the alien's military capability, "Do you have weapons on Sashoo?" she asked.

Diamond laughed. "Yes we have weapons but we have no intention of using them. We're not here to invade, we don't need to. We have the Astrosphere, it contains everything we need. No, we have come to visit, we're tourists, if you like, and we hope also to exchange information and trade with you."

"Such as?" Bing asked.

"Knowledge, art, minerals, foods and spices, sports, recipes, the possibilities are enormous. Naturally we appreciate that, like us, Earth is totally sufficient, but there's so much we can share if you so wish. Think of it as a cultural exchange." Diamond turned to the Ambassador, "You know Ambassador, we're keen to visit your country if that could possibly be arranged."

"I'm sure that can be arraigned," the Ambassador said showing great pleasure at this suggestion.

"We're also keen to establish sovereignty for Sashoo, "Diamond continued. "Naturally there are many international details to be ironed out before this can happen, but we would be very appreciative of America's support in this. It's our understanding that America has great influence on this planet."

"Yes, that is so," the Ambassador agreed. "I'll speak to the President about it personally, first chance I get," which the Ambassador knew would be the moment the meeting was over.

"I wonder, Ambassador, if you could answer a few questions about your country. I won't ask you about your military arrangements of course."

"No of course not," the Ambassador agreed.

"Tell me ambassador, the statue that stands at the entrance to your City of New York, was this some great ruler?"

"No no, that's The Statute of Liberty, she represents an idea, an ideal if you like, equality, fraternity, liberty."

"Ah philosophy, there is so much to share, and no doubt you have an advanced legal system as well?"

"We lock up our criminals," Bing said. "How do you punish yours?"

"We confine criminals also. They are not permitted on Sashoo, that is to say, if you commit a crime on Sashoo you'll be returned to the Astroshpere where we have an area for criminals."

"How many people do you have on Sashoo?" Bing asked.

"Being merely a passenger, I couldn't really say, tens of thousands probably. That sort of information only the Lowai Clan or the Captain would know."

While they were talking Bing noticed a strange kind of movement in the folds of the alien's jacket. Now she looked it seemed as if the jacket had a second set of sleeves hanging inside the armpit. Bing thought at first that these sleeves were decoration, but then she noticed the strips of cloth flicked and twitched occasionally, as if with a life of their own.

"Ah Colonel, you admire my jacket?" Diamond observed.

Bing pointed to the jacket, "These extra sleeves, are they ceremonial?"

"You are very perceptive Colonel." As the alien spoke, it's sleeves lifted up of their own accord. The smooth material slipped back to reveal a second set of arms, shorter and thinner than the upper or outer arms, and ending in child sized hands. "There are a few physical differences between us," Diamond said.

"Besides your height." The Ambassador said.

"Indeed Ambassador." Diamond replied.

"We differ from humans in another, important, way. Unlike humans we do not have two genders, we have only one. We are hermaphrodite, which is why you find us to have an androgynous appearance. We are neither male nor female," Diamond explained, "Or you may prefer to think of us as both male and female at the same time. We Langonai are able to both inseminate and conceive. For this reason, because we bare children, we refer to ourselves in the feminine."

Hence the ambiguity of appearance, thought Bing. The small heads and breasts giving them a feminine quality while the broad shoulders needed to support two sets of arms, and the narrow waists gave a masculine shape to the upper body. Because of the many layered outfit Diamond wore, it wasn't possible to learn anything further about her physical appearance.

"And the other species you travel with? What are they?" Bing asked.

"Ah yes, the diminutive Cherubim and the insectoid Vespida, naturally you would be interested in them, they are so different from us."

"We don't have anything like them here on

Earth," the Ambassador told Diamond.

"We have three sapient species on Sashoo, and two primary cultures. The Cherubim and Langonai, being primate-like mammals, have an interwoven culture. Unlike us the Cherubim are heterosexual, they are winged, and the children fly, but usually loose this ability in adulthood due to weight gain. The Vespida are entirely different. They are hive or colony beings who's intelligence is distributed amongst the colonies individuals. We communicate with them using sounds, smells and gestures. The soldier Vespida have venomous stings, obey orders unquestioningly, and to the death, because of this they are formidable close-quater fighters and make excellent body guards."

"Fascinating," the Ambassador replied.

At that moment Bing heard a familiar voice in her ear, "Hello there."

It was Bob Harding, "Mr. Harding," Bing greeted him coldly, she felt unaccountably flattered by his attention, and was annoyed with herself for doing so.

Bob gave Bing a look which said, "Well introduce me then," and before she knew it she was introducing Bob to Diamond.

"Diamond, this is Bob Harding."

"Hi, pleased to meet you, Bob said holding out

his hand. Diamond took his hand and gave it a short shake.

"I'm a businessman from England, I'm in telescopes." Bob said.

As they were talking, a group of aliens came by, surrounded by a throng of delegates.

"If it's business you're interested in then there's the person you should be talking to," Diamond said, pointing to an alien with long blond hair, and wearing a bright red sequinned jacket. "Fortune is your lady."

Diamond called out to the blond haired Langonai who came over and joined them.

Diamond introduced Fortune to Bob.

Fortune smiled on Bob with white teeth and lipstick red lips. She was shorter and broader than Diamond and looked at Bob with deep purple oval eyes, "We're hoping to be able to do much business with Earth. What kind of business are you in?"

"Telescopes, optical devices, but we're branching out into other technologies," Bob replied.

"Technology. We may have something to offer you in that field," Fortune said. "Come with me and we'll arrange a meeting." Bob left with Fortune's group.

"Mr. Ambassador, if I may arrange to meet you at your offices tomorrow morning?" Diamond asked.

"Of course, I'm at your service," the Ambassador replied.

"Ten o'clock?"

"Perfect."

"Well if you'll excuse me I feel I should circulate," Diamond said, giving the Ambassador a short bow, and Bing and the Ambassador found themselves momentarily alone together.

"I hope you found out whatever it was you needed to know," the Ambassador said.

"Some," she was troubled by a feeling that she was missing something. The aliens seemed open enough, keen to communicate, yet she couldn't shake the feeling that there was something she wasn't being told.

The Ambassador excused himself on the grounds, he was tired, and leaving for the Embassy. Bing was about to accompany him, when she was approached by a small group of humans and aliens.

"Colonel Saunders?" a tall blond man asked.

"Yes?" She replied.

"I'm Sven Erickson from the Swedish delegation? I'm science advisor to the President of Sweden, and this is Seelow." He introduced Bing to a Cherubim.

Bing smiled at the Cherubim and bending down offered her hand but the Cherubim bowed back instead.

"We prefer not to shake hands, we feel squeezing fingers like a baby is undignified," Seelow said. Close up Bing could see the creature was tiny in every respect. Seelow was less than two-feet high. His head was long, thin, aerodynamic, the ears small and flat, the nose and jaw protruding forward and, except for the ears, Bing thought they looked more like chubby pixies than Cherubim. Seelow wore a simple red and gold robe and deliciously tiny gold sandals, encasing doll sized toes. The Cherubim were, Bing thought, extremely cute. Protruding from the back of Seelow's toga were two arm-like limbs which came above his head and hung down almost to the ground. Those must be the folded wings, Bing thought.

"There's so much knowledge we can exchange which will be of benefit to both our species," Seelow continued in a high pitched melodic voice, "We're forming a scientific exchange group and thought you would be interested."

"We are arranging a seminar in Stockholm, "Sven Erickson said. "Seelow has agreed to bring a group of Sashooian scientists and we can exchange knowledge."

"I would be honoured to be included," Bing said. She doubted her bosses would be pleased to hear the Swedes were hosting the seminar. The Americans would definitely want to influence it as much as possible.

"There is much we can learn from each other," the Cherubim said, his English stilted from unfamiliarity.

"There's much we can learn from you," Bing said. "Like how you can make an island float, the barrier it's protected by, and how you make your craft appear."

"Ah, yes, I'm sure you find these things most intriguing," Seelaw said. "We will see what can be done." Seelaw was interrupted suddenly as "oohhs" and "aahhs" rose from the humans and aliens standing on the palace terraces.

People were staring at the sky. The Astrosphere had risen and a familiar image was emblazoned across it's face. There, up in the night sky, Leonardo Da Vinci's Vitruvian Man was etched onto the Astroshere's surface. The four arms and four legs of man spread to make the points of a circle, a many limbed renaissance Vishnu, symbolising the similarity between human and Langonai, as if Leonardo had known by some magical means, that they would arrive.

Chapter 12 – Extraordinary guests

Dai was very excited. Since the aliens had landed, schoolyard talk had been of nothing else. What were they like? What was their island like? What kept it in the sky? Did they all have wings? Did they have eight limbs each? Every scrap of news, every picture and television interview was absorbed and talked about endlessly. Now Dai had something no one else in school had, something even Gaku and Waku couldn't sully, something even better than a kiss from Saiko. He wasn't so keen on Saiko any more anyway, not since she had started hanging out with those two, and now he had something that would make Saiko wish she had been friends with him instead.

Dai had had little interested in his father's work. Until recently he had seen what his father did as something boring at the Ministry of Foreign Affairs. There had been a trip to Africa a few years back, but then the Saint Petersburg Summit had happened, bringing his father a promotion and leading to his inclusion in the Japanese delegation to New Delhi. Now his father was an alien expert, now that his father had met an actual alien, now he was really interesting.

Over and over again Dai made his father tell the story of how he met the aliens, every detail was repeated endlessly to his friends at school. That had been weeks ago though, now everyone at school had an alien story. Now everyone knew someone who had met one, or knew someone who knew someone who had met an alien, and no one else in school had a Dad who'd met one. As each week went by the kinds of alien people claimed to have met became stranger and more exotic.

Then Melody had arrived. She was gorgeous. All the boys fancied her, all the girls wanted to be her. She had first appeared on American television on a children's show. She was the teenage daughter of one of the Langonai who were touring Earth and had been visiting America. The aliens said they'd come to see the great tourist sights such as, the Statue of Liberty, the Grand Canyon, Disneyland, and the Lincoln Memorial.

Melody's meteoric rise to fame began the day the aliens visited Disneyland. The entire park was closed to the public and the event was to be televised by the Disney Corporation. The aliens arrived in their strange craft. Invited guests were bused in on little tractor trains. The day promised excitement and thrills for everyone.

TV Cameras panned to the sky as the alien's craft arrived. It resembled a Zeppelin without the balloon, boat shaped with a flat roof and flat bottom. The craft was white with the windows, doors and hatches mounted in brass fittings. The bowed front gave the occupants a panoramic view of wherever they were headed.

The gondola ship drifted silently down to the car park. A gangplank was lowered from the rear end of the vessel and the visitors trooped out. There were about forty of them, humanoids and Cherubim, adults and children, none of the Vespida though, which had disappointed Kanji. He ahd come over to Dai's house so they could watch the event together, and Kanji was particularly keen on the mysterious Vespida.

They watched as the aliens enjoyed themselves on the rides, watching main street parade, and being photographed with Mickey Mouse. The Mousketeers played host to the alien children and took them to see a middle-of-the-road teens band. During the performance one of the alien children asked one of the Mousketeer if she could sing a song. There was some fussing while microphones were set-up and musicians arraigned then, with an sparkling performance of Puppy Love, Melody won the adoration of every teenager on Earth. She might have been from a different world but the young alien star was signed to a performing contract before she had got out of the park and back to the gondola.

Now the shops were full of Melody's songs. She was the most pirated singer on the planet, and she seemed to be on a television station somewhere in the world everyday. Melody quickly adopted traditional Earth female teen star dress, short skirt, tight jumper and over the knee white stockings. Unlike the adult aliens she didn't hide her extra arms in folds of cloth, quite the reverse, she showed them off. She used them when she was singing, sometimes to hold the microphone and sometimes she would play with a glittering ball or trail a silk ribbon with them.

At school, some of the girls had started to stitch ribbons or even attach stuffed arms to their blouses to be more like Melody, and with her long blond hair, bleaching and wigs had become popular. Even some of the boys had taken to wearing fake arms. One at Dai's school had even made arms that actually moved, though really they only bent at the elbow. There were Melody dolls, Melody play sets, complete with Melody model gondola, a Melody drink and Melody sweets and even a Melody hamburger. Melody mania gripped the teenage world.

The thing that got Dai so excited however, was not Melody, it was much better than her. His father was going to bring an actual alien to his house, tonight, for dinner. Apparently an alien in the delegation to Japan had expressed a wish to see how the Japanese people lived and his father had offered to host them. Now, he, Dai Wakami, was going to meet a real alien face to face, he'd be the first in his school, the only one. He knew he would immediately become the schoolyard authority on all things alien.

His mother had been in a fluster all afternoon. Rushing around their Tokyo flat cleaning and cooking and getting her hair done, not only was she entertaining aliens but Dai's Father's boss and wife as well.

"Will you clean your room now Dai?" she shouted at him for the fourth time.

"No, you can't wear your Char Azimo costume or whatever it's called. You'll wear your best suit. The one we bought you for your cousin's wedding," he'd been told in no uncertain terms.

His father had come home early from work to help prepare.

"What do they eat?" was his Mother's first question. "What do we serve them?"

His father took a file from his case, flicked through it, then said, "Well almost anything apparently. I'd suggest some traditional Japanese dishes, the best of everything."

"Well what do they like?"

"It doesn't say. Only that they eat Earth food."

"How many of them are coming?" she asked.

"Four." his father replied. "Two humanoid adults a child and a Cherubim."

"A Cherubim." His mother wailed. "And just what do Cherubim eat? what do they sit on? They're the small ones aren't they?"

"They want to see us at home, experience life as we do, so don't worry dear," he reassured her. "You always make our guests very comfortable.

Everything will be fine."

The smells of food and expensive perfume, hair spray and air freshener filled the flat. Dai had his hair brushed straight by his mother only to have his Dad mess it as he got the "you'll be on your best behaviour now won't you?" speech.

The moment the doorbell rang his mother turned instantly, from a nervous wreck, into a pool of calm, tranquil Japanese reserve and politeness. His father's boss, Mr. Kasaku, and his wife were at the door. There were formal greetings, bowing and more bowing. Mrs. Kasaku was introduced to Mrs. Wakami and their son.

"I think a suit and tie might be too formal," Mr. Kasaku, who was wearing a polo neck jumper, said to Dai's father. His father went immediately to change into something similar to Mr. Kasaku.

Mrs. Wakami showed the Kasakus into the front room and offered them a drink. Dai's father came back wearing a jumper which received a nod of approval from Mr. Kasaku. Everyone stood around in uncomfortable silence. In the corner of the room Dai rubbed his shoe nervously against the back of his trouser leg.

"There are some exceptionally good seasonal vegetables available in the markets at the moment," Mrs. Kasaku said by way of small talk. For a few minutes the room filled with cautious chatter about the relative merits of locally grown carrots and lotus imported from the China. The doorbell rang again.

Everyone stood to attention in the hallway, lining up in order of importance. Mrs. Wakami as the lady of the house was to open the door, then Mr. Wakami, Mr. Kasaku, Mrs. Kasaku and, at the back, stood Dai.

The aliens entered. First a Langonai who bent her head low to come in through the door. Then a second humanoid who also had to bow to enter. They were followed by a Cherubim and finally a third Langonai who was short enough to enter without bending.

Bowing and introductions filled the small hallway and the guests were shown into the front room. The two tall humanoids sat down on the small sofa, it was clear they would be banging their heads on the ceiling lights if they moved around too much.

The first alien, Merit, wore a kimono-like outfit. Dai could see it wasn't an authentic traditional kimono, the pattern had been modified under the arms. The second alien, Forest, wore the familiar alien jacket and long skirt. The Cherubim, Kailon, wore slacks and a polo neck, Dai thought he looked like a mini version of Mr. Kasaku. But it was the fourth member of the group that Dai was interested in, Neko. She was Forest's daughter and a fellow teenager.

Being at the bottom of the pecking order Neko and Dai were the last to enter the living room.

For a brief moment the two were alone in the hallway and caught each others eye. Dia looked into the deep purple oval iris for an instant, before glancing nervously away. In the front room Dai and Neko found themselves relegated to a corner between the sofa and Dai's Father's favourite chair which Mr. Kasaku was currently occupying.

"Now you will look after Neko properly won't you," Dai's mother insisted before turning back to her conversation with Forest and Mrs. Kasaku.

"Would you like a drink?" Dai asked politely.

Neko smiled shyly at him at him and nodded.

"What can I get you? Orange juice? A coke?" he offered.

She shrugged. Dai waited. Then, in a small voice and perfect Japanese, she said. "An orange juice would be nice thank you Daisan."

Dai fussed with the drinks, getting himself an orange juice at the same time, then the teenagers stood once again in awkward silence sipping from their glasses.

"You can drink orange juice then?" Dai asked eventually and immediately realised what a stupid question that was and felt an idiot.

Neko nodded. "We can drink most human beverages." She said in a voice that was barely above a whisper.

"What about alcohol?" Dai asked. "Do you get drunk?"

"Well not me," Neko said.

"I meant your species," Dai said.

"Oh, yes, I think so, I'm not sure. We have something similar to alcohol ourselves but I'm too young to drink it."

"You're a teenager like me then?" Dai asked.

"I suppose I am," Neko replied timorously.

"What do you think of Melody?" he asked.

"I don't really know her." Neko said. "We don't understand why Earth children are so keen on her. You have so many musicians who are better."

"But she's the only alien one," Dai explained.

"Alien?" Neko asked.

Dai was embarrassed. "I mean Astrospherian."

They were interrupted by Dai's mother ushering everyone through to the dining room for something to eat. The Astrospherians had brought wine from Sashoo. Dai was determined, even at risk of death, to have a taste of this wine, to say he'd drunk alien wine, that would be so cool.

"You don't use money in the Astrosphere?" Mr. Kasaku was asking Merit.

"No, everything necessary is provided by the Clan. Beyond necessities, access is dependant on status. A clan with high status has more in it's vaults and greater access to the Astrosphere's resources, while your status within the clan determines your entitlement to Clan resources." Merit replied. "For instance, as high ranking members of the Tarakoi, we have choice in vehicles, available living and working structures, and are allowed rare or valuable things like wine stock, library resources, scientific equipment and so on."

"So everyone is in a clan?" Mr. Kasaku asked.

"Not everyone, but almost everyone. Occasionally people are cast out of their clan and sometimes outcasts breed, however the children of these exiles are frequently welcomed back into the clan in time. Anyway outcasts are provided for, no one goes without food or housing in the Astrosphere. The clan's drwa their labour source from outcasts and those who which to rise through the ranks."

"And what of the Vespida?" Mr. Kasaku asked.

"Ah yes, the Vespida, they do not mix well with other species. The relationship we have with them is one of mutual benefit. Individually the

Vespida are stupid, seemingly unintelligent, like one of your dogs or a monkey, but they're not individuals like you and me, they're a colony, a hive being. At the pinnacle of their society is the Queen. We have inserted ourselves into their consciousness as a kind of royalty, princesses if you like, who need to be helped and protected, in return for which we provide for the colony. Freed from the need to fight and scavenge for food and shelter, they are able to breed, work for, and protect us. On the Astrosphere we breed drones for domestic tasks and soldiers as bodyguards and protecting clan property." Merit explained.

"I see." Mr. Kasaku said.

"Are they the ones with wings?" Dai asked.

Merit turned her sharp eyes on Dai. "Yes, they also have a venomous sting which is lethal to most species."

"On the subject of toxicity," Mr. Kasaku continued. "How is it you are able to eat Earth food? Why take the risk?"

"In our experience life in the universe is remarkably similar from planet to planet. Life supporting planets are quite rare because life can only exist within a small band of parameters. You may say, a cold virus can exist in outer space, but it is dormant, it's neither dead nor alive, it is waiting to become alive. No complex life form has been found to exist outside the conditions illustrated by Earth. It's what I believe you call, the Goldilocks Effect."

"Every species comes from an Earth-like planet?" Dai asked.

"That is correct. All other conditions must be present on a planet. A small difference in one thing or another can leave it lifeless and barren. Too hot or too cold, too large or too small. Look at your own Mars. Just that little bit too far out and it's cold barren and lifeless. Mercury, to close and hot, has a deadly atmosphere. No, all life bearing planets share much in common, the basis of life in the universe, is universal."

"Take Kailon here for example. He is a Cherubim. His ancestors came from a completely different planet to the Langonai, he looks very different from us, but look again, look how similar he is to us. The Cherubim map to ninety three percent of our genes. Now that isn't close enough to breed, but it is close, I think you'll agree."

Their conversation moved on to comparative food types, fruits and other dull agricultural topics. Neko tugged at Dai's sleeve. I need to go somewhere private," she said.

"I'll show you," Dai replied glad to get away from the adults and the need to be on his best behaviour.

"I'm just showing Neko where the bathroom is," he told his mother, leaving the room with Neko.

"Wow, I'm glad to be out of there," Neko said. " My Mother gets so intense." She paused and looked concerned. "Can I let you into a little secret?" she asked.

"Sure," Dai said. "You can trust me."

"Can we go to your room?" Neko asked.

She sat on the edge of his bed and he sat on the chair next to the small desk which he used when doing his homework.

"I've got something to show you. I wasn't supposed to bring it..." she said, as something moved beneath her robes.

Dai thought she was going to reveal her extra arms and was about to tell her he already knew all about them when something flew out of her sleeve. The tiny creature, no more than seven inches tall, fluttered around the room. Dai almost fell of his chair in fright.

"What's that?" he spluttered.

"That's Koneko, my Cherubim," Neko laughed.

"You own a Cherubim?" Dai exclaimed in suprise.

"No, no," Neko laughed. "You don't own Cherubim, she's my friend."

"She's so cute and tiny, like a pixie," Dai said, enchanted by the diminutive creature that now sat on Niko's shoulder, holding Niko's hair for support and dangling it's doll like legs. The bat wings, half opened to help keep the Cherubim's balance. The creature leant and whispered into Niko's ear. Niko laughed.

"She says she's glad to be out of my robe for a bit. I think she was getting rather hot, but she wanted to come, she wanted to meet a human," Neko explained.

"Pleased to make your acquaintance, Koneko," Dai said, standing up and bowing to Koneko.

Koneko fluttered down, landed on Dai's desk and bowed back at him. A series of high pitched squeaks came from her, sounding not unlike those of a mouse.

"She says she is pleased to meet you, Daisan," Neko interpreted.

"She can talk? I mean you can talk?" Dai asked Koneko.

Neko translated for Koneko and they both giggled. " Yes, she can talk. Indeed, she does far too much talking if you ask me, but that's young Cherubim for you, they fly and chatter and play tricks on each other. They don't get fat and boring till they become adults."

The Cherubim squeaked again. "She wants to see your toys, your games. Cherubim love games," Neko told him.

Dai pulled some of his toys from a cupboard. A baseball bat, some model cars and aircraft, a couple of board games, a yoyo, and embarrassingly, an old teddy fell out. He didn't want Neko thinking he was childish. Koneko flew down from the desk and began rummaging through the toys that Dai had produced.

"Maybe this will entertain her," Dai said, picking up his old yoyo. He reckoned he still had the touch even though he hadn't used the thing in a long time. He wound the string carefully round the spindle, making sure it was just right on his finger, and flicked the yoyo up and down a few times before doing a couple of simple tricks.

Neko and Koneko were fascinated. "You can have this," he said, offering Neko the yoyo.

"I can? Thanks," she said. "Can you show me how it works?"

"Dai explained how to use the yoyo and soon Neko had the hang of it. "You can make it do lots of tricks," Dai said. "But it takes a lot of practice."

"This is so delightfully primitive," Neko said. Dai was a little taken aback at this remark and he defended his toy. "It's an ancient Earth toy. Apparently the Greeks used them in war over five thousand years ago."

"I have something for you," Neko said, reaching into the folds of her robe which had a pocket.

First she produced a small cube the size of the Cherubim's head, which she offered to Koneko who grabbed it in both tiny hands and started eating it. Then she produced a palm sized disc, similar in shape to the yoyo, but slightly larger and without the central groove.

"Now where is it?" she mumbled to herself hunting around in her pocket. "It won't work without the ring. Ah ha." She produced a finger ring with a flourish. She put the ring, which looked as if it were made of glass or crystal, on her finger and held the disc in the same hand. After stroking the disc with her fingers it began to glow, then it rose up from her open palm.

As the disc floated a few inches above her hand, Neko moved her fingers and the disc began to float around her. After a few orbits Neko strummed her fingers and the disc began to move in a more complex pattern, shooting back and forth in front and then behind her, dipping and weaving around the furniture as if on some invisible string.

Dai's jaw dropped. He'd never seen anything like it. His friends Kanji and Tenkou would be so green with envy. Neko gave him the disc and slipped the ring onto his finger.

"The trick is all in the fingers," she said. "Slot the edge of the ring into the groove on the side of the disc, and you'll feel the disc trying to rise," Neko told him.

Dai did so and felt a force like two magnets trying to push each other apart. "Now let go of the disc."

Dai let go and the disc began to float, just as it had done for Neko. "Good, good, you have it. Now if you wiggle your fingers the disc will begin to move," she instructed.

As Dai did so the disc shot across the room, giving a Godzilla figurine such a good crack on its plastic head it was knocked to the floor. The glow from the disc flickered then died and the disc fell to the floor.

Neko laughed. "Be more gentle in your movements," she advised. "And don't worry, the disc will only travel a foot or two from your hand before it become inactive again." She passed the inert disc back to Dai.

"How do I get it to come back?" He asked. Neko laughed. "It's all in the fingers, keeping the disc in range and bringing it back are two of the skills you need to learn. I think with practice you will master it." She told him.

He was about to have another go when his mother came in.

Koneko shot back into Neko's robe. Dai wondered if his mother had seen the creature flitting across the room, but she seemed more concerned that the two of them were alone together in Dai's room. "I think you'd both better come back downstairs," she advised. They followed her out of the room.

The conversation in the dinning room was no more interesting now than it had been when Dai and Neko left, but nothing, not even the wine he'd been able to sneek a sip of, was as exciting as having met Neko and Koneko and the yoyo disc Niko had given him as a present. Soon afterwards it was time for the Astrospherians and Mr. and Mrs. Kasaku to make their excuses.

"Can I see you again?" Dai asked Neko as she was leaving.

"I don't know." she said. "I'll have to ask my Mother."

"Mother, can I visit with Dai again sometime?" She asked Forest. Forest looked at Neko and then to Mrs. Wakami who nodded.

"I don't see why not," Forest said, in the gentle sing-song tone of her species. "I'm sure we can arrange something."

That night Dai went to bed full of excitement. He'd never been so eager to go to school.

Chapter 13 – Four months later

Several months had passed since David returned from the New Delhi reception. The last time David had seen Bob was at Delhi International Airport as David boarded a direct flight to Heathrow. Bob had stayed in New Delhi to pursue business opportunities with the aliens. So it came as a pleasant surprise when he heard Bob's voice on the phone.

"You're back from New Delhi then?" David asked.

"I am, I am. I've been travelling quite a bit lately," Bob said. "On business. Look I'm having a bit of a get together for a few friends and associates over the weekend. I was hoping you could join us," Bob said.

"Oh, sure, just let me check. This weekend you say. I'm giving a talk in London on Friday afternoon, so I should be back home Friday night and I'm free the rest of the weekend." David told him.

"That's great. I'll have you picked up Saturday morning then. It'll be an overnight stay so do bring your toothbrush," Bob added.

Great thought David, that's the weekend sorted.

The lecture in London went well, another packed room and another audience excited about the arrival of the aliens. His new role as the UK's leading television authority on aliens was keeping his new media career rolling along. He got back to Durham in good time, packed a small case for his over night stay and went to bed.

The following morning, enjoying a leisurely breakfast in the new conservatory he'd recently treated himself to, he heard noises in the street. Opening his front door it looked like a riot was happening. The street was full of people running up and down, shouting and screaming. He thought he saw a camera crew at the end of the road, and wondered what was going on. Taking a bite of his now cold toast, a shadow suddenly fell across his doorstep and the crowd went quiet. He looked up to see a large white gondola shaped object falling towards him. His immediate reaction was to duck back into the doorway, but when the gondola didn't come crashing down on to his house he looked up again. Something the size of an lorry was descending into his back garden.

He went through the house and watched as the gondola came to rest on air, a foot or so above the begonias. He noticed a small ornamental fir tree bent under the gondola's base. A hatch opened at one end of the craft which descended to the ground, forming a ramp. A small plump figure in jeans, tee-shirt and a yachting cap came hopping down the ramp.

"Bob Harding has sent me to collect you. Are you ready Mr. Shawdale?" the Cherubim asked.

"I, er, just need to, er, get my case," David said.

"No rush Mr. Shawdale, at your convenience." The convivial Cherubim appeared to be the only occupant of the gondola and was presumably it's pilot. The Cherubim then leant casually against the doorway of the gondola and began to smoke what, to David, looked like a cigarette.

While the Cherubim smoked, David grabbed his overnight case, checked the heating and the lights were off, except the one in the living room, just in case of burglars. He peeked at the crowd in the street from behind his living room curtains, and then having ensured the doors were all locked, he walked up the ramp into the waiting craft.

David had seen the alien gondolas before, on television and in New Delhi, but he'd never been close up to one let alone inside one. The hatchway ramp swung smoothly back up and closed seamlessly behind him. At the front of the cabin David saw the Cherubim stood next to a large steel coloured wheel and a variety of leavers and dials which was clearly the helm.

"Make yourself comfortable," the Cherubim called over his shoulder as he began to manipulate the craft's controls. There was no sensation of movement at all as the craft rose up above the garden and the street. Below him, David could see the amassed gawkers and onlookers, their camera phones clicking, jostling for a better look. The street fell quickly below while the motion of the gondola was imperceptible.

David sat on the red velvet coloured bench that ran along the wall of the gondola. He noticed there were a couple of small rooms near the hatchway which he assumed were the toilet and maybe storage space?

"We'll be arriving in about twenty minutes," the Cherubim said, hop-walking over. Apparently he didn't need to be at the helm the whole time. "Would you like a drink?" he said, going over to the starboard room and opened the door. Inside was a small galley. "I've got coffee and tea or whisky if you like? Or perhaps you'd like to try a Sashooian drink?"

The pilot showed David a smooth brown liquid with a purple tinge and small frothy bubbles on top. David thought he'd risk the Sashooian drink. It was served warm and sweet and tasted like nothing he'd ever had before.

"It's from a bitter bean not unlike your chocolate or coffee. Ii is believed to have an invigorating effect. Do you feel invigorated?" the Cherubim asked curiously.

"I'm not sure," David confessed. "This is all such a new experience for me. I'm already quite excited from the trip." The Cherubim shrugged and returned to the high stool in front of the helm.

David was draining the last drops of the delicious drink from his glass and wondering if it was addictive and how he could get some more, when the gondola began to descend towards open moorland. In the distance David could see the roof tops of a manor house, while below a rough line of people stood strung out across the heather.

The gondola came to rest next to two other identical gondola, sitting a foot or so above the purple tufts of heather and gorse. David felt a chill wind blow in as the hatchway opened and the ramp descended.

"Hello, David. " A cheery Bob was striding towards him through the heather and ferns. "Good of you to come. I hope you brought some walking boots. No of course you didn't, I forgot to mention we would be shooting grouse this morning. Don't know why, but I assumed it was something you didn't do yourself."

"Well I never have..." David replied cautiously.

"Do you want a go? There's time before lunch. We're just scaring up some more grouse now."

David decended the ramp and joined Bob. The heather was a little dew damp but the springy peat soil beneath was dry enough for David's city shoes.

"To be honest Bob I've never used a shotgun before," David confessed.

"Not to worry, neither had Sterling until today. Didn't take long to teach her though." Bob led David towards the group of shooters. Everyone except David was wearing shooting clothes He was introduced to a tall slender figure who, if he hadn't known otherwise, he would have mistaken for being a young man.

"Sterling has a novel way of shooting," Bob remarked. "She steadies the gun with both hands and uses her right small hand to pull the trigger." David watched as the humanoid put the shotgun to her shoulder, holding the gun with both hands on the barrel, one behind the other while a small hand took the trigger. A pair of grouse, roused from the heather by the beaters, came flapping towards the group. Stirling's gun went off twice and both birds fell. "Bloody good shot," Bob said, as a dog was sent to retrieve the carcasses.

"What do you think of that then eh?" Bob asked.

David thought he noticed a touch of the lord of the manor in Bob's tone, but he let it pass. "Good, good shot," he heard himself saying.

Bob found him a gun and showed him how to use it. More grouse came over but David's nervousness around guns, and his lack of skill in shooting, ensured the grouse were safe from him. After an hour without his coat David was beginning to feel cold. He was relieved to hear Bob tell everyone that there were hot drinks in the gondola and that they'd all be returning to the manor house shortly.

David warmed himself with another of the delicious drinks which were called Kaolate. His cold fingers slowly regained there ability to feel. Around him a general stomping of boots and blowing on hands was going on as everyone climbed aboard for the short ride to the elegant sandstone manor house that David had seen from the gondola.

After David had been shown to his room and had had a chance for a wash and brush up, he joined the others in the grand drawing room for a light buffet lunch. There were about twenty people altogether of whom David only knew one, Bob. However it appeared that amongst the humans he was something of a celebrity, many of them recognised him. The Astrospherians were understandably less interested in his star discovery, after all he hadn't actually discovered them, really, they had discovered Earth.

While eating a plate of prawn and beef vol-au-vent with fresh crusty bread and home made chutney Bob came over and said to him, "David, I must confess that I've an ulterior motive in inviting you this weekend. There is a little business I thought you might be interested in. Can we chat about it later?" With a mouth full of pastry delight, David nodded his assent and Bob moved on to mingle with his other guests.

As David wondered what the business could be about his thoughts were interrupted. "You must be David Shawdale," said a middle-aged looking man in a blue blazer. "I don't believe we've met before. I'm James Cavendish? Minister for the department of Business, Industry and Skills."

David recognised the man now, from the news.

"You known Bob long?" Cavendish asked.

"We go back." David replied.

"We're very pleased Bob Harding is flying the British flag in so many parts of the world now. Of course you'll know all about Harding Industries recent investments overseas. This is going to boost trade for Britain I can tell you. Bob was just telling me how successfully the move into Arabia has gone. Apparently the Arabs were practically falling over themselves to sell him the Dubai facility."

"Really, really," David said. He knew nothing about Bob's acquisitions. "Bob's keeping the whole thing close to his chest, apparently it's something to do with force fields?" Cavendish raised his eyebrows questioningly and David realised he was being pumped for information by the Minister.

"I couldn't say," David replied, intrigued by the Minister's line of questioning.

"No no of course not," Cavendish said, "I quite understand, it's just that, well the military is potentially interested and that could represent an awful lot of money."

"I'm sure," David replied. "I'm afraid you'll have to excuse me." David waved his glass vaguely in the direction of the food then swiftly made his way to the buffet.

Cavendish's talk of force fields interested David. What where they? Was this the same force that surrounded the floating island? Idling by the chocolate gateaux David found himself standing next to one of the Langonai.

"David Shawdale." David said holding out his hand and introducing himself to the alien.

"I'm Fortune," the androgynous alien replied. David noticed this alien was sporting a thin moustach.

"Bob Harding has mentioned you. You are his lucky star I think," Fortune said. David laughed.

"I guess that makes you Fortune from his lucky star," David joked.

"I think I will make him a fortune," Fortune replied smiling. "And he will make me one."

"Would that be from force fields?" David asked.

"Yes, indeed," Fortune replied picking up a vol-au-vent with a small hand. "We're working to create force-field technology that you can use here on Earth."

"We can't use the same technology the Astrosphere uses?" David asked.

"It is not as easy as that," Fortune replied. "The ship provides its own force fields but that would mean being entirely dependant on our ship. No, we think it better that we help you develop your own force field technology, that is why we have helped Harding Industries to acquire research centres all over the world."

"Like the Dubai one?" David asked.

The researchers in Dubai were working on a laser based technology, but we think the skills and much of the equipment can be redirected to force-field development."

"Wow," David said. "When do you think you'll have a solution and what kind of benefit can we get from the force-fields?"

"I don't really know yet, hopefully a force shield like the one that protects Sashoo," Fortune said. "I'm not a scientist myself, I'm more an organiser, a businessman like Bob. Harding Industries' scientists, tell me they're close to a solution, but you know scientists, they work on a different time scale to the rest of us," Fortune replied, smiling.

After the buffet lunch David returned to his room and set to work on some research papers, but a couple of hours later he was finding it difficult to keep his mind on science and instead found himself wondering about the aliens. Already he'd noted a change in the atmosphere brought on by the novelty of aliens on Earth and an excitement about their technologies such as force-fields, gondola flying machines, and who knew what else.

At eight o'clock David dressed in black tie and dinner jacket and descended the grand staircase to join the throng of guests. Liveried waiters carrying crystal glasses on silver trays threaded their way between brightly clad gaily chatting guests. Men in dinner jackets told each other golfing jokes women complemented each others hair and outfits.

In due course a gong was rung and people started to move in the direction of the great hall which was laid out for a feast. The guests sat down on ornate high backed chairs at the long table while the stuffed heads of long dead deer stared glassy eyed down at them from the stone walls. David found himself sat next to an attractive Langonai called Softly. She had dark green eyes, long straight red hair, and wore a shimmering figure-hugging dress, the green of which complemented her eyes, and the cut of which, revealed a very feminine body.

"I don't remember seeing you at the shoot this morning." He said.

"No, It didn't appeal to me," the alien replied. "I'm a friend of Fortune's, she invited me along."

"So, are you and Fortune partners then?" David asked Softly.

"We're very close, you don't have a word for our relationship," Softly replied.

"Your not married then or anything?" David asked.

"Langonai don't marry." Softly told him.

"Really? So you don't have a husband then?"

"No, none of us do. We're all the same sex."

"Then why do some of you dress like men and some like women?" David asked.

"It's a matter of personal choice. We have no distinction between the sexes the notion is faintly ridiculous to us. To us there's no male and female dress, just clothing. We like to look good, so we wear what we think we look good in, or like the look of, or what our friends tell us makes us look good, or what we think will make an impression on you," she smiled.

"So if your all the same sex do you pair at all?" David asked.

"No." Softly confirmed. "We don't pair like you and the Cherubim."

"Ah, the Cherubim, such an interesting name

they've chosen for themselves, except their wings aren't feathered and they don't seem to fly."

"The young ones do." Softly said. "They pair in early adulthood, after which they often gain too much weight to fly any more. An unpaired Cherubim is likely to remain single all their life. Once they mate they're bonded live," Softly explained.

"I see," David said. "Who looks after the children then?"

"The birth mother." Softly replied.

"How is the mother supported?" David asked.

"The clan is always there. The clan is extended through the generations, mother to daughter. While we inter-breed with other clans, you're born into your mother's clan. The father is nothing more than a provider of genetic diversity and has nothing more to do with the offspring. They're probably too busy having a daughter of their own."

David finished a mouthful of beef and sipped thoughtfully at the excellent red wine before saying. "So you don't have partners then?"

Softly laughed. "Oh, yes. Fortune and I are lovers. " She explained. "That's why I've come this weekend. But we're not a breeding pair nor have we had a daughter together. We're clan sisters, well, more distant cousins really."

"We're intrigued by your Earth customs. This week Fortune is being the man, and next week I will be the man, in bed and out. It's quite a laugh actually."

David swallowed, his British reserve telling him to feel a little uncomfortable with such a personal revaluation. "Do you have a job on the Astrosphere?" he asked, changing the subject.

"No, not really. To be honest there isn't a lot to be done on board, most things are automatic. Officially, the Lowai clan Pilot runs the ship, but in reality it's a motley crew of clanless and volunteers. Most of us are just intergalactic tourists, sightseers, along for the ride. The Astrosphere is quite capable of maintaining itself and our life support systems. As long as the population level remains below the maximum then there isn't a problem, and the Lowai strickly control birth rate. There's no breeding allowed on the Astrosphere without permission from the Lowai. It's why we commonly take lovers," she smiled at David.

Chapter 14 – Military failure

The Cherubim hopped across the laboratory floor and onto a stool. He looked up at Bing and smiled weakly.

"I'm sorry Colonel Bing." Jaycho said. "It's still not working."

On the other side of the laboratory a thin wisp of smoke rose from a collection of circuitry lying on a lab bench, the wires and assorted electronics giving off the smell of burnt plastic and solder.

"OK Jaycho. I guess we go again," Bing said.

"Perhaps we've not set-up the magnetic field correctly," Jaycho said hopefully.

"Sure, sure. Call me when you're ready for the next test run," Bing replied.

"We can do it I'm sure," Jaycho said eagerly, jump-walking alongside Bing. "We just need more time."

"I'm sure everyone is doing their best," Bing responded. They arrived at the science facility lobby where Bing bid Jaycho a good day.

A black limousine waited for Bing outside the thick glass doors of the science facility entrance and as she came out of the building the driver stepped smartly from the car, and opened the door for her.

"Ma'am," he said.

She climbed in to the car. God she hated being in Sweden. It wasn't anything about the country it was just where they weren't making scientific progress, that and the cold. Bing preferred the warmth of her own Southern United states.

The Scientific Exchange had been running for months. Culturally it was a roaring success. The Astrosphereians had no shortage of artists, endless paintings, costumes, music and sculptures had been exchanged. Earth had three new musical instruments, and the Astrospherians had gained violins and electric guitars.

Significant progress had been made in biology. The Astrospherians had provided detailed anatomical and medical data, including DNA samples. Scientists at the facility now knew a significant amount about the physical structure of the langonai and Cherubim. They knew their genetic structures were related enough for cross-contamination, but not enough for breeding, and it was suspected that contamination had already happened.

Interesting work was also going on in the area of mathematics through a general exchange of approaches to theoretical problems, however, technologically the humans had learnt nothing from the Astrosphereians. Despite the aliens apparent eagerness to help, it had all come to nothing.

The scientists didn't know how the force field around the island worked, they didn't know how it stayed up in the air. They didn't know how the gondola were made. It became clear to Bing and her team that the aliens they were dealing with were not trained scientists, they were keen amateurs, potting shed experimenters. Jaycho's delight at having a state-of-the-art laboratory at his disposal, and his remarks about the instruments made available to him, gave Bing the distinct impression that Jaycho and his team were as ignorant about the alien technology as the humans were.

Then there was the clan thing. Again and again the humans were told the clan library didn't have the required information, or they'd not found it yet, or they would ask other clans if they'd anything in their libraries. The Astrosphereians were unable, or unwilling, to provide any information which would allow humans to create similar technology.

The snow began to fall again as Bing's car arrived at Stockholm's American Embassy. The car moved sedately down the concrete ramp into the underground car park. A few minutes later after warming herself on the hot pipes in her office , she put in a secure satellite call to General Solomon.

"Another failure I'm afraid General," she

reported.

"I'm getting a lot of pressure from the top on this one Colonel," the General said, testily. "It's been months and we've nothing. Just one gondola, even a little one. would do right now."

"Yes Sir. We are trying, but we can't simply steal one we don't even know how to open the door. We just don't know if they would miss it, or recall it to the island, and if we got inside, we don't know how to fly them."

"Talking of which, do we have an agent on Sashoo yet?"

This was another frustration for Bing. She'd been trying to get an agent onto the island for months. Currently the aliens were in the process of flying the island across the Atlantic to Rio in Brazil. It had just passed the Cape of good hope moving westward from the Indian Ocean. It appeared aliens didn't like the Northern hemisphere winter any more than Bing did. The aliens played it by the book, before moving the island they waited for United Nations agreement, and official clearance from any nation whose territory they would pass, they even filed a flight plan. At any given time of the day or night, Bing knew exactly where the island was. The island and any gondola showed up on conventional radar, and Bing had five spy planes circling the island.

US Intelligence had measured everything they

could think of, above and below the island. Several times they'd tried to land on it, but every attempt was thwarted by the protective bubble. The only way onto the island was via the frustratingly elusive alien craft. Requests to visit the island had been politely refused. It was clear to Bing, despite the apparent openness of the aliens, humans were not to be completely trusted.

"What about these force field rumours?" General Solomon asked.

"The main source of the rumours is a British company called Harding Industries. Recently they've been buying up research facilities all over the world. We've placed operatives inside and it appears Harding Industries are no closer to a solution than we are. Our agent in their Oregon facility reports no production at the facility. The staff reconfigure and recalibrate equipment all the time, move lots of equipment from facility to facility but, nothing specific is being worked on. The whole thing strikes me as smoke screen."

"I agree Colonel. We need to know what they're up to. What are they hiding?" General Solomon asked.

"We've done some serious looking at Harding Industries. Last year it was a medium player in a niche market, it's turnover less than four million dollars. We're pretty certain funding for acquisitions is coming from the sale of alien gold and gems. There's been a small but notable increase in global gold supply since the aliens arrived. We've also identified gold with a unique signature, indicating it's unlikely to have come from terrestrial smelting techniques, so we're pretty sure it's alien in origin," Bing said.

"It's not the only way they've raised money," the General added. "There's a couple of new things I'm throwing your way. A new street drug, the papers are calling Starjoy. It's hitting the streets in a big way. It's claimed that it's non-addictive, gives a feeling of contentment and happiness, while at same time energising the user. This stuff has spread across the U.S and Europe like wildfire. We can't be sure it's alien in origin because it's being synthesised here on Earth, mainly in South America and Far East Asia and it's being distributed through established networks, so it's currently untraceable.

"However the synthesising process is complicated and requires sophisticated equipment of the kind you just don't find in remote regions, then there are the raw materials, some of which are restricted, so where are they coming from if not the island? We think the aliens are using this as a way of financing other activities."

"Like Harding Industries acquisitions?" Bing asked.

"Exactly."

"You said a couple of things," Bing reminded the General.

"Ah yes. Two days ago we pulled an operative out of Northern Cambodia. He was already dead from an unknown toxin."

"You suspect the Vespida" Bing stated.

"Right. Despite assurances from the Astospherians there are no Vespida on the planet. I'm pulling you out of Sweden Colonel, someone else can babysit the science project for a while. I need you to look into Harding Industries, get someone close to Bob Harding, and find out what's happening in Cambodia."

Well at least she was out of Sweden and could hope for better weather, if not better luck, in her new assignment, Bing thought.

"You've got to come up with something soon Colonel," the General warned her. "I'm sitting on a time bomb here. Our closest allies are the Chinese, North Koreans and Iranians, can you believe it? We need something Bing, and we need it yesterday."

Bing considered her options. She'd need to get a team out to Cambodia. She thought she might also pay a visit to her old friend Bob Harding, he'd remember her from the New Delhi reception, and she could happen to be in town. What was he up to with his new alien friends?

She called Harding's office in the UK and got lucky, setting up a meeting with him in London for the following day. Catching up with an old acquaintance, was how she'd put it. Next she looked at the Cambodian operation. She could think of a couple of approaches there. One was trace back through the distribution networks, she'd need the help of her CIA contacts for that. Another angle was send yet more operatives into the area where the agent who had been poisoned was found. All in all it wasn't much to go on.

Bing put a call through to her CIA contact, code name Night Light.

"We've got people in the chain," he assured her.

"You've located the source?" Bing asked.

"They're not easy areas for us to operate. In Afghanistan there are tribal warlords and the Taliban make it almost impossible for us to infiltrate. In South America we're up against organised criminals who've had four decades of experience fighting us and the local authorities. All I can say is, we're certain the drug's connected to the aliens, and we've got someone close to the source in South America."

An idea popped into Bing's head. "Just out of interest what about Area 51, Roswell and all that?" she asked.

Night Light laughed. "The whole thing was a

fiction invented to shit the Russians up during the Cold War. Believe me I've been, they don't have anything at Area 51, just a bunch of crap they tried to trick the Russians with, all smoke and mirrors. I can tell you categorically that we've no evidence of any previous alien visits to Earth. Nothing. Goat shit, yes, aliens, no."

"And all those U.F.O sightings?"

"Well sure, they could be genuine, but they tell us nothing. Aliens may have sent a ship to kidnap a few mid-western farmers and probed their butts or whatever. Maybe that's how the aliens know so much about us, but our analysis suggests they learnt more from the Discovery channel than from farmers anuses. They'd be able to pick-up our transmissions from as far out as the edge of the solar system. But yeah, sure they could have been hiding on the dark side of Uranus all these years."

"Yeah, right. Look keep me in the loop over South America OK?" Bing requested, before hanging up.

Fucking CIA, fucking useless, she'd have had more luck asking the Chinese.

The following day Bing was in London for her meeting with Bob Harding. After their first encounter in India, she was pretty sure he wouldn't fall for the 'young American Colonel who found him irresistibly attractive' routine. If she wanted to pull off that one, she'd have to work hard. She felt sure he'd respond to a touching-base, catching up, how are things going approach. He'd might suspect she was sniffing around, but if she could get in closer, she'd have a better chance of finding something out.

The night before she'd had an idea. She'd been thinking about putting a tail on Harding, but then decided to put a tail on anyone who was already following Harding. Within hours it become clear she was watching a farce. Harding was being tailed by just about everyone, MI6, the Chinese, the CIA, Mossad, the FSB and he was leading them a merry dance. Reports from CIA observation units detailed Bob popping up in high profile areas like London or New York, having a business meeting, usually about some proposed acquisition, he'd eat at an expensive restaurant, take-in a show or visit a club, then he'd leave town in a gondola to be whisked off to his next appointment, which would be on the other side of the world, leaving security forces scrambling to keep up.

The journey from Bing's hotel to Harding's London office was a short one. The office was centrally located just off Regent's Park, in an impressive modern building. Behind the reception desk in the lobby hung a huge painting depicting an alien landscape, the marble and mirror lifts played soft alien music.

Bing was ushered into an expensively appointed waiting room and after being offered a cup of kaolate, she flicked through a magazine from the table.

Harding Industries were proud to be partners with several other international businesses. They were moving forward into a brave new world of inter-species cooperation and benefit. They promised that the latest in technological advances would soon be available to everyone, though they failed to say what these advances would be. And they sponsored a group of orphanages in Africa.

Just glossy dross, Bing thought, casting the magazine back on the table.

"Mr Harding will see you now," a secretary with union jack fingernails and superstar glossy lipstick told her.

Bing followed the glossy black high heels into an enormous office, which Bing knew Harding hardly ever used. The CIA had bugged it months ago and he'd been in it once since then.

"Colonel Saunders," Bob Harding smiled broadly. "Good to see you again. Welcome, welcome to my humble office," he said cheerily, coming round the huge table and offering her a hand to shake.

"It's such a great space," he continued. "I just wish I could find more time to be here, but it seems that at the moment I'm having to do a lot of travelling." He smiled at her again. "It's so good of you to look me up while you're in London. I take it you were just passing?"

"It's good of you to find the time to see me Bob." Bing replied.

"Please have a seat." He offered her a comfortable chair in steel and grey fabric.

"Now what can I do for you? Perhaps you'd like a tour of the building? We have a fully functioning laboratory on the fourth floor, but then I expect you knew that already? Perhaps you'd like to chat about New Delhi, the India Government really put on a great bash don't you think?"

"Sure," Bing nodded, eyeing Bob suspiciously. She was certain he was playing with her.

"Let me level with you Bob," Bing said.

"Please do Bing. May I call you Bing? Colonel Saunders is so formal don't you think?" Bob said, settling himself in the chair opposite.

"Sure Bob. The thing is we're getting rumours about some sort of force field technology that your company is developing in cooperation with the Astrospherians." She figured she'd cut to the chase.

"I see," Bob said. "Well as much as I'd like to, I'm not sure I can help you any there. The thing is it's all a bit delicate. I mean if I tell people that we don't have anything yet, the share price will fall through the floor, on the other hand, if I confirm that we do have something, the shareholders are going to want me to produce it. Do you see the bind I'm in?"

"I understand," Bing said. "Perhaps you can give some indication of when you might be in a position to impress the shareholders?"

"Um, look Colonel I can see why force-fields are of interest to the American Government. Hell everyone's interested, I can't take a shit without tripping over an agent from one security force or another. I'd like to get them all off my back, so I'm telling you what I told the Chinese.

"The Astrospherians are not like us. This isn't some NASA-like mission to the moon, the ship isn't packed with air force pilots and scientists. These people are tourists. Look. They've all bought passage or whatever on an interstellar cruise ship. Except for a small security force they're all civilians. The galaxy's rich and idle. Any cooperation you get from them is because they see some amusement value in it. We are dealing with a species that have access to superior technology but the Astrospherians are like children, they just expect it to work, they know how to operate it, but they've no idea what makes it tick.

"Of course some of them are trying to help us figure things out even as we speak. But they're not interested in supplying humans with new types of weapons. They won't say so themselves, but I'll tell you, they don't trust the Military and they wont do business with you.

"Believe me I've tried persuading them. They're not interested in the money. They don't need it. They don't use money. What they want is to have a good time on Earth while the Astrosphere is docked here. They're tourists, they go look at stuff and take pictures and have a good time with the locals."

"You're implying that they'll leave?" Bing asked. "Any idea when?"

"Yes, and no. Yes, I think they will leave. No, I don't know when, not any time soon I think. They like it here. Look would it help if I was able to get you aboard the island?" Bob offered, surprising Bing.

"Well sure. We've been trying to get a peek inside for months."

"I can't promise anything. But I'll speak to my contact in the Lowai. I'm sure you're aware they pretty much make all the decisions up there in the Astrosphere."

"So I heard."

"I like you Colonel, I don't know why but I do. So I'll give you a tip I didn't give the Chinese. The key to these people are the clans. At the moment there's a lot of jostling for position amongst them. A sort of inter-clan war if you like, but on a status level. The clans are motivated by status, the more status they have the closer they get to the ruling Lowai clan. I'm not sure what advantage this gives them, if any, but that's what they want. Their status comes from two things, what the clan has and what it knows. The more you deposit with the clan vault or library, the higher up the clan you rise, the bigger the vault, the bigger the library the more prestige and importance for the clan."

"It all seems like a big game," Bing remarked.

"I'm sure it is, it's just another way they keep themselves amused on the long inter-galactic flights. Look at how they've adopted our sports, football, baseball, cricket, tennis they love them. That's why they cooperate with the scientific exchange, they can acquire new knowledge for their libraries, but they don't want to expose knowledge they already have to the other clans, so they're careful.

"Look I've probably said too much as it is, and I've certainly taken up too much of your time," Bob stood up.

"I do like our little chats, perhaps we can do it again some time?" he said, walking with her to the door. "I wonder if you might find time for dinner with me? Say Thursday night?" He asked with a winning smile.

It was another opportunity to gather information. Had she somehow seduced him without batting her eyelids? Was this just a trick? She supposed he might want information from her as much as she from him. She decided to play the impressed card. Fluttering her eyelids and using her most seductive smile she agreed, and added that she thought it would be a fun evening.

In the lift, when she turned her cell phone on, it flooded with text messages, several from General Solomon. As she got into the Embassy car. her driver passed her the car phone and informed her, "General Solomon is on the hotline Ma'am."

"Ah Colonel Saunders you need to get back to the Embassy immediately. Something is going down at Harding Industries."

Back in the communications suite at the American Embassy reports for Bing's attention flooded in. They all told the same story. Harding Industries laboratories had started to receive identical crates. Just one per laboratory. All the delivered crates had been stored in high security areas and no one had been allowed near them since their arrival.

An operative in a Turkish laboratory however, had managed to get a look at the contents of a crate which was damaged during arrival. The operative reported seeing a mysterious silver hemisphere, about a meter across and half a meter high, inside the crate.

It was clear to Bing, that something was going to happen. But what?

Chapter 15 – Unusual Business

After the excitement of India, Caroline felt very flat. As she and Louis disembarked from the plane at Stuttgart Airport, the first snow flakes of the year skittered across the white skies. Dark coated people huddled against the biting wind, scarves wrapped tightly round their necks, hands thrust deeply into pockets. It was a total comedown for Caroline.

The warm bright colours and excitement of India were replaced by concrete buildings, cold skies and the endless drone of orderly traffic. Caroline and Louis dragged their luggage across the street and up the steps to the flat they'd abandoned to chance what seemed like a life time ago. They didn't even know if it would still be theirs when they returned. Caroline found her door key at the bottom of her backpack under a half melted packet of minty sweets. She peeled the sticky mementos from the key's dull brass, picking off the lint as best she could, she slotted the key into the lock and turned.

Everything was just as they'd left it except for the pile of unread mail. The fridge contained a carton of green soured milk and a chunk of black spotted cheese. The geraniums in their painted plant pot had wilted and died, leaving a stark dry twig with brown crispy leaves for a headstone. The air in the flat smelt stale and damp, so despite the freezing outdoor temperature, Caroline opened a window to let some fresh air blow through.

Once the flat was tidied, aired and made cosy and warm Caroline felt able to relax. Curled up on the comfy old sofa hands wrapped round a cup of hot soup, Caroline began to feel at home again. For the first time since this all began She felt a sense of normality returning.

Over the next few days they began picking up their old lives from where they had left off. Louis went back to his job. Caroline could have had her old job back but after a visit to the office to catch up with colleagues she decided not to. It didn't feel right somehow, she wasn't the Caroline who'd worked there before, she was somehow a new different Caroline and anyway she wanted to try something she'd been thinking about since India.

In the aftermath of the beach party in Goa, Caroline and Louis had met several Astrospherians. Amongst their new friends had been an alien humanoid, Topaz, who'd made them a business proposition. Topaz had suggested setting up a shop for alien goods. At the time Caroline hadn't thought much of it and had listened to Topaz partially from politeness and partially, because at the time, she was besotted by the aliens and all things alien. On the flight back to Stuttgart however, the conversation with Topaz had risen in her mind again, and the idea had begun to appeal to her. Caroline's biggest problem now was how to get hold of Topaz.

The floating island was beginning its tour of the world and had moved on from Goa. It headed south round the Cape of Good Hope and then up the west coast of Africa, so Topaz probably wasn't in India any more, Caroline thought. In fact she had no idea how to contact the floating island at all.

Caroline wandered through the main shopping streets of Stuttgart, dreaming of owning her own shop, how she would own a brightly lit window, imagining the welcoming smile she would have for her customers. Perhaps she could somehow get a message to Topaz. There were aliens everywhere nowadays. All she needed to do was find one in Stuttgart.

A search through the local newspapers soon informed her that a group of Astrosphereians were staying at a hotel in the city centre. Caroline took a tram across town to the hotel. The usual crowd of curious onlookers and alien fans were gathered outside. Across the road Caroline noticed a three man protest group with a small placard that said "Aliens Out" in thick black marker pen.

Caroline sidled in amongst the crowd and began asking if anyone had seen any aliens that day. The general consensus was that there were some inside the hotel, but others had left earlier and would probably be back later. The talk around Caroline quickly turned to which species of Astrosphereian were in the Hotel, who preferred

Cherubim to Langonai, what the aliens were wearing today and other fan related gossip that didn't interest Caroline one bit. What Caroline needed now was to contact one of the Astrosphereians. The presence of fans outside the hotel just made the task harder for Caroline as hotel security would be tight around the alien guests.

She wandered off from the crowd and found a café around the corner where she could gather her thoughts and devise a master plan. By the time the frothy suds of her cappuccino had sunk to the bottom of her cup the best idea she'd come up with was a good old fashioned stakeout. So she went back out into the street and took up position opposite the hotel and a little way off from the protesters and their placard.

She waited and waited, marching a small stretch of pavement to keep warm. Every time there was a flutter of activity from the fans, the protesters waved their placard and Caroline watched. So far they'd all been false alarms. Then, as darkness fell and her fingers grew numb from the cold the crowd became very excited. Cameras flashing lit up the hotel entrance. Caroline saw a group of four figures, two of them very tall, coming down the hotel steps. They were aliens.

It seemed the aliens were intending to take a walk, however, the crowd surrounded the aliens photographing them, asking them questioning and requesting autographs. After a while of this the majority of fans seemed happy and let the

Astrosphereians continue unmolested, while a handful of diehards waited for the Astrospherians return.

The four aliens walked off down the street and Caroline was able to follow them for a couple of blocks at a discreet distance. Once the hotel was well behind them she picked up her pace and began gaining on them. They were in no rush, ambling along the pavement, looking in shop windows, chatting with each other. Caroline drew level to the Astrosphereians and fell into step with them.

"I do apologise for interrupting," Caroline said to the closest alien. "I wondered if you could pass a message on to Topaz?"

The Langonai she was addressing looked down at her. "Topaz? " she replied, in perfect German.

"Tall, long brown hair, silver-grey eyes? Was in Goa last week?" Caroline added hopefully.

"Well, I don't know a Topaz..." The Langonai replied.

"Is there anyway I can trace her? Get a message to her?" Caroline asked desperately.

"There is the contact website I suppose," the Langonai said.

"If you come across Topaz can you give her this note please?" Caroline requested, holding out a scrap of paper on which she'd jotted her name and number.

"If I meet this Topaz I will," the Langonai assuted Caroline, taking the note and tucking it into a fold in her robe.

"Thank you. Enjoy your evening," Caroline called after them.

So that idea had come to nothing Still now she knew that at least there was a website. Next mission, to visit the internet, something she could do on the laptop from the warm comfort of her own home. She trooped off back to the flat through the steadily falling snow.

A quick look on her laptop using the Worldfinder search engine she came across a site that seemed to promise what she was looking for. It was unsurprisingly called www.astrosphereians.com.

She joined the website, registering as a human, and left a note for Topaz on the message board. All she could do now was wait and see.

Days passed. Caroline racked her brains for some other way to get in contact, she even considered returning to India but as Louis pointed out the island had moved on and Topaz could be anywhere, on the island or off it. Then the email arrived.

"Dearest Caroline and Louis," it began. "I am so pleased you are interested in the shop idea. I have been busy helping some of my other human friends to start Astrospherian outlets but I do not have a distributor in Germany yet. I will be visiting your country in the next week or so and perhaps we could meet then to discuss further. Kind Regards Topaz."

Caroline was thrilled and emailed Topaz straight back to say she would be delighted to meet up.

The following week she was full of excitement. She'd visited all the local retail premises agents and had a big pile of available property brochures spread across the living room floor. On the day of her meeting with Topaz she put on her old business suit which she hadn't worn since her last day at the office before India. She put on some lipstick, something she'd got out of the habit of doing. She picked up the little black briefcase she'd bought specially for the meeting, and stepped out of the door.

The meeting was held in Topaz's room at the same hotel in which the other Astrospherians were staying. There were envious looks from the alien fans outside as Caroline was admitted, though there were notably fewer of them today and the little protest group had sprung a second placard. On which was written the words, "Go home now".

There were two Astrospherians in the room, Topaz, a tall and slender Langonai, and a plump middle-aged three foot Cherubim, both wore charcoal business suits. Caroline thought Topaz looked far more manly than she had in Goa, indeed she was even sporting a small goatee.

"You probably don't recognise me," Topaz said, with a wry smile. "We've found that in human business the male is often taken more seriously than the female and as I'm in the testosterone phase of my cycle right now, I've grown a goatee and adopted traditional human male business garb," Topaz explained, before introducing Caroline to the Cherubim.

"This is my business partner Chewfang," Topaz said, Caroline thought she vaguely recognised the Cherubim from the beach in Goa, but wasn't sure.

"If we may get straight down to business," Topaz said. "We could use a distributor. In Stuttgart We're able to cover any necessary start-up costs and provide the initial stock. Of course we'll want to recuperate those costs later," Topaz said.

Caroline was able to produce prices for renting commercial property and estimated sales figures based on local footfall and estimated interest in alien artefacts, which naturally Caroline felt would be great. For an hour or so they ironed out the details. It wasn't even lunchtime when Caroline came out of the hotel clutching an agreement. She went straight to the commercial property agent and began the process of renting a shop.

A few days later, having seen four or five

premises, the agent showed Caroline a vacant shop just off Koningstrase. The moment she walked in she knew it was the one. There was something about it. The stock room layout appealed to Caroline's way of organising things. She could see what she would need to do with the little staff area to keep her assistants happy in their work. All she required was shop fittings and a sign on the window and she was in business.

The next few days were hectic for Caroline. Running here and there, organising shop fitters, and arranging the myriad of little details that were needed for the enterprise. Eventually the shop was ready. It looked great, shiny futuristic shelving along one wall and along the other clothing racks, and an area at the front for displaying food and drink. The stock was neatly and attractively arranged, the foods, the clothes, the toys, all in their places and out the back Caroline had a stockroom that bulged with supplies.

Twice a week at six am precisely a lorry sized gondola descended from the sky. Caroline and Anna, her shop assistant, helped the Langonai pilot unload the boxes of goods into the shop.

It didn't take long for word to get round the City that alien goods were now available. The goods went out of the shop almost as quickly as they arrived, but when they left they were neatly wrapped and placed in a string handled paper bag and carried in the hand of another happy customer.

A particularly good seller was the kaolate drink which seemed to be popular with almost everyone. Another favourite was alien whisky which many people found to be gentler on the head than Earth whisky. She had alien jackets and alien skirts and robes which were becoming quite fashionable.

Things went brilliantly well with the shop for several months. Caroline was making her payments to Topaz and making a tidy profit for herself as well. Then, one day not long after the last snows of winter had passed and the crocus and daffodil were beginning to bloom, a man came into the shop asking to see her. Dressed in a brown coat and a cheap grey suit, carrying a serious looking briefcase, he pushed his thick-rimmed spectacles up his nose and put his case down on the shop counter. He struck Caroline as being a serious and humourless person.

"I'm Gustave Kliess from the Bureaux of Imports and Excise," he introduced himself to Caroline, showing her his identification. "I will need to see your import licence please."

"I'll just look," Caroline said, knowing full well that she didn't have one, indeed she didn't even know she was supposed to have one. After rustling around in the back room for several minutes, banging filing cabinet drawers she returned to Herr Kliess who was waiting patiently in the shop.

"I don't seem to be able to lay my hands on it right this moment," Caroline confessed. "Perhaps you could come back tomorrow?"

"I'm not surprised you can't find it," Kliess said. "According to our records that would be because you don't have one."

"Should I have one? " Caroline asked knowing the game was up. "Why do I need one?"

"You're importing goods from outside the European Union. You need an import licence," Kliess said.

Then Caroline remembered something the delivery pilot had said one day when she'd asked him how his journey had been. The pilot had said no problem, he'd come straight from the depot in Dortmund and she was the first drop of the day.

"I'm not importing these goods," she said. "They come from a depot in Dortmund."

"That may as be," Kliess said. "But there is no paperwork to say where these goods came from and we suspect them of being alien, that is to say, originating from outside the E.U."

"I have dockets," Caroline said, and a further dive into the office soon produced the delivery dockets.

"There's no address on this docket." Kliess said tapping one of the offending pieces of paperwork. "Just this logo and the words Astrosphereian goods. This will not do, this will not do at all." He shook his head gravely.

"What can I do?" Caroline asked.

"You must get a licence. Meanwhile I am forced to ask you to cease and desist in the distribution of these goods until you do. There may also be a fine for operating without a licence in the first place." Kliess snapped his briefcase shut. "I will no doubt be seeing you again," Kliess said, his parting words as he left the shop, the little bell sounding a cheery tinkling toll to his departure. Caroline had to give Anna the rest of the day off, and then she spent hours on the phone to the Bureaux while eager customers pressed their faces up against the locked door and rattled the handle till she was forced to put a small note in the window, saying "Shop closed until further notice".

She'd been in a stalemate with the Bureaux for three days when she had to turn the regular delivery away because she'd no room in the shop for more stock. By nine o'clock Topaz was on her door step. Caroline invited the tall silver eyed alien in from the chilly morning air to the sad warm glow of the shop.

"I like what you've done here," Topaz remarked.

"Thanks," Caroline replied.

"I hear you were unable to take delivery this morning?" Topaz said.

"Yes. I've not been able to open the shop for three days. The Bureaux of Imports and excise have shut me down till I can get a licence," she explained.

"Yes, yes." Topaz said softly. "We are having a problem with the local authorities. That is to say the German authorities, though we are having similar problems in other parts of Europe also. We don't know why but there appears to be some sort of movement against us. Luckily the British are always keen to do business and we are able to import into Europe through the United Kingdom. We will provide you with paperwork that shows your stock originated on some trading estate in the U.K. and that should allow you to start trading again."

Caroline was relieved." Well that's good news," she said.

"However, " Topaz lifted a finger of warning. "We believe that there is a movement amongst some of your politicians to try and restrict the import of Astrosphereian goods. This maybe in the form of higher import taxes, or it maybe the banning of certain goods, at the moment we don't know.

"We are from another world and have no political power here, so we would urge you to join with your fellow distributors and customers to put pressure on your Governments to allow us to continue our legitimate trade."

"I think I can do something there," Caroline said.

"Excellent, excellent I knew I had judged you correctly," Topaz said, smiling.

Caroline immediately got on the phone to the distributors on the list Topaz had given her, to see what was being done. By the evening Caroline found herself the self-appointed appointed leader of the distributors' movement.

The following morning the paperwork arrived from the U.K and Caroline rang Kliess at the number on the card he'd left her. It was mid-afternoon before Kliess appeared at the shop and Caroline was able to show him the papers. He nodded curtly. "Very well, you may open again. Remember there is still the matter of trading without a licence," he added.

Chapter 16 – Shields revealed

The yellow taxi cab smelt of pine scented air freshener and a hint of stale sweat as it swept David through the busy streets of New York. Downtown the sidewalks heaved with pedestrians who were swept along like leaves on the fresh spring breeze. They gathered in clumps at junctions waiting for the green man's signal. David's taxi jostled alongside Mercedes and Ford cars, motorbikes, cyclists and skaters in the urgent throng that was New York. The taxi pulled up outside the Harding Building, the New York headquarters of Harding Industries.

In the lobby he approached the reception desk where three blue-shirted security guards sat.

"Can I help you Sir?" asked the guard sitting in the middle, a young blond female.

"I'm David Shawdale," David told her.

"What can Harding Industries do for you to day Sir," she asked.

"I've a meeting with Bob Harding this afternoon, but I thought I'd pop in and see my office first," David said.

She punched some keys on the security computer. "May I see some identification please Sir," she asked.

David showed her his passport.

"Thank you Mr. Shawdale," she handed back his passport. "Would you like me to show you the way Mr. Shawdale?" The girl offered.

"Thank you. I'd be most grateful," David replied.

"Larry watch the desk will you?" she asked one of her fellow guards. "I'm going to show Vice-President Shawdale to his office." At this the two other security guards straightened in their seats and took deferential note of David's face.

He followed her slim figure to the end elevator. "This is the executive elevator Mr. Shawdale," she told him. "I'll personally ensure you have a swipe card for this elevator. " she told him, using her security card to activate the elevator which only went to five floors. The top button was marked P. The security guard pressed the button immediately below this, one marked VP.

"This elevator goes directly to your office." She explained and after a short ride the lift door slid open to reveal a vast office. Two walls were entirely devoted to a picture window which looked over the City. A huge polished oak desk dominated the centre of the room. An expensive leather sofa and designer chairs surrounded a low glass table in an attempt to create an informal space, but for all it's size and opulence, David felt the office to be rather soulless.

"Thank you," he said, to the girl, who didn't

accompany him from the lift.

"If that's all Sir?" she asked.

"Yes, thank you," David replied as the elevator doors slid closed between them and she was gone.

Vice President of Harding Industries, David thought to himself. He strode across the room, hands clasped behind his back and looked out across the cityscape through the picture window that stretched an entire wall of the office. That little bit of business Bob had wanted to talk about back in Scotland had been to offer him a Vice Presidency of the company. Bob had said it was primarily a cosmetic role and David wouldn't be required to do any actual business for Harding Industries.

David had argued it would take too much time away from his academic studies but once Bob had mentioned there'd be several Vice Presidents, and at worst, David might have to sit in on the odd meeting as Bob's representative. The main task of the job would be to attend the charity functions and dinners that Bob couldn't make himself, and the offer began to look appealing to David. When he heard how much he was to be paid for these light duties it became very appealing, so appealing in fact, he'd agreed.

This feels like the first day on the job, David thought, though he'd been a VP for several weeks, entering the office made the whole thing suddenly seem real. His thoughts were interrupted as the large maple wood double doors at the end of the room opened and a very neatly dressed woman in her mid-fifties entered.

"Mr. Shawdale," she crossed the room towards him. "I'm Doris Parker, your personal assistant," she introduced herself. "May I take you through your diary now?"

They spent some time going through his agenda, including a meeting with Bob, scheduled for the afternoon, and a charity ball that the evening. Doris then showed him the private suite, hidden behind a sliding wall, complete with bathroom, shower, wardrobe and cot. She demonstrated the executive entertainment system that slid magically from behind a large oak panel in the office. Three screens were revealed together with a fully stocked bar and a rack of media playing devices . Doris touched a button on one of the silver boxes in the rack and the main screen began to play a promotional film for Harding Industries.

The sleek black intercom on the desk buzzed and a female voice said. "A Ms. Softly would like to see you Mr. Shawdale. She's in reception now."

"Ah, right, send her up. Or is that in?" He directed this last remark to Doris who just smiled.

A moment later Softly was shown into the room. She glided across the gold and red carpet and kissed David on both cheeks. She was wearing a short pleated skirt with thick white tights and shiny ankle boots. A soft orange polo neck sweater and a short padded fluffy jacket in a rich blue.

"Hello David," she said in her soft voice. "I thought I'd welcome you to your new office. How does Vice President suit you?"

"I'm not sure I've had time to find out." David replied. "I've only just got here myself."

"I think this office works for you," Softly said.

"Thank you," he replied, flattered. "I take it Fortune is in town?"

"Indeed," Softly smiled at him. "I think you have a meeting with her later. She and Bob have something very special to show you, but I'm not allowed to tell," she smiled wickedly at him.

"Most intriguing. No hints?" David asked.

"I'm afraid my lips are sealed," she teased. "Beside which, I don't know anything myself. It was just that Fortune mentioned there was something she wanted to show you."

"I guess I'll just have to wait and see," David said. "You know I'm at a bit of a loose end until this afternoon, I don't suppose you'd consider having lunch with me?" he added.

Softly smiled. "I'd love to," she purred. "I was

rather hoping we could do something together. I'm afraid I have far too much time on my hands with Fortune so busy with business matters."

"That's settled then, let me get my coat. It's still early so we can do a little window shopping on the way."

They rode the elevator back down to reception where they were met by a large man with dark brown skin wearing a dark charcoal suit and a funny little earpiece in his right ear.

"This is Samuel, he's my bodyguard," Softly said. "I'm afraid he has to come with us, there have been incidents recently." David silently absorbed this snippet of information with typical English reserve, he didn't press for details.

They walked out together onto the street, Samuel following a step or two behind, just close enough so others would know he was with David and Softly, far enough behind so they felt they had some privacy. She slipped an arm through his.

"I find New York so exciting," she said.

This was the first time David had been on the street with a humanoid. He was quite used to them from the various meetings he'd had with Astrosphereians over the last few months, but that had always been in closed environments like the grouse shoot. This was the first time he'd been in public with an Astrospherian. Of course, for the most part, New Yorkers rushed on by with their usual, seen it all before disdain.

Not everyone on the street was a professional New Yorker, some stared openly at Softly. Often they would give David a quick look over as well. It was, David imagined, like walking down the street with a celebrity. Turning heads here and there as they walked, he kind of enjoyed the subtle attention he got, and had a feeling of, there's something a bit special about me, I have an Astrosphereian companion and you don't.

They strolled past brownstone buildings and glass fronted shops looking in the windows and behaving like any other shopper on the street. Softly spotted a tea set in a window and they went in for a better look.

The boutique assistant, a girl in her twenties with too much black mascara around her eyes and bright red lipstick on her lips, smiled nervously at David and Softly as they came in. They looked at the tea sets and coffee makers, fashionable cups, mugs and goblets that were on every shelf in the shop.

"Can I help you at all?" the emo assistant asked, while never taking her eyes off Softly.

"The tea set in the window?" Softly said to her.

"The Kathy McAllister?"

"The artistically modern one," softly said.

"That's a genuine McAllister, she's only made ten of these sets they're very rare," the girl said. "Would you like to see it?"

Softly said she would and the girl carefully took the teapot out of the window and handed it to Softly. Softly turned it around in her hands, her third hand steadying the bottom of the pot.

"Would you like to see a cup too?" the girl asked, devouring every aspect of Softly's appearance.

"I would, thank you," Softly, handing back the tea pot. A tea cup was inspected. Softly seemed satisfied and said to the girl. "I like it, I think I'll take it."

The girl bustled about taking boxes and paper and reaching the set from the window. As the girl was packing the tea set the owner of the boutique came out of an office at the back of the shop. A short round woman in her fifties with greying hair, wearing sensible tweeds.

"I see you're buying the Kathy McAllister," she said to David.

"I'm not. My companion is," he told the woman.

"You have very good taste my dear," the woman said to Softly. "That's a rare piece. Do you collect?" she asked.

"Oh yes," Softly replied. "I have acquired a few

sets recently, but I think this probably is the nicest."

"Well if you're interested I pick up the odd exceptional piece from time to time. Let me give you my card and you can call to see if I have anything in. In fact, I don't know if you're interested, but I have a rare Japanese set that I was thinking of using in the window when the McAllister had gone, would you like to see it before it goes in the window?"

Softly indicated she would be interested, so the woman led them into a small office that smelt of paper and dust and gas heater. She picked up a box and opened it reverently. Reaching inside, she pulled out a ball of paper and carefully stripped it away to reveal a delicately decorated blue and white porcelain teapot in the Japanese style.

"This a Miskagori Matagaki," the woman said. "It is a one off, he only ever makes one of anything he does. Note that while the decoration is a traditional pattern the teapot is porcelain not iron as is normally the custom. Matagaki believes that his tea sets represent the core of the Tea Ceremony. That each identical action is in itself a unique moment that though repeated a thousand times, is always ultimately unique and unrepeatable."

Softly didn't need to be sold any further and bought both sets, arranging for them to be delivered to her hotel. The shop assistant almost curtsied as she held the door open for them. David couldn't tell if it was because Softly was an alien or because she'd spent so much money in the shop.

They decided it was time for a spot of lunch. A little further up the street they came to a popular restaurant, the Oaks. A watering hole for New York's most wealthy, famous, notorious and powerful inhabitants.

"Monsieur, Madam," the Maitre d' greeted them in French as they stood at the entrance to the elegant dining room. "You have a reservation no?"

"I don't think we do," David said.

"I'm afraid then we have no tables available Monsieur," The Maitre d' told them.

"I wonder," Softly said softly. "If you couldn't just squeeze us in? You would be doing Mr. Shawdale and I a big favour."

"Monsieur Shawdale?" The Maitre d' said slowly, taking a closer look at David. "Ah Monsieur Shawdale, le hom d'etoile. But of course, of course, do forgive me. Naturally you understand that we do not normally seat people without first the reservation, but I can make an exception in your case Monsieur Shawdale. Please follow me." The Maitre d' led them across the room to a table near the window.

"This will suit you?" the Maitre d' asked.

"Thank you, this is excellent," Softly said. "We are most grateful."

"You are welcome Madam," the Maitre d' produced two menus and left them to make their decision.

"Wow," said David. "I've never had my name dropped before to such effect. It got me into the BBC canteen once in London, but that was impressive. I'm impressive?"

Softly laughed. "It would seem your name now opens doors."

"And gets tables," David joked.

The food was exquisite, the service exceptional. As they tucked into a light cod mornay with glazed red cabbage terrine and mashed potatoes, David got the feeling that they were attracting some attention. A man came across from another table.

"David Shawdale? I'm Michael Longs, economics editor for the New York Times." He smiled. "Sorry to interrupt your meal, but I was wondering if you had anything to say about your appointment as Vice President of Harding Industries?"

"Michael is it?" David asked. "I've not been in the job long enough to comment I'm afraid."

"Could you tell me anything about the announcement Harding Industries will be making tomorrow?"

"As I said I can't comment." David told him.

"Well, I have to ask, it's my job. Sorry for interrupting your mea," The editor said. "Thanks and good luck with the new appointment."

During dessert a little girl came up to their table, shyly asking for Softly's autograph, which Softly was happy to give. The girl skipped away, all smiles and giggles. They had coffee with handmade chocolates, then David thought he should be heading back to the office for his afternoon meeting. Softly kissed him on the cheek and he smelt her perfume on his face all the way up in the lift.

Doris had a couple of items for his attention, an invitation to a charity ball and an invitation to dinner with the Mayor of New York. David felt he'd been catapulted from being a S-list celebrity straight to C-list maybe even B. He found he was enjoying his new status.

"You have a meeting scheduled with Mr. Harding," Doris told him. "You can take the elevator up to his office."

Bob's office was even more impressive than David's. It felt like he had to walk across a football field to get to Bob's desk at the centre of a sea of dark green carpet.

"Hi David. Glad you decided to accept my offer." Bob said as they shook hands and greeted each other. "Fortune should be here any moment and we can go down to the labs, there on the fifth floor. Have you had a chance to look round the building yet?" he asked.

David confessed he hadn't, that he'd spent the time enjoying lunch with Softly. Just then the lift pinged and its doors silently slid open, Fortune stepped out.

"Right," Bob rubbed his hands together. "Lets go see what we've got for the shareholders then," The three of them stepped into the lift and began to descend.

"Have you two actually met before?" Bob asked, he made the introductions.

"I feel I know you David." Fortune said. "Of course we met briefly in Scotland, and Softly has told me all about you."

David wasn't sure what to make of this so he smiled politely and said nothing. The lift arrived at laboratory level and they stepped out into a chrome and white room. Technicians in lab coats were absorbed in various tasks and took no notice of the new arrivals except for a short plump Cherubim in a too-long lab coat who came hopping over to meet them.

"This is Vigsoo our head technician," Fortune introduced them.

"We're all set up and ready for the demonstration," Vigsoo said, as he led the way. His wings were now so old they looked like two hinged sticks with little of the flight membrane left. As he walked he used these appendages as if they were walking sticks or crutches.

The little group passed lab benches with all kinds of equipment, wires, lenses, small steel tools, silicon chips and robot armatures, before coming to a sealed door that stood at one end of the room. Vigsoo ran a security card through a reader and placed his palm on a biometric lock. With a hiss of air the steel door slid open and they stepped inside. The door slid shut behind David with an ominous clunk.

The room was large and white and seemed empty at first. Calibration and measurement lines were painted on the walls in various places in black or yellow. Vigsoo lead them to a control podium near the door.

The podium contained an array of buttons and leavers and assorted lights none of which David could see any obvious use for. A small wooden, black lacquered, box with the DaVinci logo, inlaid in gold on the lid, sat on a corner of the control panel.

Vigsoo picked up the box and opened it, first offering its contents to Bob, then Fortune. David peered inside the box. It contained five money clips, each lay, glinting, on the red satin lining. He picked one out as the door hissed open and a woman in a lab coat came in.

"This is Gemma," Vigsoo introduced her. He picked a money clip from the box and handed it to Gemma who walked out into the middle of the test area.

"If you would please Gemma," Vigsoo said to the woman. She clipped the metal grip onto the pocket of her lab coat and activated it. A brief flash of blue lightening ran across her body so swiftly David wasn't sure if he'd really seen it.

Vigsoo opened a draw and taking out an automatic pistol he shot Gemma several times in the head. David was momentarily deafened by the noise, startled by the suddenness, and completely stunned, by the fact that Gemma just stood there, smiling back at Vigsoo.

Chapter 17 – Sweet revenge

The Kasaku Maido Cafe on the corner of Shengshi Road was one of the oldest Maido cafe's in Tokyo, and a favourite hangout of the local cosplay community. Dai Wakimi sat waiting for his friends at a table covered with a yellow and white chequered cloth. The maido's, waitresses dressed in Victorian maid outfits, served tea from chintzy teapots and fancy iced cakes on doily covered plates.

While waiting for his friends to arrive Dai's thought's drifted to the previous day, which he'd spent in Neko's company.

The Astrospherians were currently occupying the entire top two floors of the hotel. Neko and her mother Forest had a room on the lower of the two floors. Neko's mother welcomed Dai into the suite which comprised a main reception room and two bedrooms, off to either side.

Dai thought Neko was looking particularly cute that day. She'd obviously been influenced by Dai's talk of manga and cosplay because she was wearing a fetching manga style outfit in white and blue with gold piping. She had gold and blue ribbons in her hair, which she wore in long flowing locks.

Dai and Neko sat side by side on the sofa drinking coke from the refrigerator, their knees occasionally touching, her thin blue stocking rubbed against the rough denim of his jeans. Forest sat across from them on an easy chair and they chatted about the weather and which restaurants in the area they had visited, a subject on which Forest seemed to have an endless opinion and Dai almost none.

After a while Forest asked if they'd be all right on their own, as she needed to go down the corridor to see someone.

"I'll just be next door," she told them.

"No Koneko today?" Dai asked Neko after her mother had left.

"Oh she's probably down in the ballroom. " Neko replied. "The Cherubim children love it in there, they can really fly around there's so much space and it gives them a chance to show off to the hotel guests. They get a great kick out of doing tricks and flying amongst the guests," David and Neco laughed together at the thought of the Cherubim's antics.

"How are you coming along with the yoyo disc?" Neko asked. Dai showed her some of the tricks he had learnt while Neko encouraged him with 'oohs' and 'ahs', complimenting his on his adroitness.

Niko produced a yoyo disc of her own and they began to have a battle. The little discs swooped and clashed, a shower of sparks flying off them as they collided with each other. After a few minutes of disc smashing Niko produced a white sphere, about the size of a table tennis ball.

"This should make things a bit more interesting," she said, throwing the ball up in the air where it hung patiently over the glass-topped coffee table. She flew her disc at the ball which hit it with a satisfying thud, sending the ball scudding across the room towards Dai. He immediately sent his disc in pursuit and hit the ball back. Laughing they whacked the ball back and forth across the room with their discs, scrambling over table and chairs to keep the discs in range.

"You try to get it into that bedroom and I'll try to get it into this one," Neko said. The game achieved a new vigour as the discs whizzed back and forth around the room, Dai and Neko chasing the ball and each other, breathless with laughter and the excitement of it all.

Neko was getting closer to her doorway goal and relentlessly pressed her advantage against the more inexperienced boy. Not to be beaten at any cost, Dai dived at his opponent in a desperate attempt to avert defeat. They fell on the floor together rolling around as he tried to wrestle her control ring from her finger and make her disc fly off. Suddenly she was sitting on his chest pinning his arms to the ground and tickling him with her extra hands.

"Hey, that's cheating, Dai protested, through bursts of laughter as he wriggled around making Neko lose her balance. Their faces were close now, he could smell her breath.

"Do you want to kiss me?" she asked, nuzzling his nose with hers. "I'll let you up for a kiss."

Dai paussed filled with indecision. Neko sensed Dai's hesitation and sat up, her attitude suddenly cold and huffy.

"Don't you want to kiss me? Afraid you might catch some sort of alien disease from me?" she asked.

"It's not that," Dai said, sorry he'd upset his friend. "It's just, well, its difficult to explain." He moaned.

"Oh, I get it, it's the boy girl thing isn't it. Mother said it would bother you."

"Well I don't know if it bothers me... but then, I don't know anything about it."

"Oh, you want to see? You want to see if I'm a boy or a girl. I tell you what." She challenged. "Lets play kiss and tell."

"Really? Should we?" Dai asked. It all seemed very naughty and exciting. Neko leant forward and offered her lips and without thinking Dai found himself responding in kind. Her soft lips tasted of the bubblegum cherry lipstick she was wearing. They kissed for a minute then she rolled off him. It was a nice kiss, nothing different from the occasional kisses he'd had from the girls at school.

Neko sat on the floor, her back leant against the bed, her legs stretched out before her, feet crossed at the ankles. She looked at him, then slowly lifted the blue and white sailor suit top she was wearing.

"See. I have breasts just like an Earth girl," she pouted. "Now show me yours."

Dai obediently lifted his shirt to reveal his hairless chest.

"No breasts," Neko said. "Just like a child." She pulled her top back down, then nodded at Dai's jeans. "Now show me your you-know-what," she said slyly.

Dai pulled his shirt down. "What if your mum comes back?" he protested.

"She wont, anyway we'll hear her, we've got plenty of time."

"Well show me yours first," Dai said.

"I showed my breasts first," Neko argued.

Reluctantly and not a little self-consciously he undid the button on his jeans and unzipped the fly. He pulled his jeans down to his knees. "And the rest." Neko teased sliding across the carpet and gently tugging at the band of his y-fronts. Dai had never shown his penis to anyone before.

The only other people who had ever seen it were his mum and the doctor who delivered him, and his mum hadn't seen it in a few years. As a red glow of embarrassment spread from his face across his body he lowered his pants for her to see his penis and testicles and the few pubic hairs he had managed to grow.

Neko inspected him for a minute, then said. "OK, you kept your part of the bargain," she lifted her short pleated skirt and slipped her knickers down her thighs.

Dia was a little taken aback. Neko had what looked like a small penis where a clitoris would be and below that her vagina. Her labia were more extended than in a human female.

"See," she said. "I have a vagina just like a human girl, and a little penis, but it's only a tiny one."

"I only have a penis and human girls only have vaginas." Dai said. Neko looked sad and it occurred to Dai that Neko might want to be thought human, to be seen as being as human as possible.

"Look," he said. "It doesn't matter. You're only a little bit different. I'll kiss you again to prove it." They tidied themselves up and then he knelt next to her on the soft carpet by the bed and gave her another kiss.

"I am very different," Neko said, somewhat appeased. "It won't stop us from being friends though will it?"

"No it won't," Dai assured her firmly.

"And we can have another kiss sometime?" she asked.

"Of course. You can have one more right now." Dai said, and they kissed again. Suddenly his recollection of the day with Neko was interrupted by the arrival of Tenkou and the girls at the Kasaku café. He stood and bowed as they came over to join him.

That afternoon Dai held court at the corner table. The maido in knee length pinafore dress and ruffled petticoats, over the knee stockings and little lace apron, knelt at the table as she served Dai and his guests with tea and small traditional cakes, as is the fashion in Tokyo's Maido Cafés.

Tenkou had arrived with two girls from their year in school. Akina who up until recently would never have hung around with someone who previously had been as uncool as Dai, and her friend Keiko. Now the four of them sat together wearing the psychedelic coloured majorette uniform jackets, they'd bought earlier at a nearby market, as a way of introducing the girls into the fun world of cosplay.

When the maido had finished serving them, Dai took out the yoyo disc that Neko had given him and made it hover round the edge of the table.

He flew it above his friend's heads and around the lampshade. He manoeuvred the colourful disc above the cups and plates on the table, and brought it to a halt, hovering just in front of Tenkuo's nose.

"I wish you wouldn't do that," Tenkou complained, as the others laughed. Dai flicked the yoyo disc back into his hand.

"Lets see it again," Akina demanded, and because it was Akina he made the disc float slowly over to her where it hovered above the table just within arms length. She reached out to grab it and it dodged her grasp. They laughed.

"Tell us about your alien girlfriend," Akina said.

"She's not my girlfriend," Dai said defensively. He felt the need to be clear about this, it was only fair to Neko after all, and he'd been bullied by Waku and Gaku over his shemale boy friend.

"They're all men you know," Gaku had said as the two boys pinned him against his locker in the school corridor. "That makes you a poof boy. A dick sucking homo," Gaku taunted.

"Oh arg, you probably fancy me, don't you nancy boy?" Goku teased, punching Dai on the arm. "Erg, you want to kiss me and suck my nob. I should make you do it too you alien loving freak." He punched Dai in the stomach and walked off laughing with Waku.

"Well, whatever.," Akina was saying.

"What's' she like? What's her Cherubim like?" Keiko asked.

"She's very sweet and generous," Dai said. "And Koneko is just so cute. She sat on my hand and ate cake," he told them. "And her wings are bright like a dragonfly's."

"Neko and Keneko, that's sweet," Akina said. "Cat and her kitten. Are those real names?"

"I doubt it," Tenkou said. "They've all taken Earth words as names."

"What about the girl boy thing they've got going?" Keiko asked.

There was quite a bit Dai knew about it but he wasn't about to tell them. All he said was "They're all female, they can all give birth."

"But they can all sperm each other as well," Tenkou said. He wasn't being any help in getting Dai out of this. He began to regret his trick with the yoyo disc.

"Yetch," said Akina.

"So I've heard," Dai had to admit. "But I don't know how they do it."

"I've heard they have a special tentacle to do it with," Keiko said.

"Do you know Cherubim have two sexes?" Dai said, trying to subtly change the subject. "Apparently the females are smaller than the males, which gives them a better chance of finding a mate because they keep their ability to fly longer. When they do mate they lose the ability to fly, so they mate for life. If one becomes your friend then it will likely be your friend forever."

"So I can't buy one then?" Keiko asked.

"They're not pets," Dai objected. "They're very clever little people. Sure, the young are unruly and disorganised, which is why they don't go to school till they're adults and don't usually learn to read or write as children."

"How great, not having to go to school," Akina said enviously.

The atmosphere around his table suddenly changed and Tenkou gave Dai a funny look, rolling his eyes towards the door.

A cold gust of air made the hairs on the nape of his neck stand on end. He knew without looking around that either Gaku or Waku or both had walked into the Maido Cafe. He heard voices behind him and heard the scraping of chair legs on the floor as someone sat at the next table. Dai flushed hot and cold. He steeled himself, but for once he wasn't afraid. No he actually wanted this, he was glad they had come in, he had a little surprise for Gaku and Waku.

Loud talking came from the table behind him as the maid brought tea for the new arrivals. Dai was certain that one of the voices was Gaku's. When the maid had finished serving, Dai heard Gaku saying something about ladyboy lovers.

Someone tapped Dai on the shoulder. He turned to find himself looking right into Gaku's eye.

"You could get a job in here as a maid," he scoffed at Dai. "Then I can be your master. Mind you'll probably be rubbish at that too."

Dai looked Gaku directly in the eye then deliberately turned his back on him. "As I was saying seeing the Cherubim flying round the ballroom is quite a sight," he said, making pretend conversation so that Gaku would know he was being ignored.

A hand gripped Dai's shoulder. "Oy, maid, don't ignore me when I'm giving you orders," Gaku snarled at Dai while Waku sniggered in the background.

"And what are you going to do about it?" Dai snapped back angrily.

"I'm going to punch you in the stomach is what I'm going to do," Gaku announced.

Dai looked at Waku sitting behind Gaku, sniggering at his oafish friend's bullying tricks.

"Yeah, whatever," Dai said bravely, tucking his hands into his belt and even taking a moment to crack the best smile he could muster at Tenkou, as if it were all a good laugh amongst friends.

"Think this is a big joke do you?" Gaku was almost shouting and his face was flushed with anger. "I'll show you what a big joke it is." He swung a hard fist into Dai's solar plexus. Dai didn't move. His face didn't flicker. Gaku stood confused, rubbing his bruised knuckles.

"What the fuck," Gaku swore and grabbed at Dai, but was unable to get a grip on him. He swung another punch, this time at Dai's head, again without any effect.

"What the hell's going on here?" Gaku wailed, his attempts to harm and humiliate Dai failing fast. "You're fucking weird, weirdo," Gaku said, backing nervously away and tripping over a chair. He fell flat on his arse much to Dai's delight.

Getting back to his feet Gaku told Waku to hit Dai. Waku wasn't sniggering any more. He half stood, unsure whether to carry out his orders or retreat. Dai took a step towards Waku who promptly fell back off his chair and onto the floor.

The bullies picked themselves up and started to leave. Their hurried exit was interrupted by the maido who wanted payment. Gaku threw a handful of notes at her and the two bullies rushed out, casting fearful glances over their shoulders.

"What happened there?" Tenkou asked, barely able to keep his mouth from hanging open.

"Just one of the perks of having alien friends," Dai said proudly. "A little gift from Neko."

He unclipped something from his belt and showed it to the others. A small metal clip with a tiny silver stud on it.

"What is it? How does it work? Can I have a go?" Tenkou asked in a single breath.

Dai threw the clip to Tenkou. "Put it on your belt or pocket then press the stud," he instructed.

Tenkou did this, then said. "Nothing's happened."

Dai picked up a cake fork and threw it at Tenkou. It bounced off him. "Try to grab him." Dai told Keiko.

She tried. "I can't." She laughed, her hand unable to hold onto Tenkou. "He feels all slippery."

Tenkou took the clip off and reluctantly returned it to Dai who tucked it firmly onto his belt.

"It's a personal force field shield," Dai said. "The stud generates a force field that covers your entire body, protecting you from attack. You can be shot wearing one of these things and you wont even feel it."

"Wow. A personal force field," Tenkou was almost drooling at the thought. "Think what you could do with one of those. You could rob a bank or anything., He mused. "Can Neko get me one? I'll do anything for it."

"I think that might be arranged for my special friends," Dai said.

"Can we be special friends?" Akina asked, fluttering her eye lashes at him. "I'll give you a kiss."

"A kiss now, and one when I get you the shield," Dai bargained.

Akina leant forward and taking Dai's head in her hands she kissed him on the lips. A good long kiss. She tasted different from Neko, but also good. She stroked a finger along his chin when they'd finished. Tenkou looked positively green with envy and Dai thought it a good idea to spread his fortune.

"If you want a shield Keiko, you should give Tenkou a kiss," Dai said.

Keiko looked a little doubtful but her eyes kept glancing back to the clip on Dai's belt. Overcoming her reservations she gave Tenkou as good a kiss as Akina had given Dai.

"Very well ladies you have a deal," Dai said smiling.

"Sealed with a kiss," Tenkou added, grinning from ear to ear.

Chapter 18 – Unfair advantage

The large grey pantechnicon truck came to a gravel crunching halt, at the side of the main road, leading to the Harding Industries Mount Fairview facility. Hydraulic pistons hissed and popped as the mobile command centre deployed. A satellite dish rose from the roof of the truck and with a clunk, locked in place.

Two unmarked black SUV's with tinted windows followed the lorry off the road onto the gravel and came to a sliding halt. The car doors flew open and eight people in dark suits leapt out and disappeared into the command centre, through a door at the back of the truck. The black SUV's swung back onto the main highway and shot back down the hill.

Inside the command centre, officers took their assigned places with Bing at the communications post. Monitors around the walls sprang into life, consoles lit up, and every officer donned a communications headset. The big digital clock at the end of the room read five thirty five am. One of the officers began calling out. "Delta Squad in position. Alpha Squad in position."

On a bank of monitors Bing could see the live feed from the squad leader's cameras. Several feeds showed woodland and hillside views and one monitor covered the Facility. As she watched the first rays of daylight began skipping brightly across the silver roofs of the buildings.

In the loading area a row of trucks waited under the arc lights as the last few pallets were fork-lifted on to them. Drivers and loaders could be seen moving about the loading bay. A puff of exhaust from a lorry told Bing they were ready to move off.

"All squads in position," an officer called out. Green lights flickered beneath the monitors.

"Air Support is now on line," another officer confirmed.

"We're good to go," a third announced.

Bing waited for the first lorry to move out, this would be a little payback to Bob for the merry dance he'd led her these past few weeks. She was still steaming about the meeting they'd had in London. Making a fool of her like that, inviting her to dinner at the very moment Harding Industries were making their move. He was laughing at her.

Bing was pretty sure the bastard had beaten her to the force field technology. Over the last few days incidents had been reported, isolated incidents, but it was clear from the intel that some sort of personal security device had gotten into the civilian market, while the military had nothing.

What really galled her was she liked Bob

Harding. She was fooled by his sophisticated ease, his charm. He made her laugh and there was something about him that she admired. She hated herself for it, for being so stupid, for being such a girl. She'd played the 'catch me if you can' card at dinner hoping to penetrate his defences. She'd let her hair down and worn a slinky emerald green dress that shimmered as she moved and showed off her athletic body in a way that was almost obscene. He hadn't fallen for any of it and now she was afraid, she had.

The Mount Fairview convoy reached the Facility entrance. The large electrified gates slid open and the trucks rolled out. She wasn't worried about them, she wanted them outside the facility, not trapped inside when the action started. The trucks would be meeting a road block further down the road and then she'd have several thousand of the security devices. But what her superiors really wanted was a production facility, the ability to turn out endless amounts of shields for the military to use.

"It's time," Bing said to the officer standing behind her.

"We have green light. We are go go go," the officer said into his headset.

On the monitors the images began moving as squad leaders started the assault on the facility. More black SUV's roared up the road past the command centre as the squads of soldiers approached the facility across the fields that lay on all sides, the net was closing in. The first helicopter flew overhead.

Yeah, Bing thought, there was no way she was going to let some alien or a smarmy stuck up Englishman get the better of the US Army. This was American soil and things would be done the American way here. The US Army would make sure of that.

The operation had to be swift. They knew the facility staff were likely to have personal shields and therefore conventional weaponry probably wouldn't work. But she had one or two tricks ready.

Black SUV's drove straight through the facility gates onto the front lot and fanned out around the entrance to the main building. Heavily armed dark suited officers flooded out across the tarmac covered ground.

Bing felt her ears popping, as if she were in an aeroplane. The air pressure had changed.

"Do we have weather change?" she asked an officer.

"No Ma'am, clear skys," came the reply.

A thought crossed her mind that this was not the best strategy, but the ball was in play now and there was no going back. She hoped her worst fears were not about to be realised. This could cost a lot of American lives if it all went horribly wrong.

The first team of agents approached the main building at a jog, and stopped a few feet from its gleaming steel and glass entrance. There was a strange moment when, to a man, their progress was arrested as if by an invisible wall.

"We're meeting strong resistance," a voice crackled from the communications system.

"Continue to advance," the order was given.

"Unable. Repeat meeting resistance. Some kind of barrier," the voice on the radio reported.

Right, thought Bing, lets see if we can't do something about this. "Send in the Energy System Unit," she ordered.

The agents outside the facility and the squads, of soldiers in the surrounding countryside waited ready for action, weapons pointing at the Facility's windows and doors, behind which there was no sign of life. Several helicopters circled overhead. A massive flat-bed truck slowly manoeuvred up the road and onto the Facility front lot. The ESU sat on the trailer, a huge green tube with silver pipes coming out of both ends. Technicians fussed round it's large green form like ants around a rotten apple, as they readied the ESU for action. Two long dark cables were rolled out of the side of the ESU and up to the edge of the invisible barrier.

"Now lets see what happens when we hit them with a burst of energy," Bing said. "Fire the Capacitor."

A great crackle of electricity forked out as the entire might of the capacitor was released through toroidal coils and the seething power, amplified and focused through the electrolytic crystal was fired into the shield. A semi-circle of flickering blue light grew from the point where the cables connected. They smoked and burst into flames. The ESU shook violently on its mountings. Agents were thrown onto their backs.

"Advance," the order was repeated, the agents approached the shield again, and were repelled again.

"We have negative impact. I repeat negative impact."

"Power up the targeted EMP System" Bing ordered.

The Electro-Magnetic Pulse system took a few minutes to charge up, during which a unit of soldiers probed the shield. With the EMP ready to fire, the area was cleared and all electrical equipment turned off.

"Fire EMP," Bing ordered.

A massive pulse of energy was released at the shield, following which, the agents approached the shield once more and again met with resistance.

Shit, thought Bing, what now? It was a stand-off. They couldn't get in, and whoever was in there, couldn't get out. There were no signs of the occupants. From the moment the first SUV had crashed through the gate barrier the loading bay workers had disappeared.

Outside the command centre the day began to warm up. California sunshine shone through the trees and it looked like being another beautiful west coast day.

"General Solomon on line one," an officer said.

"Bing, what the hell is going on down there?" Solomon demanded down the line.

"We're at an impasse General." Bing reported. "We're unable to take the facility, they've some sort of giant force field in place."

"This is turning into one almighty crock of shit," the General said. "We're gonna have the media all over this any minute now, this is California, there's no way we keep this under cover for long. Get it cleared up immediately," the General broke the connection.

"Ok Guys, we're pulling everyone out except the penetration teams," Bing told them.

The officers began issuing orders. The assault

squads disappeared back into the surrounding countryside. The ESU truck began backing out of the Facility entrance and down the road. Two new SUV's and four police squad cars arrived in the front lot.

"Phase two is now operational," Bing announced. They'd been prepared for the media attention, after all this was the land of the free, and the American media felt free to report on anything it liked, no matter what the Army told them. The cover story was simple, a hostage situation. Not many details, an armed person or persons had entered the facility during the night and were holding staff hostage.

Where was the call from Bob Harding? Bing asked herself. Surely he must know that the American's had attacked one of his facilities. She'd expected him to have been on the line to her by now. The bastard was holding out on her, making her sweat. Yes, she was sure that's what he was doing.

The minutes ticked by with no solution to the stand-off presenting itself. The predicted media press pack began arriving and soon their dish topped vehicles were parked in grounds at the rear of the facility. Dark-lensed cameras appeared and hair sprayed anchor people began their usual litany. "This is Amy Carter reporting for Channel Twenty news." The CIA's fake FBI agent delivered her counter intelligence to the salivating journos.

Luckily for Bing and her team, the so called 'hostage situation' was not the hot topic of the day. Harding Industries itself was providing the diversion. From Harding facilities all over the world the first truck loads of personal shields were being delivered to the major supermarkets and department stores. Kilometre long lines of eagerly queuing shoppers formed in front of the stores waiting for stocks of shields to arrive. As the lines grew longer and the day heated up patiences grew thin and fights broke out.

People waiting to buy shields became edgy, feeling vulnerable, as newly shielded shoppers threw baseballs, stones, even tins of food at each other, delighting in their own invulnerability. Desire intensified and the shields became not just the next must have thing, but the ultimate, must absolutely have, at any price, thing and the rioting started.

Bing watched the news coverage from the back of the command centre. Rioting in a Fresh Buy parking lot in Jacksonville, Ohio, flooded out onto the main street. Cars were attacked and burnt, people ran down the street shouting, throwing bricks and smashing shop windows.

Bing noted one or two unusual aspects to the riots. Both shielded and unshielded individuals were participating in the riot. So while some people were reacting to fear, others were taking advantage of their new toys. It was not long before the bank raids began and bank after bank reported incidents. Drug dealers began working in broad daylight, gangs formed and roamed the streets with impunity.

As the day wore on police with personal shields appeared on the streets. It was unclear whether these had been supplied directly by Harding Industries or if individual police had bought their own, either way the increased police presence had the effect of calming the people down. Now they were left with the problem of the bank robbers and the injured.

Bing was both relieved and horrified by it all. At least the heat was now off her operation. No one was going to notice the botched assault on the facility. As if to underline this all but one solitary news crew had abandoned the facility grounds in a rush to cover the hysteria in towns and cities all over the US. As day broke across the planet the same reaction was seen again and again.

Bing was interrupted as an officer brought a brown cardboard box into the command centre. IT was an ordinary packing box with the Da Vinci Vitruvian man logo on the side.

"We've got the shields from the delivery trucks," the officer said. "There was some initial resistance, the drivers were all shielded, but they're beginning to grow tired of being trapped in their cabs and we've begun commandeering the contents of the trucks."

Bing looked in the box. There were thousands of little silver hemispherical button badges with pins on the back. Each button had the Vitruvian man image embossed on it. Bing picked one up and twirled it thoughtfully between her fingers, then she pinned it on her lapel.

"Do we know how these work?" she asked.

"Just touch the button," the officer replied. Bing tapped the button badge but nothing seemed to happen, was it working? How would she know? She thought she felt a tiny bit colder but wasn't sure. She glanced down at the badge on her lapel, it looked as if it had a faint glow to it. She tried picking up a pencil, but it rolled away from her. She tried again traping the slippery object between two fingers and slowly, she was able to grasp the painted wood surface of the pencil and picked it up. She tried to snap the pencil. Nothing.

"I've a forensics team report for you Ma'am," An officer said, passing a file to Bing. "The team have been experimenting with these for the last hour."

The report was slim. As Bing had found out, you could pick things up while inside a force field, if you did it slowly. The team had also learnt a gun could be fired at someone who was shielded without doing them any harm. Conversely a gun could be fired by someone wearing a shield. Shields didn't muffle sounds or suffocate the wearer, so they were gas permeable.

Simply touching the button a second time

deactivated the shield. After turning hers on and off a few times Bing decided there was an almost imperceptible feeling of her skin tightening and cooling when the shield was on, but other than that the only visible sign was a faint glow from the button itself.

Bing ordered all personnel under her command to receive a button shield then returned her attention to the news.

In New York criminals had taken to drive-by shootings in broad daylight. Early in the day gangs had successfully wiped out opponents, entire organisations had been dispatched. But by midday gang wars had become farcical, comical even, with the whiff of cheesiest Hollywood movie. Turf crews machine-gunned each others' cars into blazing fireballs, only for the occupants to walk unscathed from the wreckage returning fire with equal vigour. Once all ammunition had been fruitlessly expended, they took to whacking each other with anything that came to hand machete, knives, pieces of wood and bricks.

The first indication that shields had been smuggled into prisons occurred when rioting erupted in several penal facilities. Clearly this was a day for settling old scores amongst criminals, many felt totally invulnerable and set-out for revenge. A prisoner thrown from a cell block roof didn't get up and walk away. While the shield had saved his life from the fall, his internal organs had impacted against his bones and he was taken away in an ambulance, unconscious and untreatable, as he was still secure behind an impenetrable shield which the paramedics were unable to deactivate.

Daylight began to fade and as evening fell and Bing had still not received a call from Harding. It began to occur to Her that she might have played somewhat into his hands. How did the facility attack benefit Harding? It couldn't be as simple as embarrassing the American military, Bob didn't work like that, there was no advantage in it for him. He didn't make enemies where he didn't need, so what was his game?

She thought about withdrawing the penetration team and announcing the hostage takers had given up, killed themselves, it was all over, and if it hadn't been for the solitary news van sat in the facility grounds, she would have done so there and then.

At nine pm she gave in and called Bob Harding.

"Colonel Saunders. Bing. Hello. I've been expecting your call. How's the weather in California?" she could hear him smiling down the phone at her.

"What's going on out here Bob?" she asked.

"I would have thought you had a much better idea than I from where your sitting." Damn him, she thought. "You know what I mean Bob."

"If you're referring to what's going on inside the

Mount Fairview facility then I can't help you beyond saying that they've raised a limited area shield against a possible incursion on the facility. Apparently the grounds are not yet considered safe enough to turn the shield off. May I also add a note of personal gratitude for the excellent advertising the U.S Military has given Harding Industries' latest product, the limited area shield. We're expecting major orders from corporations and Cities around the world. I though the electrical attack was just spot on, nicely demonstrating the capabilities of the limited area shield, the big one, the kind protecting all our facilities."

"You bastard Bob." Bing screamed at him down the line. "You've hung me out to fucking dry here. "

"I didn't encourage you to take this action," Bob replied calmly.

"You knew we needed those shields." Bing replied hotly.

"And I warned you, the Astrospherians don't want to play ball with the military, the military doesn't play nice. Besides if we supply the Americans we have to supply the Chinese, the Russians, the North Koreans and the Iranians, otherwise it wouldn't be fair. We're doing deals with local law enforcement agencies, giving them every assistance we can. If you want more shields than the seven truck loads I let you have this morning, rather nice of me I thought, I didn't have to let those lorries out this morning. Then you'll have to send your troops down to Fresh Buy to get them like everyone else."

"If you want my advice Bing, think about getting out of the war game, it's just changed, war isn't going to be the same again. By the end of the year you are going to be looking for a new job. Tell you what, why don't you resign your commission and come work for me, tomorrow?"

"Fuck you Bob," she spat down the line.

"Well if you reconsider there's a good job waiting for you at Harding Industries," Bob replied, laughing.

Furious Bing cut the line. Her temples throbbed, her head felt like it was going to burst. She crashed out of the communications centre and punching the aluminium truck side with all her might.

"Fucking limey stuck up lying la-di-da fuck," she shouted at the two moons. "British jerk-off with your commonwealth, colonial attitude, fuck him," she seethed.

When she'd calmed down again she went back into the command centre.

"Recall the team, the operations over., she ordered. The black SUV's left the facility. The command centre lowered its satellite dish and antenna. Several more SUV's crunched onto the gravel and picked up the officers. Soon the road to Mount Fairview was empty and the sounds of the crickets returned. The lone news van pulled out of the lot and disappeared down the road.

The facility seemed to shimmer for a moment, perhaps just the heat of the day, and an imperceptible blue flicker ran up the building. A minute or so latter the tiny figure of a Cherubim came out of the depot doors and stood on the loading bay dock smoking a cigarette and watching the thin plume of smoke rise up into the blue Californian sky.

Chapter 19 – Unforeseen consequences

David was beginning to grow tired of his rooms on the fifth floor of the Metropolitan Hotel. He'd not been able to go home, or even out of the hotel for over a week now. Not since the release of the personal shields. His home, his office at the University of Durham, his office in New York and the lobby of the Metropolitan were all under siege from the media. David had not made himself available for comment.

He slumped dejectedly in an elegantly upholstered chair, staring at the newspapers on the coffee table. To be fair, no one seemed to think he was directly responsible for the riots, but as a Vice President of Harding Industries people had questions and he didn't have any answers.

He considered the newspapers lying on the table in the room. The story about the bank robber caught his eye.

A thirty five year old man from Brooklyn had been one of the first to get his hands on a personal shield. John 'Gonzo' Charlton had fallen early and easily into a life of crime. In and out of reform schools and handed from one uninterested relative to another throughout his childhood, he'd celebrated his adulthood with a prison sentence for burglary and this seemed to set a trend in John's life. At thirty nine years old John had spent just over half his adult life in prison.

His latest stretch in the big house had ended a few weeks earlier, when he bumped into an old friend, Rusty, from an earlier prison stay. They met in a seedy bar downtown and got drunk together. Rusty had a business proposition for him. He knew about a planned hijacking and they needed some trusty crew, he knew John was the man for the job. Jobless and living in a roach hotel, John didn't take much persuading. Two nights later found John and Rusty sat in the back of a dark blue car with a nervous jumpy boy called Flash and a large silent Moroccan called Momo. Flash, despite his youth, was the gang leader and he filled the rest of them in on what was going down.

The plan was simple. Flash's gang were to wait near an abandoned dockside warehouse for the hijacked truck to arrive. Someone who Flash called Franky, knew people and one of them knew a guy in the trucking business who had heard Harding Industries were hiring as many independent truckers as they could, to haul some alien stuff. The whole thing was supposed to be secret, but Franky had paid the driver off and now the delivery was going to come to the warehouse where Flash and the gang were waiting.

They sat in the car, smoked cigarettes and talked shit. Flash appeared agitated and jumpy, his knee twitched incessantly which made John feel nervous. "Don't mind Flash," Rusty told him. "He's just, you know, a bit sparky."

As dawn broke they heard the rumble of an

engine coming along the deserted wharf leading to the warehouse. A large white unmarked truck drove round the corner. The gang sprang into action, opening the warehouse doors for the truck. The sound of the dying engine echoed in the vast dusty space as the driver climbed down from the cab, the harsh crack of a gun shot rang out. Flash had shot the driver.

"We have to cover our trail," Flash explained to the gang, just before he died.

The second shot had come from the truck driver who waved a large automatic at the remaining members of the gang. Flash lay dead on the floor, blood oozing from a hole in his head.

"Little fucker, try to shoot me would he?" the driver swore and kicked Flash's corpse, before picking Flash's pistol from the floor. "Right, you lot work for me now," the driver told them. "Get this stuff unloaded."

The sudden, violent ,change of boss left the gang reeling. To start with they did as they were told, opening the doors at the back of the lorry and piling the boxes onto the warehouse floor while the driver stood over them with a gun. John was getting a bit pissed off at the way things were turning out. Heaving boxes was not the kind of work a self-respecting hardened criminal like himself did, normally he was the one pointing the gun. None of them were keen on the labour and their work was sloppy. It wasn't long before Rusty failed to catch a box and it fell, split open, and its contents scattered across the floor. John saw what looked like hundreds of shiny sliver button badges.

"What the fuck's this?" John said picking up a handful of the buttons.

"You just keep moving those boxes," the driver said, motioning with the gun.

"This is fucking rubbish. What you gonna do with all these buttons?" John asked the driver, picking up a box and shifting it as he spoke.

"Got a contact with the Hells Angels? Running out of studs are they?" He taunted.

The driver laughed. "Don't you know what these are? How do you think I survived our friend's little attack?"

It had puzzled John. He'd assumed Flash had simply missed though he'd been so close he didn't see how.

"These are alien shields," the driver laughed. "I'm wearing one. All the drivers were given one before we left. In case we were hijacked," he laughed again.

"Shields, what are you talking about?" Rusty joined in the conversation.

"See, I'm wearing one of the little buttons," the driver explained. "You just put it on, touch it and *you're shielded."*

"What does that mean? " Rusty asked.

"Nothing can hurt you. Not axes or bullets or fists, nothing," the driver said.

"Like this?" John asked, activating the button he'd pinned on his t-shirt. The driver shot him. Nothing happened.

"Fuck me," Rusty said, staring from one to the other.

"Forget about that," the driver said, "Get on with unloading." He turned the gun on Rusty. "And don't get any wise ideas about the shields."

"Fuck that," John said. "I'm out of here," at which the driver shot him again, with no effect.

Momo, who until now had been in the back of the truck throwing boxes out, jumped down to the ground. "Fuck you," he said, carrying off a box of shields. The driver shot him, then Rusty then John again for good measure. John and Momo watched as Rusty's body fell lifelessly to the floor. They looked at each other then rushed the driver knocking him down. They set about him with fists and boots but soon realised their blows had no effect, so picking up a box of shields each, they walked out of the warehouse.

David put the article down and crossing the room poured himself a coffee from the heated pot. Was this what it was coming too? He asked himself. What was probably the most significant advance in peace, and what use was it being put to? Protecting the weak and innocent? Saving lives? No it was being used for crime. He returned to the chair and continued to read.

Throwing the boxes of shields on the back seat John and Momo jumped in the car and drove off. After a while Momo asked, "What now?"

John thought about this. He hadn't intended to become the gang leader, in fact, he'd thought the gang was finished, but now, here was Momo, this lump like giant of a man, asking John what they should do, that, to John's mind made him the boss of a very small gang, more a team or partnership really. They had several hundred shield buttons in the car, but neither being salesmen the only course of action John could see was a visit to a fence he knew across town.

He gave Momo directions to the pawn shop on Earl and third and slumped back in the lumpy old passenger seat. He flicked the glove box lock open and closed, open and closed with impatience as they sat in slow moving traffic. Suddenly the glove box flew open and a pile of parking tickets fell into the foot well, joining the burger wrappers and drinks cans that were already there.

Sitting in the glove box half wrapped in a bit of oily cloth lay a dark black glock semi-automatic gun, it's muzzle gleaming under a thin sheen of gun oil.

"You've got a gun in here," John said. Momo nodded.

"Does it work? Is it loaded?" John asked. Momo shrugged, "Not my car," he said.

John picked the gun out of the glove box and examined it. He guessed it had been Flash's gun and it appeared to be in good order. The clip was full and the breach slid smoothly when he pumped a round into the chamber.

"You know I've just had an idea," John said. "Pull over here and I'll tell you the plan over breakfast. Momo parked the car and they entered a dinner which smelt of cheep fat and burnt coffee. They took a table next to the window and while they waited for coffee and waffles John outlined his plan.

"Seems to me," he said, "that we've got the new toy on the block. You saw the buttons save me, hell, and you from being shot. Now think about it, while we can't get shot, other can. I'm thinking this is as good a chance to rob a bank as any. You in? Cause if you are there's an Agricultural Credit and Loans bank just across the road that should be opening, say, oh, about the time we finish breakfast."

Momo sat a while in silence, perhaps thinking, perhaps just being Momo, then he said in his thick Moroccan accent, "Sure, you are the boss."

They'd finished their waffles and were paying the waitress when the manager arrived at the bank and let in waiting staff and early customers. John gave the waitress a large tip, which he thought a lucky thing to do, then he and Momo got back into the car. John took the glock and tucked it down the front of his jeans as Momo pulled the car across the road and parked right outside the Agricultural Credit and Mutual bank.

The pair walked casually into the cool marble and steel bank. John fired the glock into the air to attract staff and customer attention.

"This is a stick-up, everyone on the floor," John ordered while Momo relieved the security guards of their weapons and locked the bank doors.

"Everyone does as they're told and no one gets hurt," John told the confused and frightened customers. The tellers and other bank staff were all lying on the floor as they were supposed to but three customers were just standing and watching the scene.

"On the floor," John screamed at them waving his gun in their faces.

The group, two young men and a young woman, laughed at him. One of the young men said, "Just carry on, this is great man."

John shot him.

"Wow, cool," the young man yelled, dancing

around. "Look, not a scratch."

This remark caused a stir amongst the other customers and staff.

"Shit they're wearing shields," John called out to Momo, a gesture which saved the life of a have-a-go security guard, who had been about to tackle the robbers thinking John's gun didn't work.

"So?" Momo replied.

"So, how we gonna shoot them?" John shouted. He span around pointing his gun at everyone. "No one move," he ordered.

"Get them," an elderly customer shouted out to the young man who, with a smile, smashed a chair over John's head.

"Not working," the young man informed the hostages in a matter of fact voice. "I think the robbers are shielded too."

"What's a shield?" a female teller called out.

"Shut up, shut up the lot of you. You don't have shields so you can be shot," John screamed.

"Don't worry," the shielded girl cried out. I'll got get shields for everyone," she began walking towards the door.

John fired again. "You leave here and I'll be forced to kill someone," he threatened the girl, then *grabbed a female hostage by her hair and pushed the gun muzzle into her mouth. The hostage's eyes bulged in terror, her sensible brown shoes skidded on the marbled floor as John forced the middle aged hostage to her knees.*

"She isn't wearing a shield. You wanna make me paint her brains all over the walls?" John threatened. "You stay right where you are or she's dead."

This had the desired effect and the shielded girl returned to her position next to her friends. The group now looked far more serious, the girl on the verge of tears. She kept glancing at the poor woman, pulled half up on her knees, with a gun in her mouth.

"OK people this is what we are going to do now," John said, thinking on his feet.

"We're going to wait for the police to call. Then they're going to give us safe passage out of here and we can all go our merry ways, if, you all behave yourselves."

Silence fell in the room. Everyone waited, tense, nervous, jumpy. Tellers cast glances at the black phones which sat on each desk, willing them to ring. Someone coughed dryly. The hostage wept quietly. Momo tapped the tips of his boots on the polished concrete floor, tap, tap, tap, as the minutes ticked by.

The entire bank jumped when the phone on the

manager's desk rang. John still holding his hostage, signalled Momo to answer the phone, then thought better of it. Momo didn't seem to be the brightest he'd met, perhaps he, John, should negotiate with the police.

"Get her," John said to Momo indicating that he should hold the female hostage. There was a brief struggle as they exchanged places and guns, then John went to answer the phone.

A cool voice spoke down the line, "We'd like to send Ms. Bartlett in to negotiate, she's coming over now."

John said OK and hung up. Momo looked at him. "She wants to come in and negotiate." John said crossing to the doors and peering out. Ms. Bartlett, a neatly dressed blond haired negotiator in her early forties was walking towards the bank. John let her in and locked the door after her.

"I'm Sarah Bartlett from the District Attorney's office. I can make you a deal."

"Go ahead," John said.

"Mr. er..."

"You can call me Gonzo," John said.

"Mr. Gonzo, the District Attorney is prepared to make you a deal. If you leave all the hostages behind, you and your colleague can walk away with me, as your hostage. After all, we can't stop *you, your wearing shields."*

John thought about this a moment, "And we take the money," he stated.

Ms. Bartlett frowned a moment then said, "Very well and the money, but only two bags each agreed?"

"Agreed," said John.

The three of them left the bank with Ms. Bartlett leading the way, John pointing a gun at her back. Momo climbed in the front seat and John and Ms. Bartlett climbed in the back with the money. That was when the police car hit them. Now they were jammed in the car.

"What the fuck," John cried, trying to put the gun to Ms. Bartlett's head.

"She's wearing a fucking shield," John moaned and lowered his gun.

"Now gentlemen, just how long are the three of us going to sit here like mugs?" Ms. Bartlett asked.

David tossed the magazine back onto the coffee table. Just what was it he was involved in? Had Bob been levelling with him when he'd said he'd had no idea there would be a reaction like this. Was Harding Industries to blame for the civil unrest and deaths as some politicians and journalists were claiming? or was it more complex than that, as Bob had claimed. Harding

Industries had done nothing to excite people about the product, and people's reactions had come as much of a shock to Bob as it had to David. He couldn't help agreeing with Bob about one thing. The shields were changing the world.

He flicked over the pages of the magazine and found an article by the London Times Foreign Correspondent, who'd recently interviewed front-line villagers in Helmand Province, Afghanistan. The journalist wrote about the experiences of one young woman in particular, Hami, who had returned to her village after finishing her degree in agriculture at the University of Kabul.

"At first it was hard being back here," she said. "Others in the village don't always agree with the way I was educated, that I am an educated woman. Men in particular don't like to take orders or advice, from women. So I mostly work with the women here.

"We grow mainly wheat and maize, but I've been experimenting with cash crops and have had some success with tobacco and coffee. A lot of the fields further up in the mountains are opium or cannabis and are controlled by the warlords. Every year they try to persuade us to turn fields over to these crops also, but we're too low down the mountain and if we do, the Army come and burn the opium fields.

"In the autumn the Taliban come from the mountains and try to take our food and

sometimes destroy our crops, sometimes they execute people who have upset the local Mullah. Life is very difficult here in the mountain footlands, both the land and our neighbours are hard and unforgiving.

"That has all changed since we got the personal shields and the village has a limited area shield of it's own."

One building at the edge of the village stands either side of the shield wall. One half of it is in ruins from the mortar shelling this village underwent only two days ago, a reprisal from the local warlord for having a limited area shield. Half of the building stands untouched. Just one dramatic example of the change the shields have brought to this remote village in Afghanistan.

Hami went on to explain how personal shields are making a difference here.

"We received shields from UNICEF for the whole village. At first people were a bit afraid but after the UNICEF workers demonstrated them we all took one. Now people can travel safely to surrounding villages. They have learnt that if you're wearing a bag when you activate your shield, the bag is shielded too. Whatever you're carrying is shielded.

"Taliban and Warlords are still a problem. We've had our livestock shot and they blow up trucks and buses, destroying peoples' goods and property, but now it just makes people here angry

with them and they are keener to help the Army find them.

"I have tried experimenting with the shields on our livestock. I found if you put a shield on a chicken and touch the button with the chicken's wing, the shield activates, but unfortunately I was not able to turn it off again, and the chicken died of starvation several days later."

As we are talking a truck piled high with goods arrives at the village and Hami takes me over to the shield entrance to see them unloading. "This is the only way in or out of the village now, " Hami explains to me. "At night we can close the shield completely and are safe from attack."

In a building in the centre of the village Hami shows me the shield controls. A simple silver dome about the size of a half grapefruit sits on a shabby desk in the mud lined room. Hami shows me the five finger sized dimples on the sphere's surface. "The dimples control the shield entrances, pressing this one turns the shield on, and this one opposite, turns it off," she explains.

We go to drink more coffee outside Hami's hut and she tells me about the attack she witnessed the day before I arrived.

"We saw the Army early in the morning coming up towards us. Not long after some Taliban appeared in those rocks over there. The usual firing and shouting happened for a while. Then they noticed no one was getting killed, so the

Army advanced. The Taliban kept firing and shouting at them till the Army were almost face to face with the Taliban. Now the Taliban have retreated up into the hills and the Army is blocking them in."

Here in the Afghani foothills the face of war is changing forever. While there's almost no aircraft activity, military ground forces are pouring into these foothills and chasing Taliban and Warlord alike, back up their mountains, where they'll be imprisoned in their strongholds. As Hami and I sit sipping our coffee and the sun dips over the Afghani mountains high above us, the first lorries carrying cement and iron reinforcement drive past the village on their way up the mountain to seal the insurgents into their mountain strongholds.

Today Afghanistan is Changing, tomorrow it will be a different place. Hopefully a place with far less to trouble it than has been the case in the past.

David's moral debate had kept him in the hotel all week. Was he to blame? Was there any blame? He'd been badly shaken by events, but the articles he had read helped him put things in perspective.

Chapter 20 – Alien lover

Several weeks had passed since Harding Industries launched the personal force-field shields and David was able to return to his home in England. He'd bought himself a manor house in the Yorkshire Dales which he felt was very much in keeping with his status as Vice President of the world's most powerful company.

He'd something else to be pleased about. Bob was sending the Langonai, Softly, to Yorkshire to brief him on the next big Astrosphereian product to be launched. They weren't going to make the mistakes they had with the personal shields, Bob assured him. This time they were going to get it right.

David had had some misgivings about the launch of the shields. The riots and the crime sprees, not to mention the collapse of great chunks of the military supply sector, primarily in armoured vehicles, artillery and missile production. Hundreds of military hardware companies had gone bust over night, but here in the remote Yorkshire dales that all seemed a world away.

He put the final touch to the room prepared for Softly. While his housekeeper had made the bed and aired the cupboards, he wanted to make a personal gesture. He brought the vase of flowers up from the kitchen and placed them by the bed. Pink roses, her favourite Earth flower, she'd mentioned once.

David looked out of the bedroom window at the beautiful Yorkshire moors rolling off to the distant horizon. Dry stone walls marked out fields. Here and there the odd hardy tree stood guard over flocks of sheep and herds of cattle. The soft warm sunshine of early autumn gave the scene an enchanting glow. The beauty of the Yorkshire dales, that was the view he was giving her from the bedroom window. He checked his watch. She should be arriving by gondola any minute now. David went downstairs and waited in the living room for her arrival.

He didn't have long to wait. A red and gold gondola began its descent into the lavishly large, though wind swept, garden at the back of the house. David rather liked the look of the resplendent, brightly coloured gondola sat in his garden, it straingly gave the old place a royal feel, a touch of the old Empire. He hurried across the grass to greet Softly.

She stepped gracefully down the ramp in tight black jodhpurs and expensive riding boots, a long green silk shirt specially tailored for her extra arms, belted at the waist, and a cream coloured fur-lined sleeveless jacket.

"Hi, hello, welcome to Chez Shawdale," David said, greeting Softly at the bottom of the ramp and kissing her on either cheek. She smelt faintly of Chanel number 5. "Can I help you with anything?" David asked.

"What a lovely place you have," Softly replied. "You can help me with my bags." She handed David a loop of pink leather with a leather strap which was attached to a large pink trunk and when David pulled the strap, the luggage followed obediently, bobbing along in mid-air.

David and Softly began the walk up to the house, the luggage following along behind them. "That's rather nifty," David said of the luggage.

"Bob is thinking of launching a floating luggage line," Softly said. "Amongst other things. We must have a chat about that later, but first please show me around your beautiful home."

They lead the luggage up to Softly's room. David was pleased to see she noted the roses and the view. Then he took her on a tour of Shawdale Manor.

The wood panelled grand entrance hall with it's main staircase built in aged oak gave access to the upper floor and the ground floor reception rooms. On the left a spacious living room and on the right a dinning room. Behind the staircase a stone flagged passageway led to the kitchen.

After Softly had been given the grand tour they sat down to eat a simple lunch of cold meats and cheese. "This is all local produce," David said. "I was thinking we could go for a walk over the Dales this afternoon,. See some of the local countryside. It can be quite beautiful."

Once they'd eaten, they strolled across the garden and along the lane which led into the countryside, and the view from Softly's window. The single track of tarmac wound it's way over hill and dale a thin dull ribbon of dark grey threading between dry stone walls. Large tractor tyre prints and hoof marks were stamped into the mud at either side of the road. David opened a large wooden gate and they entered a field.

A warm sun shone in the pale blue sky as they walked over tight springy grass cropped short by sheep. At the top of the field they came to a stile snicket cut into the stone wall with two large stones to help them climb over. As they began walking down the far side of the hill with the sun filled valley spread before them, Softly slipped her arm through David's.

"It is beautiful," she said, looking into his eyes.

"I used to come up these hills as a child," David said. "My parents would rent a small stone cottage near Kettlesing and we'd spend the weekend rambling through the Dales." They came to a small stream bubbling along the side of the field. David straddled the stream, his solid walking boots planted firmly on the bank either side as he offered Softly a hand across. They continued walking along by the side of the stream looking for a way into the next field.

"I suppose you've spent your whole life in the Astrosphere?" David asked.

"Oh no, not at all." Softly said. "I was born on a planet, not unlike this one. Slightly less gravity so trees and grasses grow taller than they do here, and you wont recognise the species. They use chlorophyll though, so they're green in the summer and brown and red in the autumn. The part of the planet I was born in is white with snow all winter. I come from a particularly mountainous region which we're only able to populate because of the gondola. I remember my childhood rides flying home from school on winter days when everything was covered in snow and the whole world looked like one giant white snowball, all clean and new."

"We're you ever snowed in?" David asked.

"No no, the gondola are always available and capable in any weather," Softly told him.

They walked further, now uphill again and at a slightly slower pace than David was used to because Softly was used to lighter gravity. For a while they walked in comfortable silence, watching each foot placed in front of the last, the gentle sound of bird song pleasing in their ears.

"Still it must be nice being out in the open again, after all that time in the Astrosphere," David said.

"It's not at all bad in the Astrosphere," Softly replied. "But yes, it is nice to step onto solid land as it were. To have a far horizon to look at."

"How long were you in the Astrosphere for?" David asked.

"About forty earth years," Softly said.

"You don't look like a forty year old woman," David remarked. "You look much younger."

"That's because I am," Softly replied to David's surprise.

"How can you be younger?" he asked mystified.

"I'm not younger in the sense that I'm..." She had to stop and think about it. "I'm eighty three Earth years old."

"Wow, you don't look a day over thirty, how is that possible, do you live a lot longer? Are you naturally young looking all your lives?." David was astonished.

"No. No, naturally, that is to say 'in the wild', we would live about fifty years, much as your species does. However, we've extended our natural lifespans with a medicine that keep us alive for hundreds of your years. We age much as you do, our muscles sag our skin looses its elasticity, it just happens much more slowly than nature intended, and we have surgery and youth drugs that combat these signs of age."

"So your youth and beauty is thanks to youth drugs and surgery?" David asked.

"No no," Softly laughed. "I'm far too young for that. Physically I'm a thirty six year old, but I've lived eighty three years, that's all."

"It's an anti-generic isn't?" David exclaimed. "You're using some anti-ageing drug."

"Yes. We have a drug that arrests ageing. It can't make you younger, but it makes growing old take a lot, lot longer," Softly explained.

"How much longer?"

"Oh, five or six times longer," Softly said casually.

"Five or six, so you could live to be four hundred years old?" David calculated.

"Well many people stop taking the drug once they're physically over eighty or when physical enfeeblement sets in, and of course children don't take it so the first twenty years of our lives we age at a natural rate, so most people live around three hundred years."

"Does it work on humans?" David asked. This was an exciting thought.

Softly smiled at him. "Oh yes."

"We must start supplying the world with it. Everyone wants to live longer. Surely it's everyone's right to," David insisted.

"It's one of the things Bob has sent me up here to

discuss with you. You know he feels some mistakes were made with the launch of the personal shields. We should have considered the possible reaction. Of course things are better now because of the shields. As I undersand it organised crime in the Mafia sense is almost completely wiped out, physical threats are no longer, well a threat. The shield isn't a gun, it's purpose, its use, is completely passive. It's defensive not an offensive.

"No one need worry about being blown up by terrorists anymore, though a fall from a plane would be fatal, but that will change too we hope. We want to bring the gifts we have to humanity, but you guys don't make it easy.

"Take the anti-ageing drug for example. We want Harding Industries to distribute the drug world wide. It's already got the infrastructure with facilities round the world, but your drug laws prevent us from introducing the drug for seven to ten years. We don't think people will wait that long. You see the dilemma we have? Not withstanding that at the moment we're not capable of the production levels needed."

"Can't the Astrosphere supply us?" David asked.

"No, the Astrosphere is capable of providing for its population, but there's no extra capacity. The Astrosphere has a highly balanced ecology. It's not natural like a planet and we have to be very careful what we introduce. It's why no human has been allowed there and no Sashooian allowed back. First we must see what incubates on Sashoo. If there is a serious health risk the Astrosphere will be forced to abandon us here."

"Wow you'd all be stuck here then?"

"Not everyone would complain. Already several hundred Sashooians are basically living on Earth permanently. I'm one of them. I like it here. I like it better than home and I like it more than the Astrosphere. Like everyone else from Sashoo I was aware of the risks of making planet fall, of landing on your planet."

By this time David and Softly had made it to the bottom of the hill and along the valley floor. Beside them the stream had become a flat bed river lined with massive chunks of slate grey stone that despite having lain for hundreds of years had not been worn by the ice cold crystal clear waters that rushed over them.

The sun began to dip behind the hill tops. It grew colder as the hills shadow fell across the valley.

"We should think about getting back," David said. "Lets get home and warm up in front of the fire."

"Yes. It has been a good walk," Softly said, fiddling with her watch.

"It's still a good hour's walk back from here even if we stick to the main road," David said.

"Oh, you want to walk back?" Softly said with

surprise.

"How else are we to get home?" David asked, as a dark, red and gold object floated into view and headed down the valley towards them.

"I can send it back." Softly said.

"Ah, well now your gondola is here it would seem churlish to refuse the ride. Besides which, I think I'm quite glad to be going home now," David replied. Softly slipped her arm through David's and they walked up the ramp into the gondola.

They strolled over to the helm as the ramp closed behind them and they looked out on to hills and dales which shrank before their eyes. The gondola rose about two hundred feet and now the fields below them looked like they were filled with toy sheep and pipe cleaner trees. Here and there a miniature tractor or land rover moved across fields near farms which looked like dolls houses. In the distance, a bright ribbon of headlights and red glinting tail lights flowed along the motorway, strung out like a giant, Christmas tree fairy light.

The gondola floated down into the garden and David and Softly went inside the house to see what the housekeeper had prepared for supper. "I think this occasion deserves making a little extra effort," Softly declared. "I suggest we dress for dinner."

"You brought evening wear? I guess I can find

mine in the back of a wardrobe somewhere," David said.

He waited in the living room, leaning nonchalantly on the large marble mantelpiece wondering if a pipe would make him look more distinguished and lord of the manor like, when Softly entered the room. She wore her hair down with a small band of silver to hold it back from her face. A figure-hugging long blue silk halter neck dress that trailed to the floor with three inch high heel strapy blue sandals underneath. At her throat she wore a diamond choker, and on each of her four arms she wore a matching diamond bracelet. She seemingly floated across the carpet to join him by the fireside.

"You look stunning, beautiful," he told her.

"Why thank you good Sir," she smiled and curtsied. "That is right, calling you Sir?" she asked.

"Indeed, it's most appropriate to my sex," David replied.

"Ah good good, I find all that a bit confusing and I'm always afraid I'll get it wrong," Softly confessed.

David gave her a glass of champagne which she held in her upper hand by the stem, while her lower hand gently ran a finger around the foot of the glass. They chatted about the walk before going into the dining room to enjoy more wine and a sumptuous meal of chicken in white sauce , dauphinoise potatoes and mixed vegetables, followed by a chocolate orange desert, cheese, biscuits and liqueur coffees. They talked mostly about David and how his discovery of the Astrosphere had changed things for him. She laughed at his jokes, lightly touching his hand or knee when she did so.

As they got up from the table she tottered momentarily on her high heels and held him for support. They staggered back to the living room, where they fell laughing onto the large soft sofa which sat in front of a roaring fire. Sipping his liqueur and looking at Softly in the flickering fire light David felt himself falling in love. It seemed she felt the same, as she took his glass with a small hand and kissed him. He felt the stickiness of her lipstick on his lips and the taste of her in his mouth and the touch of her hand on his thigh.

David paused suddenly. Softly sat back and looked at him. "Are you all right?" she asked.

"Can we do this?" he replied feeling puzzled, confused. "Is it right? I mean you and me, we're different species."

"Yes we are," she replied, keeping her small hand on his thigh and he didn't remove it. "But we are also so very similar in so many ways."

"What about your lover Fortune?" David asked.

"She wont mind if we become lovers for a while.

I can stop seeing Fortune if that makes you more comfortable," David wasn't sure what would make him more comfortable, this was the weirdest experience of his life.

"I don't know, It's all so strange to me," David said.

"We like each other. Lets be adult about it, we're sexually attracted to each other, it's only natural that we would want to express that with each other." She leant in close to him and nibbled at his earlobe as her hand drifted up his thigh. David found himself once more in her embrace.

The ribbon holding up the top of her halter neck came undone and the front of her dress slid down revealing large round breasts cupped by delicate pale pink lace that allowed a hint of the firm nipple behind. She took his hand and placed it over her breast. Little gleams of sparkly dust stuck to his fingers as he softly caressed her. She pressed him back into the sofa and straddled him. Holding his head in her hands and kissing him, small fingers tugged at his trousers.

She pushed back on him and levered herself into an upright position, pulling him on to his feet in front of her, she pulled his jacket off and unfastened his shirt. He pushed at his trousers with his feet pulling them off. Softly wiggled her slim hips and the rest of her flimsy dress floated down round her ankles and she stood in blue high heels, blue lace top stockings and pale pink lace panties which contained a surprising bulge at the top and an inviting crease below. Softly pushed David back on to the sofa and straddled him with her knees.

She held his hands behind her head and kissed him violently while small hands guided his hardness inside her. As always when with the aliens, there was something both strange and strangely familiar about the sensation. Softly held his tongue gently with her teeth and rocked back and forth in his lap and David let himself go with the moment. Soon they were both moaning with pleasure as they rose to a crescendo of inter-species orgasm.

As he lay there with Softly across his chest, her large breast under his chin he wondered if what he had done was technically bestiality? But he let that one float by while he stroked her hair.

"We should go to bed," David said.

"I thought you'd never ask," Softly replied, stirring from on top of him and draining her champagne. They staggered up the stairs together and into Softly's room where they fell on the bed. She raised herself up on her elbow and said. "Oh yes, before I forget, I've got a gift for you." She rolled of the bed. Kneeling on the floor in her lacy underwear she wrestled with the trunk before it clicked open. She rooted about inside and came up with a small silver tube.

Triumphantly bearing the phial above her head

she sliped across the carpet on her knees to the bedside.

"It's something very special. I want you to drink it for me," she said, unscrewing the top of the phial and handing it to him. "Trust me it will do you good."

David drank. It was mainly tasteless, a tiny bit sweet and runny like honey. It clung to the back of his throat for a few seconds.

"Now you'll stay young, like me," Softly smiled up at him and stroked his chin.

"That was the longevity drug?" David asked collapsing back on the bed.

"Did you like it? " she replied, running a finger down his chest. "Did you like your first taste of eternal youth?"

"Um, I thought you said three hundred years..." David mumbled as she began kissing him again.

The following morning they woke up in a heap of entangled limbs and bed clothes and staggered down to the kitchen for breakfast.

"I've brought a case of the longevity drug for you darling." Softly said over the top of a big white coffee cup.

"How are we going to distribute the longevity drug to the people?" David asked.

"We have to be very circumspect at the moment," Softly said. "At first it will only be available to a select few, our little secret. But we expect to spread it, and this way we can keep pace with production. It's going to be seven years before your governments makes it legal for everyone, and some people need it now."

David thought about this as he bit into a piece of buttered toast covered with thick chunky marmalade.

"You know what we could do after breakfast?" Softly smiled coyly at him. "We could go back to bed?"

Chapter 21 – Change of heart

The rooms at the Maharajah Hotel in New Delhi still retained some of their glory from its former heyday, hidden beneath a veneer of shabbiness. The high ceilings, corniced and fluted with bunches of plaster grapes at each corner, flecked with the gold and purple paint of the glory days. The tall French windows with peeling white paint had dusty glass in the frames. The carpets, richly woven in dark reds and greens, were now faded, worn threadbare in the doorways. The upholstery on the oak and mahogany regency-style furniture was lumpy, the petite point animals and leaf patterns worn thin. Still what do you expect for the price? Bing asked herself.

Despite its run-down appearance the Maharajah Hotel still had the ability to impress one with the Majesty of the Raj, and for some odd reason its shabbiness created an acceptably modern face. It was comfortable and the service was excellent. Bing's room on the third floor had once been magnificent, now it was shabby chic. The sounds of the busy streets below floated in through the window on a light warm Delhi wind that teased playfully with the long net curtains which hung from the cracked ceiling to the scuffed oak-tiled floor.

There was character and charm by the bucket load. Contrary to the hotel's run down appearance, the rooms were clean, pleasant and richly appointed. The bath taps were a little corroded and stained and the white bath enamel chipped in places, but the water was hot and fresh and whilst lying in a mountain of bubbles staring at the marble walls there was still a great sense of ostentatious sophistication which, despite herself, Bing couldn't help liking.

It was about four in the afternoon Delhi time and Bing could hardly believe only five hours earlier she'd been standing on the White House lawn as a part of the American President's entourage. Whisked through the streets of Washington in a black Pentagon car, she'd seen nothing of the White House, instead she was led straight to a group of delegates waiting on the lawn's green grass. Before them stood the now familiar shapes of two Astrosphereian gondola each sporting the American flag on the side, and one gondola proudly carried the Presidential seal. For the first time in history an alien craft was to be Air Force One.

But then this was a day for historical events. The president and the representatives of fifty states were going to New Delhi for the first World Congress to begin discussing how they would continue discussing the business of establishing a world government. No one thought it would be a quick or short process, not every nation had elected to attend, but it was a beginning, an historical beginning. It was becoming clear that the world needed to come together if it was to deal with the issues the aliens' presence raised.

Delegations from all over the US and the world,

had been departing in Astrosphereian craft all day long from their homelands. For the representatives of the people, normal aeroplanes were now considered too risky, too vulnerable to attack and capable of mechanical failure. A personal shield might save you from a bomb, but it wouldn't save you from a twenty thousand foot fall, gondola were the only craft to guarantee safety and luckily Bing's old adversary Bob Harding had stepped in with an offer of gondola rides to all World Congress delegates. Only the few countries who didn't trust the Astrosphereians sent delegates on conventional aircraft.

Bing had a half hour wait before Air Force One rose sedately from the White House lawn. The second gondola with Bing in it followed Air Force One up into the clouds above Washington. The gondola quickly floated up to thirty thousand feet giving Bing the stomach churning sensation of being in a high speed lift. She had the feeling of being only just on the comfortable side of fast as the gondola accelerated across the sky. Through the large front windows of the gondola the black starry sky of space hung above them while the whites and blues of sea and sky lay below.

The speed of the gondola was not the only disconcerting thing about the ride. The lack of pilot, helm or controls was also discomforting. The lack of apparent control to the craft gave Bing a feeling of unease, of not being in control, though she supposed that in reality the sensation was little different from any other transport where you're not the driver yourself.

Five hours after leaving Washington the Presidential gondola began their descent towards Delhi International Airport. They weren't going to land at the Airport, what would be the point when the gondola were able to land directly at the American Embassy? However the Astrosphereian craft were using regular flight paths for their descent over the city to prevent posing any danger to regular air traffic.

Below Bing could see regular aircraft landing and taking off, but at the gondola altitude several hundred gondola of all sizes and colours arriving and leaving. Those leaving from the Airport bore the Harding Industries logo and carried executives, businessmen and the wealthy. So much more convenient and safer than the old aeroplanes. No need for baggage security, no holds, so no need for check-in, simply carry or wheel or lead your luggage on board. No delays or space restrictions. As gondola filled with passengers new gondola materialised out of nowhere on the tarmac. The only thing preventing the entire world from flying by gondola was the price. Harding Industries had a deal with the world's major airlines and airports to keep gondola prices at luxury levels.

Never the less many airlines were beginning to feel the pinch. Unable to compete on comfort, speed or convenience meant loosing the highly lucrative business class and all airlines were quickly becoming budget. A brief golden age of budget flights had begun. Meanwhile as quickly as airlines went under, Harding Industries bought them up and stripped their assets. The aeroplane manufacturing sector was already in meltdown, facing the inevitable supremacy of the gondola as air transport orders for new aircraft were drying up. Again Harding Industries stepped in, bought up the companies and tore them apart.

At Delhi the Presidential delegation received the luxury door to door service. Instead of descending at the international airport or the freight area with the other gondola the Presidential gondola continued towards the city of New Delhi. The city shield was just visible to Bing as light danced off dust falling from the atmosphere onto the massive force-field dome which now protected New Delhi. The Presidential gondola headed for a sky entrance, a gap in the shielding allowing gondola traffic to pass through. Somewhere in New Delhi there'd be a control room where the entrances could be either sealed against attack, configured for prevailing atmospheric conditions or simply switched off. These days it only rained in the city if the Mayor wanted it to rain, and of course, as long as it was raining on the dome. Rainy days, weather permitting, were announced two days in advance and were now only ever for a maximum of three hours.

The positioning of the sky entrances in the shield allowed a soft warm breeze to cool the citizens as they went about their daily business and on the hottest days the shield was darkened at its apex to provide shade across the city. It also created a new economic division. Land prices inside the dome shot up as it became the most desirable place in the area to live, while a massive shanty town grew up against the back wall of the shield. Entry to, and exit from, the city was now restricted to highways and rail links. Wide tree lined boulevards had been provided at every entrance to prevent the unmitigated level of accidents that had been caused by pedestrians using roads and railway tracks to enter the city.

The Presidential gondola began the final descent to the American Embassy, where everyone disembarked and the gondola performed their final disconcerting trick of dissipating to nothing. The gondola, now empty of people and luggage, simply stopped being solid, its edges becoming soft and fluffy as if viewed through a cheep plastic filter. As it lost definition it became a drifting rain of dust to be blown away on the wind, and it was gone. Anything left inside dropped to the ground. Bing watched as some coins fell and a drinking glass smashed,scattering glass across the dusty ground.

Half an hour later Bing was booking into the Maharajah Hotel after a bumpy jostling taxi ride across the city from the Embassy. She enjoyed the faded grandeur of the old Maharajah, it's seen better days façade and grandiose rooms. She was glad she'd taken Bob Harding's recommendation, but felt some resentment towards him, in that, he'd predicted her tastes so easily.

Sitting in a pure white fluffy bathrobe with the hotel's crest embroidered on its pocket, Bing studied the documents that lay on the carved oak desk. The first report was intelligence from the Afghanistan-Pakistan border.

Apparently the US military weren't able to get enough cheep vehicles to carry troops to the area. Construction work had started on a car factory at Keshem but it would be at least three weeks before it came on-line. There were issues with roadside bombs destroying equipment intended for the factory and further delays looked imminent. Meanwhile a specialist team at the US Embasy had begun buying up every cheap vehicle in Kabul to the point where old cars and trucks were becoming expensive. The lack of co-operation from Harding Industries to provide troop transport was seriously hampering the Americans' activities in the area. This was one of the reasons Bing was in New Delhi, to try and persuade Bob to help with the Afgan war effort, though Bing knew, he'd not move on the issue.

A second report needing her attention outlined a field agent's failed attempt to gain access to Sashoo. This had been a constant frustration for American Intelligence. The agent had managed to board a gondola bound for the floating island which was currently off the coast of Madagascar. The agent had managed to disembark onto the island but as happened previously, the human agent had been immediately detected and returned to land.

The disembarkation bay on Sashoo was one of the most documented places on the planet, it was also one of the most boring, and frustrating. Little more than a vast hangar with cute carts scooting about loaded with passengers and cargo. The only thing of interest was the high number of Vespida reported to be in the hangar. Why had Bing's agents not managed to penetrate further? How were her operatives always so easily detected?

Yet more reports needed her attention. Jaycho and his team of Astrosphereian scientists still hadn't come up with anything of any use to her. This was yet another report that the US military didn't have the shield technology. It was clear now, that she was never going to get the answer from the Astrosphereians. Either they didn't know or they weren't telling.

They had however, been able to ascertain how the shields worked. They not only created force fields but each shield generator button was a tiny force field itself, and at the same time, a force field generator. In other words, Force field generators were made entierly out of a force fields. What Jaycho described as nano-field technology. By using forces to bend and control other forces they could create machines made from energy and free particles . These 'machines' could conceivably be anything, gondola, cars, houses, weapons, even floating islands.

Shield technology contained a further advancement. On activation a detection field was created that scanned the individual it was to protect, before the surrounding protective field was generated. The shields allowed atmospheric gasses to pass through them so they didn't suffocate the wearer to death.

A knock at the door interrupted Bing's reading. A Cherubim wearing an expensive black suit stood in the corridor. Was that a security earpiece he was wearing, Bing wondered, seeing a tell-tale clear plastic cord tucked behind its tiny ear. The Cherubim handed her a note before gliding off down the corridor on wide flexible wings. Bing took the note back to her desk.

Suspecting who it might be from she flicked open the neatly folded and expensive looking paper, As she'd thought, it was Bob Harding, inviting her to dine with him that evening. She'd only been in town for two hours and already Bob had found out. She was beginning to think his intelligence sources were even better than hers. She hoped he didn't want to gloat, which would be unlike Bob, so what did he want?

They hadn't really spoken since he'd infuriated her so over the Californian shield facility farrago. He probably thought she was still mad at him, which was true. Still, an expensive dinner would go some way toward making up for it and nowadays, according to her intel, Bob only did expensive dinners.

At eight o'clock in the evening Bing was waiting in the hotel foyer wearing a seductive shimmering blue dress and high heels. She'd spent a bit of time on her hair and fought it into shape, which in her case was a single plat at the back with a velvet and silver pin clip to keep it in place. She held a ludicrously impracticable clutch bag which went with her dress. The Cherubim who'd delivered the note entered the foyer and spotted her. The few people in the lobby watched politely as he hopped over.

"General Saunders, your carriage awaits., the Cherubim said. So Bob knew about her promotion too. Bing began to realise the power Bob Harding had in being able to use Astrosphereians to send his personal messages.

The Cherubim hadn't been poetic when he told Bing her carriage was waiting. Standing in front of the hotel was a gilded Cinderella carriage straight out of the eighteenth century, sans horses. At least he'd drawn short of having the Cherubim dress in full livery, Bing thought. The Cherubim opened the carriage door for her then followed her in. The carriage rose gently into the dusky sky and floated off, bobbing over roof tops and domes. She looked down at the evening bustle, the press of people in the crowded streets below. She could see the expressions of amazement on the faces of the people who looked up and pointed excitedly at the carriage. After a few minutes the carriage began descending into the hubbub below.

A large crowd was gathering in front of the restaurant to see the unusual craft arrive. Liveried waiters rushed out the doors to clear a space for the carriage and to greet its occupants. The Cherubim jumped out and held the door for Bing. A waiter stepped forward and offered her his hand as she climbed out of the carriage feeling like a queen. As she mounted the steps and entered the restaurant with the Cherubim, the crowd pressed in on the carriage and it dissipated behind her. Bing hoped she'd not left anything in it.

The restaurant's interior reflected the former glory of the Raj everything was in perfect condition, as if freshly decorated every morning. In the main eating salon large golden chandeliers shone and sparkled over a field of white cloth, covered tables, and gold and white chairs. Bing was shown to a table by the Maitre d' and left with the menu. She noticed the Cherubim had disappeared. A waiter came over with a glass of champagne and the menu.

"Mr. Harding offers his apologies, he'll be a few minutes late," the waiter told her.

Bing sipped her champagne and wondered how she was going to handle Harding. The last few attempts she'd been too direct, which was her way, and as much the fault of military training as personality. He always seemed to be one step ahead of her, she needed a way to throw him of his game. Would sleeping with him do it? Probably not. Sleeping with him, assuming he'd sleep with her, was unlikely to make him any more trusting, and was an idea born primarily from desperation.

There was a stir of excitement in the room, Bob had arrived. At that moment a brilliant idea hit her. Not without risk certainly, but workable. Perhaps she could play both ends against each other with her in the middle. Her plan however, depended on Bob making her an offer.

"General Saunders," Bob smiled at her, his face tanned, his simple black silk suit expensively cut, his cuffs showing just the right amount below the jacket sleeves. He seemed relaxed and in good humour, but that was Bob, you never knew what he was thinking.

"Congratulations on the promotion. I take it US Intelligence has seen fit to reward you for your work," he added.

"Thanks Bob." She replied rising to offer him a kiss on the cheek. "You know how it is, now I'm based at the Pentagon they had to make me General."

"And a ravishing one too." Bob said giving her an admiring look.

"Why thank you." Bing replied, she couldn't help a small smile of appreciation at the compliment.

"You know, I can't help wondering," Bing said. "Why you keep inviting me to dinner. Is it just to gloat on your latest triumph over me? Or is there something else, because I can't keep doing this with you if it's just to satisfy your ego."

Bob paused, holding a fork full of white fish raised ready to eat. He completed the manoeuvre thoughtfully, and when he'd swallowed replied. "Do I seem to be gloating? I hope I'm not. I'm a little hurt Bing that you'd think of me that way. I like your company. Your a challenge, something different from the people I so often meet, and if I'm honest I'm attracted, even though I know your tastes lie elsewhere and you only meet me as part of your job."

Now it was Bing's turn to pause fork in air. She coughed. "It's true, previously I've been seeking information, but over time I've come to like you too."

Bob laughed. "I can't see why, it seems to me that I'm more of an annoyance to you. I wasn't sure you'd come today, the last time we spoke you were so furious with me."

"And I haven't forgiven you yet," She replied. "Though this meal is taking things in the right direction," she added with a smile.

"As to my tastes, well lets just say I have wide, liberal interests and I'm prepared to try new experiences, sometimes I find I like them too," she smiled coyly at him.

"Indeed," Bob replied slowly. "And what was it you thought you might try now?"

"I've been thinking about what you said last time we met, about the military being finished. Well, it's probably not as drastic as that, but things have started to change and I'm no longer sure what sort of role the military will have in the future and what role I'll have in it."

"Don't tell me you're thinking of taking me up on my job offer? Which is still open by the way," Bob offered with a smiled.

"Well, as a mater of fact, I was thinking about it," Bing replied.

Chapter 22 – Airball match

Dai was very excited. Today he was going to see a truly rare event, the first ever Airball match on Earth. He and his parents had been invited by Neko and her mother Merit to a Cup game. One of the Clans competing was Neko's clan, clan Tarakoi. Dai knew which side he was rooting for, he had the hat, the shirt and the foam wings all in Clan Tarakoi team red and gold.

The match wasn't the only exciting thing of the day.Tenkou and Kanji were already green with envy over Dai's impending ride in an Astrosphereian gondola. Neko and Merit were to collect the Wakami's directly from their home. With an hour to wait for their arrival Dai was ready and sat with his foot tapping impatiently against the leg of his chair.

Dai didn't care that some of the kids at school were saying gondola were bad and put people out of work. Notably these were the kids who had relatives who worked in the aircraft and tanker industries, the businesses where gondola transportation was having the greatest impact. Dai wasn't about to give up his ride just because a few people had lost their jobs. They'd find new ones, he was sure. Indeed the days' sporting event was sponsored by Harding Industries job initiative program.

Eventually Dai's long wait was rewarded. The Wakimi family who lived in a flat, in a housing block, had no garden for gondola to land in so the red and gold liveried craft which had come to collect them hovered off the Wakimi's third floor balcony, while a crowd of intrigued onlookers formed in the street below. Nowadays such crowds usually harboured the odd malcontent shouting anti-alien slogans.

The gondola lowered its ramp over the balcony rail. The climb aboard was a little tricky due to the steep angle of the ramp which had formed small steps in its surface and a safety rail along both sides. Dai though this terribly exciting, looking down at the crowed below as he crossed the little bridge into the gondola. His mother however seemed rather agitated by the experience and had to take a quick sit down on a cushioned seat and catch her breath while his father greeted everyone on board. Dai rushed to the picture window situated at the front of the gondola in time to watch his house recede away as the gondola rose into the sky. Neko came over and joined him, her hand touched his as they held onto the brass handrail that ran along the curving window.

"Wow this is so cool," Dai said to Neko, with a massive grin on his face. "Tenkou and Kenji are going to be sooo jealous," Neko smiled back at him. She was wearing a tight little cheerleader's outfit in the clan colours and a pair of foam Cherubim wings which she was able to slip her lower arms into to make them flap. She wore red and gold make-up on her face and had had her finger nails painted in red and gold. Dai thought she looked hot.

"Where's Koneko?" Dai asked, noticing the Cherubim's absence. "Surely she won't want to miss this?"

"No, no," Neko laughed. "She won't be missing the match. She's in it."

"Wow, isn't she a bit young?" Dai asked.

"Only the children fly, so Airball is played by Cherubim children. That's why the rules are simple and the careers short. Adult Cherubim actually prefer your Earth game of foot kickball."

"It's football, or soccer if you're an American, though the rest of the world calls it football." Dai quickly informed her, and only just managing to prevent himself from going on to explain the offside rule.

Dai's father wandered over to join the teenagers by the window. "This is fantastic isn't it Dai?" he said.

"Yeah Dad," Dai replied enthusiastically. "It's brilliant. Out of this world. I can see the whole city below."

"It is amazing floating along like this., Mr. Wakimi agreed, then added. "We want you kids to have a good time today but we expect you to behave yourselves."

"Yes Dad," Dai droned.

"You can rely on us Mr. Wakimi," Neko assured him.

"Your Dad's funny. How does he expect us to behave?" Neko asked when Dai's father had wandered off to rejoin the other adults.

Dai wasn't completely sure, though he had a idea. He reckoned a repetition of the day they played with the yoyo discs at the hotel might be one of the things. Not that he'd have time for investigating the mysteries of kissing or anything like that today, he had an airball match to watch.

The alien craft began to descend towards a large park where a number of other gondola already hovered in a rough circle around an area marked out on the park grass. They slipped alongside another gondola and seemed to click into place. Dai felt a slight sensation of bobbing as if on some gentle unseen wave.

In front of the gondola the airball pitch was marked out, a large white circle painted on the grass, a football sized solid circle marking the centre. Two grand old oak trees stood opposite each other across the circle. The circle had clearly been marked to include the trees which bore white circles around their lower trunks.

More and more gondola joined the hovering craft and an ad-hock stadium made of floating gondola began to form around the pitch. There were spectators on the ground as well as in the air. Tension in the crowed began to mount as gondola opened their roofs and lowered their front screens, the sounds of the crowd flooded in.

"See the bench up in the trees?" Neko pointed it out to Dai. She indicated a narrow platform mounted high up in each tree, about fifteen meters from the ground. "And the goal on top of the tree?" Each tree had a pole strapped to it's trunk that stood a meter or so above the tree top. The poles had a small t-bar with a white knob at each end.

Floating down between the trees appeared a kind of lit score board with a small umpire's pod hung beneath it. An adult Cherubim in a purple leotard stood in the pod.

"That's the umpire," Neko explained.

"There will be a slight delay before the match begins while we create a safety field for spectators on the ground," the umpire announced. As he spoke two similar craft descended either side of the pitch. These had larger pods hanging from them which held the commentators. The floating commentary boxes released a swarm of small tubes, which were in fact cameras, and these took up position around the pitch. The boards above the commentary boxes displayed the images from the miniature cameras they'd just launched.

"Sports fans of all ages, species and gender, welcome to this presentation match between team Clan Tarakoi, in red and gold, and team Clan Quwai, in blue and white. This is the first Harding Cup match," a commentator announced. "But first, let me introduce the Harding Airball Majorettes." A tinny fanfare played from the loud speakers. Silver and blue flashes shot across the middle of the pitch before hurtling down towards the grass in a line which curved up again just before it hit the ground.

Dai reckoned there had to be at least thirty tiny Cherubim in silver and blue leotards, each about the size of a seagull, each with wings painted in silver and blue, each trailing a meter-long silver or blue ribbon.

The flock of Cherubim flew nose to ribbon in a high circle, forming a vertical ring above the pitch. The ring of flying creatures slowly tipped until the ring was horizontal to the ground, then the ring sank downward only to explode outward like the splash of water when a rock is dropped into a pond. The tiny winged flecks of silver and blue fell again toward the ground in bunches of threes, then shot up into the air spliting like little living fireworks.

At the apex of the manoeuvre, they suddenly played dead, dropping towards the ground as the crowd held its breath. At the last moment they all fluttered back to life, flying up and over and around in a seemingly random fashion till four rings of circling Cherubim formed above the corwd.

The rings became stars, which interlocked with each other. The Cherubim burst apart, flying to the edges of the pitch, then diving back towards the centre point in a whirl of spectacular, near misses. They rose again, and dove again, coming up in a large chevron and like an arrow without a shaft they flew off. The crowd was ecstatic, shouting and applauding the spectacle.

Once things had quietened down a little the announcer said. "Team Clan Tarakoi."

Seven small streaks of red and gold shot across the pitch and came to rest on the bench in the Tarakoi tree. The crowd applauded.

"Team Clan Quwai." Blue and white Cherubim streaked toward the vacant bench. Again the crowd cheered. There was a certain amount of good natured jostling amongst the diminutive young athletes as they settled on the bench. As with the display team, these Cherubim were dressed in leotards and had painted wings.

The umpire's pod rose above the tops of the trees where the umpire held out what looked like two luminous yellow cricket balls tied together with a piece of string. He held the bolas out of the pod with one hand and put a whistle to his lips with the other. On the benches the waiting Cherubim got very excited. One team Quwai member fell from his bench and had to clamber swiftly back through the branches to regain his position.

The umpire dropped the bolas and watched it fall. As it hit the ground he blew his whistle and three Cherubim from each bench swooped in for the grab. The remaining four from each team took to the air in a more leisurely fashion and began circling. A streak of blue and white shot up from the pitch floor headed straight for team Tarakoi's hoop. Immediately the defenders swooped down.

The leading Quwai player held one of the balls in her hands while other players snatched at the ball which trailed behind her. Red and gold Cherubim swooped and grabbed at the loose ball. Suddenly the Quwai player lost control of the bolas as a Tarakoi player pulled it from her grasp. He flew past her performing a barrel role then a loop-the-loop and headed back across the field of play towards the Quwai goal.

As he flew the Tarakoi player tried to reel in the spare ball, but now three defenders were on him. One successfully grabbed the free ball and for a moment they both held on trying to fly in different directions. The Cherubim, being unable to hover and needing forward movement to keep them aloft, began to tumble towards the ground, seemingly tangled in the bolas rope. The bolas fell free as the two Cherubim flapped away from each other.

Immediately four waiting Cherubim dove down to the ground and snatched up the bolas. This time two opposing players held a ball each but were forced by the nature of the bolas to fly in the same direction, neither wanting to let go and both heading off the pitch between the goal trees and out of play. The umpire blew his whistle and the Cherubim were forced to drop the bolas. It was snatched mid-air by a team Tarakoi player who dove, weaving and rolling towards the Quwai t-bar.

A Quwai defender knocked the bolas from his hands and it went flying into the Quwai tree. It was like instant Yule tree decoration, suddenly the tree was full of bright colourful clambering Cherubim. Now the action was amongst the branches. A Couple of Cherubim circled the tree in case the bolas fell out but the rest ran helter skelter along the branches and up the trunk. They were as skilful in the trees as they were in the air and seemed just as much at home there. The colourful flashes of team outfits flickered along the branches and occasionally the luminous yellow of the bolas balls could be seen some times higher and some times lower down the tree.

It looked like a fight might have broken out in the tree amongst some of the Cherubim, but it was difficult to tell. Suddenly a red and gold Cherubim shot triumphantly from the tree heading directly up. He stalled himself mid-flight and dropped toward the t-bar swinging the bolas as he came down so it wrapped itself round and round the bar. The scoring Cherubim flapped his wings and did a backwards somersault roll.

Joined by his companions they performed a celebratory aerial acrobatic manoeuvre before returning to their bench.

A slightly older Cherubim in purple flew heavily to the top of the tree, retrieved the bolas, and returned it to the umpire. The score board now read one nil to team Tarakoi. The first goal had taken less than two minutes to score.

"Wow, this is a fast paced game," Dai exclaimed.

"It's fast," she agreed.

"Were they fighting in the tree?" he asked.

"Oh probably," Neko responded, as she watched the umpire drop the bolas back into play.

"Is that allowed?" Dai asked.

"Can't really stop them," Neko said without taking her eyes of the action. "They fight all the time anyway. I said the rules were simple, besides which the umpire can't see what's going on in the trees any better than we can."

The crowd roared, drowning out Neko's words as team Quwai scored a goal.

"Cherubim parents can't control their children. The very attributes that have allowed an arboreal species like the Cherubim to avoid predators in childhood, by climbing and flying, equally prevent their parents from catching them and chastising them. The Cherubim have very free childhoods with no real authority over them at all."

As if to underline her words a new fight seemed to have broken out, this time mid-air. The combatants fell swiftly towards the grass but the fight split up just before the pair smashed into the ground and they flew apart. Dai noticed the Cherubim weren't terribly good at fighting, in-flight the main technique was to wrap a wing around an opponent which invariably sent both plummeting downward. In the tree the action was more tugging and pulling at each other with the occasional slap thrown in. But then what did you expect from a species who's natural defence was flight not fight, arboreal omnivores, hunter gatherers like humans, only with a greater appetite for insects. It was well known that the Cherubim considered locusts to be a great delicacy and were even creating a growing market for the insects.

After forty minutes the umpire called half time, with the score at a fairly even five to six in team Quwai's favour. The Cherubim teams flew off and the acrobatic team returned with a new routine. The spectators began their picnics. Dai and Neko found themselves eating egg and cress sandwiches and drinking orange juice from cartons with a straw.

It was not long before the second half started. Team Tarakoi came in hard and fast trying to catch up to their opponents one point lead.

About half way through the second half the players were beginning to flag. The extra burden of point zero two gees more than they were used to, was starting to tell on them. The play fell more and more to the trees.

"Normally we can see better than this," Neco said. "Championship goals are made to a specific design with the same number of branches on each and of course no leaves. But traditionally trees were where the game was played and even today Cherubim children will have a dive-about match using two trees as goals. At its most basic all you need is two trees and a piece of string with a rock tied on at either end."

"And the ability to fly," Dai added.

"Yes," Neko laughed. "And the ability to fly." She fluttered her foam wings.

The match entered it's final minutes with the score at nine to ten in favour of team Quwai. The Tarakoi had trailed their lead throughout the second half and it didn't look like there would be a comeback at this late stage. Suddenly a team Tarakoi broke for the Quwai tree and made it into the lower branches.

"That's Keneko! Go Keneko," Neko shouted, as the spry young Cherubim scurried up the trunk of the tree using hands, feet and wing hooks to speed her. It seemed Keneko had found a new source of energy to boost her. The other Cherubim followed her, but there was only one lone defender higher up the tree than Keneko. Just one small Cherubim to get past. The pursuing Cherubim snatched at the trailing ball that swung from Keneko's hand. For a moment it looked like the bolas would wind itself around a branch which would inevitably cause another fight and cost team Tarakoi the match, but the free ball bounced off the branch and Keneko was able to continue scrambling upward.

As she came close to the waiting Quwai defender she had two choices, either dive for the t-bar now, or try to dodge past the defender. In Dai's opinion, with her energy clearly low the dodge looked like her best option. She feigned, starting a dodge and then twisted it into a launch for the t-bar. The defender was caught off balance, but even this momentary hesitation in her rise up the tree had cost Keneko ground to her closest pursuer, who launching straight after her caught her by the foot and they both came tumbling down into the branches.

Keneko quickly recovered herself but the others were all over her before she could climb again. A massive scuffle broke out amongst the players, then the final whistle went.

"That was a great effort," Neko told the disappointed Cherubim when Keneko returned to the gondola.

"It was a magnificent match," Dai said. "Everyone in it deserves to celebrate."

He wasn't sure, but he thought he heard the disgruntled Cherubim mutter under its breath. "Lousy Earth gravity."

Chapter 23 – Three years later

Caroline had opened a shop on Koningstrase and for three years it had been a roaring success, providing her with a comfortable living, turning a tidy profit month on month. Recently however, business had become difficult in the prevailing anti-alien atmosphere.

The introduction of Astrospherian craft into the private market had had a serious impact on employment. The automotive industry collapsed overnight, affecting a vast swathe of workers. The makers of cars, lorries, buses and trains were forced to close plant. Rail workers, car dealers, component manufactures, road sign makers, Traffic wardens and parking attendants, were all laid-off, while vehicle licensing agencies, petrol stations and motorway cafés closed their doors for the last time. millions of people all over the Earth suddenly found themselves unemployed, and so the protests began.

For two weeks now Caroline had been unable to open her shop door. A permanent protest of angry placard waving people was camped outside her shop. She'd been forced to put her staff on holiday pay and board up the shop windows.

Today she was visiting with Chewfang in his apartment in little Sashoo, the Astrosphereian quarter of Stuttgart. As Caroline's gondola drew level with Chewfang's apartment it deployed the ramp and she crossed the short bridge, stepping onto the fourth floor balcony before dismissing her gondola.

"Caroline. How good to see you," Chewfang greeted her, opening the balcony doors to let her in. He was wearing a black business suit and tie. The rear of his jacket had been expertly tailored to allow his wings to fit through. Now middle aged, his wings were useless for flying and he kept them folded behind him most of the time, only spreading them to help when walking long distances. Besides which, with an adult wingspan of almost two meters, he couldn't unfurl them fully indoors anyway.

"Hi Chewy," she called him by his familiar name. "These damn protests are really hurting business."

Chewfang commiserated with her. As the principle distributor of alien products for Germany, Chewfang was well aware of the issue. All over the country his outlet owners were complaining about the same thing.

"How's Topaz?" Caroline enquired about Chewfang's business partner.

"She's fine, on business in Berlin at the moment," Chewfang replied.

Caroline had learnt that Topaz and Chewfang were life-long partners from childhood. As Chewfang had never bred he'd not formed a life partnership with another Cherubim, and as was often the case when this happened, had remained loyally attached to his humanoid friend. It was perhaps Chewfang's greatest regret that he'd never found a breeding mate.

"Any idea how long it will last?" Caroline asked, settling into one of the chairs in the apartment.

Chewfang hopped bird-like over to the kitchen. "Cup of tea?" he called.

A few minutes later, tea poured into delicate china cups, Chewfang took his saucer in one hand and without spilling a drop, swung himself up on to what looked like a modern art sculpture made of iron. It was Chewfang's chair. Despite resembling an accident at a coat-hanger factory the chair, for Cherubim, was the height of comfort. A neat little shelf on one of the upright struts gave Chewfang somewhere to rest his tea cup and keep his spare reading glasses.

He stretched his wings carefully, spreading them three quarters full and giving them a little shake. Caroline could almost see through the thin bat-like membrane of pink and brown skin that stretched between the elongated fingers. She knew that Cherubim wing structure was primarily the same as a bat wing. In adulthood the membrane receded somewhat as long thin finger tips protruded from the wing. While the fingers formed wings, the thumbs were hook like. With the wings folded the hook-thumbs were used to walk on and helped when climbing trees.

"To answer your question about the protests Caroline, I'm afraid I don't know, but as always with these things I think we can expect things to quieten down again eventually."

"But how long?" Caroline asked again.

"We can't worry about that. We've been doing good business for a long time, I think we can weather the storm," Chewfang reassured her.

"This all blew up when we introduced the new line of personal gondola," he continued. "We thought high pricing and limited availability would create a slow growing market and that the changes brought by private gondola ownership would be gradual too. Unfortunately we misjudged the fervour with which people want the gondola and as you know the pressure of demand forced us to lower prices and increase availability faster than we wanted."

"I remember," Caroline said. "The first few days were fine, I was selling everything you let me have and at prices above those you were recommending, then the lines of customers started. I had people outside the shop all day long, I had customers who'd waited all night, then two days, then three and then things got ugly."

"Quite so," Chewfang agreed. "A difficult position. However by alleviating that situation we have created another, potentially more dangerous one. Indeed the very situation we were trying to prevent, well at least minimise, was the collapse of the transport industry."

"Well you can't blame us if people would rather use gondola than cars or buses," Caroline said.

"perhaps you can't reasonably blame us, but when you've lost your job and there's no clear alternative, people tend to get anxious and angry," Chewfang replied. "There are no other jobs for them to go to, it's not as if the transport industry has been replaced by another industry which people can retrain for, gondola production requires an extremely minimal workforce.

"It is one of the differences between our cultures," Chewfang warned. "We Astrosphereians live in a society where only those who want to work do so. Your society demands that everyone who hasn't sizeable capital, has to work, whether there is work or not. You might have thought your leaders would have seen this coming," Chewfang mused. "With an ever-increasing population and limited resources, your planet, you can see there'll be two results; population size limitation and unemployment."

"Even before we arrived, you'd careened through industrial and technological advancement at a socially destabilising speed. You people were riding through the streets on horses less than two hundred years ago, do you realise that's within my lifetime?" Chewfang spluttered. "When I was born you had no car industry, no oil tankers, aeroplanes, TV, radio or computers.

"When you improve farming and industry to the point of minimum workforce for maximum output and continue to increase the population you are going to face a situation of increasing unemployment. The issue is not one of unemployment however, it's about lack of employment opportunities. If you deny access to capital, what you create is a situation where you have enough resources for everyone, but let people starve to death because they don't have a job."

Chewfang, now totally eased into his theme, continued. "What you call a capitalist economy is not capitalist at all, it denies access to capital, it's a labour economy. From your point of view we Astrospherians are trust fund babies. We all have a capital amount and live on the interest."

"What stops you all from simply cashing in the principle and going on a spending spree?" Caroline asked.

"It's a trust fund system," Chewfang replied. "The clan retains control of the principle not the individual. On death that principle becomes available to another citizen, who may well be a grandchild, but who could be any clan member. You can't spend the principle, but you can add to it. You can also maintain a private principle if you make money, though we tend not to use tokenism for goods transfer any more, it's considered very old fashioned, like using a cheque book is for you.

"Perhaps the best way to put it is we all have a pension from birth."

"That's nice," Caroline said, thinking how different her life might have been if she'd had a pension from birth. No money worries, ever.

"Anyway," Chewfang continued, "the upshot of this cultural clash is we've inadvertently put an eighth of the world's population out of work over night and we can't think of enough things to help sort the situation out. Progress always comes suddenly and violently, imposing its effects on society. You ask me how much longer the protests will last. I say how long will it take your governments to sort it out? Your service sectors can't absorb the existing workforce, so I guess they'll have to absorb the rest into the military, education and health. It's a mess and it's going to take time to clear up," Chewfang sighed.

They both sipped thoughtfully on their tea.

"Look we've got a couple of short term solutions," Chewfang said eventually. "I'm not saying they're perfect but they'll keep us in business for the duration. The thing is..." He shifted uneasily on his bar, gripping on to it with the hook on the elbow of his wing and gave Caroline a look. "Though this is not entirely legitimate."

"What do you mean?" Caroline asked.

"Have you noticed how the reports of Vespida sightings in Myanmar and Brazil have increased recently?"

"Now you mention it..." Caroline hadn't thought about it, what with the protests and everything, though she had seen the TV news reports.

"We think they may have established nests," Chewfang said, "and of course they're beginning to range."

"Are you saying we've got feral Vespida on the planet? How did this happen?" a shocked Caroline asked.

"The thing is some Astrosphereians have been supplying a drug, well several actually. It's rumoured these drug dealers have been using Vespida to guard their illegal jungle factories. I'm sure this is all forbidden by the Lowai Clan, but they have no jurisdiction on Earth so they can do little about it.

"Anyway, that aside, the result for us is there's an established underground distribution network which we can use temporarily to supply our customers with gondola."

"Um. I'll need to think about that one Chewy, I'm not sure I want to get into bed with criminals,"

Caroline replied thoughtfully.

"Of course, I understand your reservations. I mean, we've been turning a tidy profit these last three years and I'd be surprised if you didn't have the capital to ride this one out," Chewfang said, then laughed.

"What's so funny?" Caroline asked.

"I was just thinking of the irony of it," Chewfang explained. "The human prohibition of drugs is most confusing. If it was legal think of all those jobs which would be created. Think of the tax revenue that would be raised to help those who fall foul of drug use from a lack of education about it. It's not as if prohibition works to prevent addiction or even exposure, your societies are full of drug addicts. No, it creates a black economy which provides funds to criminals and terrorists. Sure they also make money from robbery, kidnap and other crimes, but drugs are very lucrative. The drug wars are your most expensive stupidity by far."

"I suppose there is kind of irony there," Caroline agreed politely.

She had heard enough of Chewfang's rantings. Clearly she was out of business for the foreseeable future. Thanking Chewfang for his time and the tea, Caroline stepped out onto the balcony. She fingered the charms on her silver charm bracelet. Her fingers closed on a charm which resembled a car without wheels. She stroked the car charm and a moment later a gondola in the form of the car-charm materialised next the balcony. It drifted for a moment as it positioned itself, then lowered its ramp.

On board, Caroline stepped over to the small control console that sat on the brass rail which ran along the bowed front window of the car-gondola. She entered the coordinates for her house, just outside Stuttgart, and the car shaped gondola drifted lazily upwards. She began thinking about her situation. It was lucky Louis hadn't given up his job after they married last year. There had been some debate about it at the time, but in the end Louis decided he wanted to continue working for his firm, retail wasn't really his thing.

Well it was good Louis had kept his job, because they'd be living off his wages for a while now as the shop not only failed to bring in income during the crisis, but was actually costing money. They would have to rein in their personal spending quite a bit.

As she mulled things over, the gondola began to descend towards her home. It set her thinking how lucky she was. She had the house and her savings, a considerable amount of stock that, even if she didn't take up Chewfang's offer, she could start house calls to her best customers, or what about parties like the underwear and the Tupperware people did? Or sell over the internet? Yes there were ways and means. She'd have to move stock from her shop to the house, probably in the middle of the night to avoid attention, but it was all possible.

Her best customers, the alien-loving xenophiles had already bought top-of-the-range gondola at top prices and many of them would want their supply of alien foods and drink as well as the gadgets and gizmos, like the yoyo discs, hover boards, and hover luggage which were as popular as ever.

She thought for a while, then called her Assistant Manager Anna, "Hello Anna, it's Caroline. Look I've been talking with Chewfang and he's no idea how much longer this protest is going to go on, so I'm keeping the shop shut for the foreseeable future. Now this would normally mean I'd have to let you go." At this there was a muffled cry from Anna. "But I've an idea that might keep us in business if you're interested." Anna was interested. "You know those underwear parties? I thought we might try holding alienwear parties, you know, get everyone round to someone's house and sell stuff over wine, cheese and chats. We would need to use your place though, until we can get the support of our customers. You would of course act as the agent and get a percentage of the sales. What do you think?"

Half an hour on the phone and Caroline and Anna had sketched out a plan. Caroline turned to her customer contact list and began making calls.

By the time Louis got home she had received confirmation from forty enthusiasts for her first party, to be held later in the week and was beginning to work out how she was going to handle the stock. Louis dropped onto the sofa in their designer living room and listened to the araingments she had made. She mentioned her conversation with Chewfang's and his offer.

"That Chewfang is an odd fellow," Louis remarked. "But then he is an alien. Interesting ideas, I wonder if any of them would work."

"Who knows," Caroline replied. "I'm not going to use his criminal contacts though, too risky."

"Yes my dear," Louis agreed. "Too risky. We don't need to take that chance, We'll do just fine with your plan," he kicked off his shoes.

Caroline thought to herself how lucky she was, she'd made the right decision marrying Louis. She put down her paperwork and went to sit by him on the arm of the sofa. She stroked his hair and kissed him.

"You know in time people will start new business and find new jobs," Louis said. "Job losses will eventually be forgotten. We move on. You remember how we travelled to India? The waiting at the airports, security checks, sleeping on the train, carrying everything we needed in our backpacks."

"Those were good times." Caroline said.

"They were good times," Louis agreed, "it was a great adventure, but today, my god, we have the luggage lifters and the gondola. We can take as much luggage as we want. We can travel in a flying sailing boat, or a carriage or whatever else you have on that clever little bracelet of yours. In fact we don't really need to take any luggage, we can fly to India now, from our front door, have a curry in Madras and be back here by bed time."

"I don't really feel like curry tonight," Caroline joked. "But I know what you mean. The gondola are going to change a lot of things. Food can be transported anywhere in the world for virtually nothing."

"Or people can be transported to the food," Louis exclaimed.

"No more cars, or car tax, or waiting in line at the petrol station," Caroline bantered back.

"Or waiting for buses, trains or planes."

"No car parks or parking problems."

"No traffic wardens, parking attendants, lorries blocking the road."

"No more roads or rails."

"Surely there will still be roads." Louis objected.

"For what?" Caroline asked.

"Pedestrians and cyclists."

"No more cycling or walking, everyone will go everywhere in a gondola." Caroline proclaimed.

"I think people will still like to exercise," Louis pointed out. "I say the roads, or at least the pavements and cycle lanes stay."

"Oh very well then, but no roads."

"Ok no roads," Louis laughed.

"You know I quite fancy Japanese food tonight," Caroline said. "I know a nice little place in the Gardens of Tranquillity in Tokyo. So you fancy a bit of sushi tonight then?"

"I know what I fancy a bit of," Louis said, pulling her off the arm of the sofa into his lap.

Chapter 24 – Thirty years later

The slim figure in the long black coat and wide brimmed hat entered the bar on twenty third street. She shook the rain from her coat and looked around the poorly lit room. It was mid-day outside, but the place had a midnight air about it. Yellow light poured feebly from faded red and blue lampshades onto the chipped table tops that stood in the booths lining the wall.

Bing hung her hat and coat on a battered coat rack which stood by the door, before taking a seat at one of the booths. There was only one other customer sat on a stool at the bar. The bartender who was diligently polishing a whisky glass looked up.

"Coffee." Bing ordered. The barman nodded, continuing to polish his glass for a few moments more, before turning to the barista machine sat behind him. As the machine began to hiss and steam, wheezing in its exertions to make something coffee like, the door to the bar opened again and a woman walked in.

"Make that two coffees." Bing called to the barman.

"Good to see you again Bing," The woman said, seating herself opposite.

"Hi Karen, glad you could make it to our little get together," Bing replied dryly. These days she felt ambivalent about the clandestine meetings with her American Intelligence contact. She'd started with relish and enthusiasm for the work. She'd become a field agent and that had excited her, but over the years she'd changed, it had worn thin and now she wasn't sure which side she was on any more.

Karen was Bing's third contact since she'd accepted Bob's job offer at Harding Industries. Three contacts in thirty years wasn't bad, didn't represent too much exposure. Thirty years in which she'd barely aged five.

"How are things?" Karen asked.

"Not bad," Bing replied. "I've made progress on the Brazilian issue. I think our mutual friend is in the Brazilian Government, Gozalez Perateago, Minister for Transport. He's been holding meetings with a certain Cherubim we're interested in," Bing reported.

"And the Vespida?" Karen asked.

"Nothing to substantiate the nest theory, but they're definitely out there in the jungle. I'm also beginning to think they're the reason we can't get close to Sashoo, I don't know how they're doing it but they seem to be involved every time an agent is detected. Anyway there's nothing connecting them to Harding Industries. All the evidence points to clan Lowai involvement."

"Those secretive bastards," Karen said. "We

know nothing about them after all this time."

"In thirty years the only Astrosphereian who has admitted having contact with the Lowai is the Lowai Agent on Sashoo. Bob meets with the Agent every now and again but it's always a courtesy call, never business. The problem is we just don't know what the likes of Fortune and Chewfang are doing, we've never been able to get anyone close to the centre of their operation."

"What about the Cherubim? I thought we had an angle on him?" Karen asked, slowly stirring sugar into the muddy brown fluid that pretended to be her coffee.

"Oh he's cooperating, but he's not having any more luck than we've had. Even though he has access to Sashoo," Bing said. "Look this is long running, much longer than we thought it would be when I started thirty years ago. Back then we thought there was a risk of armed invasion, the possibility of hostilities, but what we seem to have here is a trading post situation."

"And we're the Indians," Karen added.

"Now that we have alien enclaves, they'll soon be asking for a homeland of their own. It's been an invasion by stealth, spearheaded with technology."

"Technology we have no control over," Karen remarked.

"We've tried but never successfully obtained a shield generator. They always dissipate when we get them out of the facility, and in any case, this is force field technology, we could never get it open, even if we got one back to a laboratory.

"Meanwhile we have access to shields and the field-generated atmosphere craft through Harding Industries, and we're now synthesizing the longevity drugs for ourselves here on Earth. We've come a long way in adjusting to our new world. I just can't help feeling that we're missing something. We have aliens who've become citizens of Earth but there's something that feels temporary about it, I can't quite put my finger on it.

"It's been thirty years and nothing since has arrived from the star. When is a supply ship going to arrive? " Bing slid the usb drive, with her report in it, across the table to Karen then stood up. "Till next time," she said.

Walking back up twenty third street Bing was thinking about the way things had changed since she'd started spying for both sides. She'd come to respect Bob Harding for his directness and purpose, the way he handled things met with her approval. Sure to begin with things had been a mess, the world economic crash brought on by the collapse of the traditional transport industries had eventually been over come. Harding Industries had put a lot of money into sports, arts promotion and small business funds to create employment. Perhaps that was the plan, to turn Earth into a giant factory, making macramé plant pot-holders for the rest of the galaxy.

The introduction of the eternal pension by Harding Investments had also had an effect, admittedly taking its time to filter down through the economic system, and now there was talk of the Government taking it over. The brilliant economist Vlad Kavistky had developed the Sashooian concept of capitalism into a commercially viable financial tool. Simply put, people were encouraged to place money in a scheme whereby they built up a capital sum of their own, just like savings, and like savings the capital remained guaranteed.

Governments already running unemployment and health schemes quickly saw the advantages of the system and began to establish citizens capital schemes of their own, providing the initial capital for their citizens and allowing them to 'pay off' the capital over time. This sea change in economic policy had had the added bonus of bringing unparalleled stability to the world markets. As these new schemes were unable to invest in high risk ventures, the guarantee being that the capital remain, the schemes were forced to be ultra-conservative about investment and the spread of industries they invested in. This coincided with a revolution in traditional life insurance and pension plans. With a population now likely to exceed it's life span by as much as eight times, pension and life insurance companies had simply packed up and gone bust overnight. The Capital Pension scheme was there ready to step into their place.

She had one herself. A nice tasty little pot of capital that currently fed its earnings straight back into itself, a nice tax contribution rebate that fed into the investment and it was all guaranteed by Harding Investments, and soon to be underwritten by the American Government.

On the downside there had been all the upheaval, the rioting, the aliens might not have invaded ray gun in hand, but they'd caused a lot of trouble, unwittingly perhaps, but trouble never the less.

Her own life as a double agent had had some ups and downs. She should have retired over five years ago, but the longevity drug, which she'd had access to long before it became available to the general public, meant she was going to live much longer than the military had anticipated when she first signed up. Secondly it had long become a matter of understanding between Bob and her that he knew she reported to her old employers and that they knew she reported back to Bob. She had in many ways become just another conduit for Bob to communicate with the American intelligence community.

She still held hope that one day she'd get an agent onto Sashoo, or even onto the Astropshere itself, but in thirty years she hadn't come any closer than she had the day the Sashooians arrived. Getting to the Astrosphere was easy, she could take a field-craft any time, they were perfectly capable of space flight, though they were intended for atmospheric travel and didn't have the insulation needed for deep space flight. Several teams had been sent in the past, but hadn't been able to penetrate the sphere.

Another change was obvious in the very streets she was walking. Thirty years ago the road had been full of cars, today the road was a single lane with wide sidewalks and a sports lane for cyclists, skateboarders, hoverboarders, rollerbladers and so forth. Occasionally a Maserati, Lamborghini or a Ferrari would pass by, the only road traffic left, the classic classy car companies were the only ones still in business. In a world where anyone could afford a field-craft only the luxury car market had survived, driven by the status-obsessed and the uncompromisingly petrol headed. Now pedestrians ruled the streets walking on wide tree lined boulevards, an array of different shaped field-craft floating down from the sky to deliver people. Above her regular lines of field-craft crossing the city a thousand feet above the road like a strange long cloud that not only rained field-craft to street level but also back up to the skies, bearing passengers and cargo.

Bing checked her watch. Plenty of time to walk to her meeting with Bob, no need to summon a field-craft. Her relationship with Bob had changed over the years. At first she had made great effort to seduce him, which she'd successfully done and they had become lovers for almost a decade. But then she'd given birth to their daughter Penelope. That had changed the dynamic between them, now related through child, Bob had used her motherhood to downsize her role at Harding Industries. He hadn't cut her pay, he'd given her a rise, but he'd begun to cut her out of the information loop.

To be fair being in the loop had hardly answered the questions she'd been asking, but it had made things very difficult for her with her other employer as her reports became slimmer and slimmer.

Bing entered the restaurant where she was meeting Bob. He was already there, sat at a white clothed table with a lunch time Martini. He was alone as usual.

It had been several weeks since they had last seen each other, "Bing, good to see you. Your looking as young and radiant as ever." Bob greeted her, kissing her on the lips.

"Bob, good to see you too," She replied.

"How's Penelope?" he asked.

"Enjoying University, I thinks she likes it at Cambridge," Bing replied. "She's still not sure if she wants to start the longevity drug this year though," she told him.

"Well it's a big decision and there's no reason she shouldn't get a few more years maturity behind her first," Bob said.

There was nothing that girl could do wrong in her father's eyes. Couldn't he see for every year she delayed taking the drug she was losing five or six more off her life? But he didn't see it that way.

"We're not sure of the long term effects yet, we don't know if the human synthesis of the drug is completely stable," he argued.

"It's had plenty of time," Bing retorted.

"Other than that she's doing well?" Bob asked, diverting from the contentious topic.

"She's fine. The usual stuff about boyfriends and that sort of thing, and probably partying too much. You really should make the time to go and visit her yourself. It would do you both good."

"Yes I think I will. That's a good idea," Bob replied. "Perhaps I should take her on a little break next holiday, the Caribbean perhaps."

"Don't take her away from her studies," Bing insisted.

"Sure, sure," Bob agreed, as their starters arrived.

"I almost forgot to ask," Bing said. "How's your new political career going? I heard you were to be appointed British representative to the World

Government."

"Yes, next year. It should be good, the World Government is beginning to shape up. Of course there's a lot of work to be done yet. It's in no way a formally accepted Government even by its supporting countries, but it's only a matter of time now. Hell, it took the U.S. a hundred years to federalise the States, and Europe took over fifty, we've only had thirty and this is the whole world we're talking about." Bob said.

"Hey Bob, I'm not knocking it. America is one of the big backers," Bing replied.

"We really need the Chinese to come fully on board though. You know they are still one of the few countries in the world that has always refused Sashoo visiting rights, and their twenty year ban on alien technology has really screwed their environmental targets. They ran petrol cars for almost two decades longer than the rest of the first world."

"I can't believe we've not been able to adapt force-field technology to power production for industrial and residential use," Bing said.

"You worked with the International Science Group. You know that even with Sashooian help we've never been able to develop anything beyond what they already have. We understand the principles, that by using a small amount of energy, a filament field is created, which collects energy from the surrounding environment from light, temperature, pressure, even from the electrons they encounter. When enough energy is gathered it the fields form in to a shields or field-craft, which then grow more energy collecting filaments. But we can't manipulate these fields ourselves. The generators are made from force-fields, we can't open them, so we can't reverse engineer them.

"What we need, and what the Sashooians are unwilling or unable to give us, is the instructions for building a field generator of our own which we can use to create the fields we want.

"Again, it's the same with the anti-gravity technology. We know it's a reversed polarity gravity field, which works like two magnets repelling each other and by strengthening or weakening the gravity field in the field-craft they float up and down. But we can't replicate this technology because it's wrapped up in the force-field generator technology. Without their cooperation we're stuck," Bob concluded.

They ate in silence for a while, then Bob asked, "I suppose you're investigating the Vespida reports?"

She nodded in agreement, her mouth full of fresh water salmon with lemon and black pepper.

"Those rumours have been going around for years. There's never been any evidence of a Vespida nest here on the planet."

"It's kinda unpleasant thought though, those giant wasps introduced into our ecology," Bing said, dabbing at the edge of her mouth with a napkin.

"I think the higher gravity would probably force them to evolve into a smaller species. Besides which, they're bound to the Lowai. You only ever see them with Lowai agents, never with any other clan. It means that there's two or three Lowai agents here on the planet who haven't made themselves known to the local authorities, that is to us, almost certainly because they're involved in the manufacture of party drugs."

"Or worse," Bing said.

"Like mind control drugs? Are you still pursuing that old idea?" Bob smiled.

"There's nothing wrong with the idea. Yes, they might be doing that," she insisted indignantly.

"They could, but they're not," Bob shot back. "You still don't get it do you? It's that military background of yours. We've already been 'invaded', we invited them in. Now they're here living amongst us, two new species. Hell, they even brought their own homeland with them, the Peripatetic Sovereignty of Sashoo Island. The U.S. alone has over four hundred thousand aliens registered as citizens. They've colonised us, our way of life has been changed irrevocably by their arrival. Ask yourself why hasn't another ship come from the Shawdale-Huxley star? I know you ask that question. I've asked that question, and I get the same answer every time. We're a long long way from the next habitable planet, we're a small uninteresting backwater. And like you, I don't buy it.

"I've worked with you to get agents onto Sashoo, unsuccessfully. The Lowai hold the key to this and we've not seen a single one."

"What do you mean?" Bing asked. "I've met their agents."

"Their agents yes, but not the Lowai themselves. There are no Lowai Clan members on Sashoo at all or at least if there are, no one is admitting it. Sashoo is an independent group, Sashooians lived on Sashoo island inside the Astrosphere, the Lowai live on another island. Anyway, like us, they've only ever had contact with the Lowai through their agents. When the Astrosphere arrived the Sashooians made the decision to leave the Astrosphere and come down here, perhaps there was a deal with the Lowai, which is the feeling I get, but no one is admitting it."

"So what are they doing?" Bing asked.

"I can't answer that, only the Lowai know, but you know as well as I what Harding Industries has been doing. We've been selling alien technology for thirty years and they've been buying gold, diamonds, art, spices and the such like. I'm certain these things are going into the Astrosphere. I can't be sure because the goods are collected from us, but I have the books, every ounce of gold we've handed over. It's more than four times the amount they pushed into our system to finance their operations when they first arrived. It can't all be sitting around Sashoo adorning the necks and wrists of Sashooians."

"So they're collecting stuff," Bing replied.

"Don't you see what that means?" Bob asked.

"Not really. They like our stuff. Mind you, stock piling gold and diamonds, maybe they intend flooding the market to bringing it crashing down," Bing suggested.

"I doubt it," Bob replied slowly. "It's just as likely that once they've fill up with Earths riches they'll be off on their way. And what will we do then?"

"Do you really think they'll leave?" Bing asked.

"Do you think they'll stay for ever?" Bob replied.

Chapter 25 – Fifty years later

Dai Wakami stepped from the gondola straight into the living room of the twelfth floor flat he shared with Neko and Keneko. He closed the sliding windows behind him, walked through to the kitchen and put his briefcase down on the table.

Keneko sat on a stool by the breakfast bar drinking an orange juice while Neko busied herself at the kitchen counter preparing the evening meal. When she heard Dai come in she wiped her hands on her apron and went over to kiss him. "How was your day at the office dear?" she asked.

"We were just discussing the arrangements for your sixty fifth birthday next week." Neko told him. "Keneko suggested we hire out the Matsisho hotel ballroom."

Dai shrugged, and picked at the carrots his wife had been slicing. He selected a slightly crooked one and began nibbling on it.

"I wasn't thinking of doing anything for it really," he said. "Our Ruby wedding is in a few months time and I thought we'd concentrate on planning for that."

"Your so sweet," Neko replied kissing him.

"Well we were the world's first inter-species

marriage and I think people will expect us to do something. I've had two television companies contact me already." Dai said.

"But it's not just for them," Neko exclaimed.

"No it not, we deserve a good party, it's been forty years, forty years of our love for each other, that's got to be worth celebrating. Forty years and you look as cute as the day I met you," Dai replied.

"He knows all the right things to say," Neko said.

"I can't believe it's been almost fifty years since the Astrosphere arrived and delivered you, my angel, from the stars," Dai said.

"Ug, now he's overdoing it," Keneko said. "He's right about your looks though, you barely look five years older than when we landed." Keneko looked young too, though as she was no longer a child, she'd lost the ability to fly . Now she perched on a kitchen stool gripping the edge with her wing hooks. Wings that would no longer bare her aloft in Earth's heavy gravity.

"There's something else." Dai said.

"Oh?" Neko said, returning to her vegetable chopping before Dai ate it all. He reached out for another carrot and she gently slapped his fingers away with one of her small hands.

"There's something going on at work , but I'm

not sure what," he said.

"I don't see how anything can go on there without you knowing dear," Neko said. "You are Director of Harding Industries Shield Division for Japan."

"I know but something is definatly going on in Storage Division."

"Like what dear?" Neko asked.

"They're being very secretive about it, but I'm hearing rumours the warehouses are empty."

"Oh, does that mean there will be shortages of Zarango leaf and Charpmal?" Neko asked.

"Not Charpmal!" Keneko shrieked. "I don't think I can live without my Charpmal chip cookies," she lamented.

"No no, it's not Distribution, it's Storage. Goods held by the Storage Division are destined for Sashoo. Distribution is good arriving from Sashoo. Distribution warehouse are full, in fact they're talking about turning some of the empty storage warehouses over to Distribution," Dai told them.

"That is strange." Keneko said. "Why would they do that?"

"Um and the Chingans from two doors down moved out last week," Neko said. "I wonder if there's a connection."

"The Chingans?" Dai said.

"You remember them dear, the Langonai who live at number 45? They came round last Christmas? Three of them? Well Journey said she worked for Storage, I'm sure."

"Where did they go?" Dai asked.

"I don't know, I just assumed they'd got work somewhere else and moved."

"I think I need to go and visit some old friends," Keneko said, hopping down from the stool. "I'll be back later." She went into the living room to summon a field-craft.

"Looks like it's just the two of us for tea tonight then," Dai said as he sat on the recently vacated stool and admired his wife's behind as she stood chopping vegetables in her white stockings and short black pinafore dress. "perhaps we can make a night of it." He suggested. "We've not yet tried on our Astralman and Astralwoman costumes," Dai said smiling at Neko's back.

She half turned. "Um, that would be fun, but we don't know when Keneko will be back."

"She doesn't mind us dressing up," Dai said.

"No, but we didn't warn her. It might be bit of a shock to her if she comes back and were 'at it' in full costume," Neko replied.

"You have a point. So what's for dinner?" Dai responded.

By the time the vegetable flan was ready Keneko still hadn't returned so Dai and Neko sat down to eat without her. They were just clearing up the plates when someone knocked unexpectedly at the door.

"Must be a neighbour," Dai said, getting up from the table. "I'll see who it is."

It was Cadillac the Langonai from the flat next door. "Hi Dai," she said. "Is Neko in?"

"Sure we've just finished supper," Dai said, letting her into the flat.

"Hi Cadillac," Neko greeted her cheerily. "What brings you over?"

"I was wondering if you had any boxes you weren't using?" Cadillac asked.

"I'm sure I can find some. Why do you need boxes?"

"Oh we're moving out."

"Moving out? Why?" Neko asked. "Where are you going?"

"I have a little bistro in town,. Well rather I did

but I've sold it and we're moving back to Sashoo."

"Back to Sashoo?"

"Everyone is, well not everyone, but lots of Astrosphereians are. You don't see many Astrosphereians these days do you?" Cadillac said. "Mind you with a human husband it is going to be quite a difficult time for you I'd think."

"What are you taking about?" Neko asked. Dai could see she was beginning to get angry with Cadillac's attitude.

"The rumour is the Lowai are planning to move on. Nothing's been confirmed yet of course, but the advice to those who don't want to get left behind is begin preparing."

"The Astrosphere is leaving?" Neko asked.

"That's the rumour." Cadillac confirmed. "Anyway I've grown tired of running the bistro, the first twenty years were a good laugh, but its all become a bit of a drag, I don't need the money so I'm off back to Sashoo."

"Oh, well let me see about those boxes for you," Neko said.

"Are you sure you won't be needing them yourself?" Cadillac asked.

"No, well, er, I don't know. I can easily get some

more," Neko replied, and piling a bunch of boxes into her neighbour's hands, she gently pushed her out of the door.

"Well what do you make of that?" she asked Dai, once Cadillac had gone.

"If it's true we need to think about what we're going to do. Do we stay or do we go?" Dai replied.

"But an we go?" Neko asked. "Human's have never been allowed on Sashoo. They may not let you go with us."

"If I can't go with you, will you stay here?" Dai asked.

Neko thought about it then said tearfully. "I don't know, I don't want to be the only Langonai left on Earth. I feel I should talk to my mother and find out what she thinks about this."

"Sure, I understand," Dai said. "It's too late to do that tonight she'll be in bed. You can take a field-craft over to California in the morning and have brunch with her."

"If you can go, would you?" Neko asked Dai, as they sat curled up on the sofa in front of the living room screen half watching a sitcom half lost in their own thoughts.

"I don't know, I guess so, it would be exciting to travel to the stars, to see the galaxy. I guess I need to speak to my parents and see if they need me here. I'm their only child after all."

"They would miss you."

"I could come back some day."

"Perhaps, but how long will it be before you can return?"

"Well, where will the Astrosphere go next?" Dai asked.

"Only the Lowai know that, assuming they do know, maybe they just fly where they feel like." Neko said.

"Why do the Lowai have so much power?" Dai asked.

"I don't know, It's just the way things are. Mother says it's because they own the Astrosphere, but there are rumours. Some say that the Lowai are themselves controlled by another Clan that no one has heard of, others that they're a sort of galactic secret service sent to spy on Earth, or their space gypsies. Every Sashooian has a theory, but no one actually knows."

"Well how did you and your Mother come to be on the Astrosphere?" Dai asked Neko.

"I was too young to remember. Mother says she bought a holiday package, a kind of life cruise to see the stars, but she's always been very cagey about where she got the money from and why she wanted to go on such a cruise. I never thought much of it. I grew up on Sashoo and accepted that things were the way they were, since then we have had such a lovely life here in Tokyo I've not really thought about it." Neko replied.

They were just about to go to bed when Keneko returned. She was all flustered as she hopped down the field-craft ramp and into the living room. Once the doors were closed and the room had warmed up a bit she began to tell what she had learnt.

"I went to see some friends in Hong Kong who I haven't seen for a long time, old friends from the airball team. Anyway one of them has connections with a Lowai Agent and he was saying that the Astrosphere will be leaving soon. He doesn't know how soon it will be but an official announcement will be made shortly. I'm afraid, he doesn't know whether humans will be allowed on board the Astrosphere, nor could he tell me if Sashoo will definatly leave with the Astrosphere or stay here on Earth. And of course he doesn't know where the Lowai intend going next."

"So it really is happening then," Dai was shocked.

"Looks like it," Keneko replied.

The next few weeks were strange for Dai and Neko. Alien neighbours and colleagues began packing up and leaving. A Langonai here, a Cherubim there, another empty desk, silent flats, fewer field-craft flying overhead.

The Lowai were not quick to confirm the situation and the steady trickle of people leaving continued, till one day, about two months later, Keneko came in with some news. Dai and Neko were in the kitchen considering the final touches for their ruby wedding celebration. The possibility of the Astrosphere leaving hung heavily over their plans.

Keneko hopped excitedly across the kitchen and perched on her favourite stool. "I've just heard that the Astrospherian agent has confirmed," Keneko announced.

"Confirmed what?" Dai asked. "Give us some details here."

"The Astrosphere is leaving. Apparently all consulates to Earth are being closed. All the Sashooian administrative staff who are leaving have returned to Sashoo and only the permanent mission to the world government is now manned. All aliens who hold Earth citizenship are now the sole responsibility of the nation they have joined."

"So we're all Earthians now?" Neko asked, as both she and Koneko had taken Japanese citizenship.

"Looks like it. Looks like we might be stuck here.

The Agents are saying a petition process might be set-up. I don't have any details but it looks like we might be able to join some kind of lottery for those who wish to return to Sashoo," Koneko told them.

"Also all non-citizen residents are being advised to either obtain Earth citizenship or return to Sashoo."

"My Mother doesn't have citizenship," Neko wailed.

"Will she apply?" Dai asked.

"I think she'll go back. I've had a few chats with her about it, and I don't think she wants to stay here forever," Neko said.

"Ok well lets take things one step at a time," Dai suggested. "I've spoken to my parents and while they would miss me very much, they understand my desire to explore the universe in the spaceship that's hung over our heads most of my life, they have each other and their savings," Dai said. "So how about we put ourselves up for this lottery thing and see what fortune sends our way. If we want to go, it's not as if we have a great deal of choice in the matter."

Neko tearfully agreed.

"That's if there is a lottery," Koneko pointed out. "That's not confirmed, it maybe wishful thinking."

"I guess I shouldn't go handing in my resignation too soon then," Dai said practically.

For the next few weeks Dai, Neko and Keneko were in limbo. The Astrospherian district of Tokyo grew quieter and quieter as non-citizen aliens moved out and returned to Sashoo. The Lowai failed to provide any substance to the lottery rumour, though it was clear from news reports that the Lowai agents were in negotiations with the World Government over population issues.

A few weeks later a Lowai agent announce a lottery system allowing fifty thousand individuals to travel on Sashoo. The important part ,from Dai and Neko's point of view was, while aliens were first pick, humans with alien mates or consorts would also be considered. There was ten days allowed to apply to the lottery.

Early the next day Dai took a field-craft downtown to the application office in Tokyo city and put in an application for all three of them. The paperwork done Dai went home and began packing, not knowing if he would be unpacking in the same flat, or on Sashoo.

Halfway through their ten day wait Neko's mother returned to Sashoo. They had a small quiet reunion the night before she departed. Dai's parents came and the six of them had a tearful evening reminiscing, exchanging parting gifts and expressing their affection for one another.

With the departure of her Mother the whole thing became more imminent and urgent for Neko. She no longer cared which way the lottery fell, but she wanted to know what their fate would be. The waiting put a great strain on her and she became irritable and weepy. Dai tried to keep things as cheerful as possible, in his playful way, but his efforts were clearly frayed by his own worries.

Although no official figure was put out it was estimated that on the morning of the lottery results eighteen and a half million individuals were waiting eagerly for the results. The method of selection as with so many things controlled by the Lowai was a secret. Dai had had to file an extensive report with each of their applications, but the selections might just as easily be chance. Dai imagined a giant loto machine with everyone's name on it whirling round before popping out onto a long tray.

The results were listed on several internet sites, and each successful applicant would receive written confirmation in a special letter.

At ten thirty in the morning Neko saw the postal field-craft make its visit to the postboxes in the apartment block lobby and she took the lift down to the ground floor. Nowadays she felt like it was her own private lift, she so rarely met anyone else using it, there were so many empty flats in the building. The postman had already been and gone, not many letters to deliver to now.

As she approached her mailbox it looked empty and her heart was already sinking as she slipped the key into the lock and opened. A brown bill faced her, but behind it a long white envelope with the Astrospherian logo on it. She barely dared to open it. Of course she knew that they must have won a place because they'd been notified, but had they all won a place?

In the kitchen her hands shook as she held the envelope out to Dai.

"No you open it," he said.

"I'll open it if neither of you will., Keneko squeeked. "I want to know just as much as you do."

Neko pushed back the flap and tore the envelope with her finger before extracting the folded paper within. She spread it out on the kitchen table as if laying out a treasure map. Dai half expected her to weigh a corner of the letter down with a salt shaker.

"We're in," Neko said, with a shaky voice.

"We're all three on board, Dai you've been granted Sashooian citizenship." She wept for joy.

For Dai the moment had both sadness and joy. In

that instant he knew he was to say goodbye to his parents for perhaps the last time. But he was going on a voyage of exploration like none other in the history of mankind.

The following day Dai's parents came over to help pack. He gave them a watercolours picture he had painted, and gave his father a document allowing him to settle any affairs Dai had on Earth.

His Mother and Father stayed overnight and the next morning Dai summoned a removal field-craft. With the help of gravity field lifters the work of loading the large blue removal-craft was quickly done. Then they sat around the kitchen drinking a farewell cup of green tea from cheap cups. They sipped in silence, sadly enjoying their last few moments together. Dai's Mother softly crying into a delicate handkerchief.

Then it was time to go the removal-craft ramp began to close leaving Dai with a final view of his parents, standing hand in hand waving goodbye. His heart both exited with anticipation, and sad with loss. Parting such sweet sorrow, thought Dai.

The journey around half the globe to Sashoo island was a muted affair, the three of them each lost in their own thoughts. The islands of the Caribbean came over the horizon and shortly after that Sashoo itself and Dai began to get excited. As far as he knew no human had ever set foot on Sashoo before. Their removal-craft began to curve towards the Island, which was currently floating some one thousand feet above sea level.

The removal-craft headed for a point at the front of the island just below its rim. Dai saw what looked like a big square hole cut into the earth in an area clear of trailing plant tendrils. A shield entrance opened allowing the craft access to the landing bay.

They joined a line of waiting field-craft in the vast landing area. Below them field-craft of all shapes and sizes were moving purposefully around. Several lines of such craft floated along one massive wall. It was clear these were being unloaded and their contents moved on in smaller craft. People were transferring from removal and transport field-craft to personal conveyances. A steady stream of these small sleek flying car like vehicles were leaving the bay.

After half an hours wait Dai and Neko's removal-craft finally floated into a large hanger like structure, one that all arrivals were passing through. The ramp door opened and an official looking Cherubim entered their vehicle. He inspected their lottery letter and their Earth Identifications. Then he began informing them.

"By accepting the terms and conditions of residency on Sashoo you forfeit any rights to return to the planet Earth. That is to say if you continue on from this point you will not be allowed to return to Earth. Do you understand?"

It was clear to them all. the Cherubim handed Dai a form. A knot formed in the pit of Dai's stomach as he leant over the document that gave him Sashooian citizenship. He hesitated, pen poised, then taking a deep breath, he signed.

"Very well. Welcome aboard Sashoo Citizen Dai," the official said. "You have been allocated accommodation through your wife's Clan, Clan Tarakoi, of which you are now a member."

The official made some notes on a wrist computer and left their craft. A moment later the craft moved on through the check point and began to descend towards its place on the deck below, where a further official asked them to leave the vehicle.

The removal-craft shimmered and changes shape before moving off, their things were once again on their way, this time without Dai and Neko. A flying-car field-craft materialised with enough room for three, and they climbed in. The flying-car rose up heading through a short tunnel which was cut directly into the Sashooian soil and led to the island's surface. They skimmed over an expanse of Sashooian grass warmed by the Caribbean sunshine and headed for Sashoo City.

As they approached Dai could see it was unlike any city he'd ever seen. There was no cohesion between the styles of buildings. Some buildings were joined by bridges which defied the laws of gravity, other buildings didn't reach the ground at all. Signs in strange writing floated between the many-coloured structures.

Dai felt lighter because of the lower gravity on the island. Something about the Sashooian buildings suddenly occurred to him. "These buildings, are they force field buildings?" He asked Neko.

"Most of them are, including our new apartment," Neko said.

"I'm going to live in a force-field building," Dai laughed, as the flying-car they rode came to a halt next to a wall that rose eight hundred feet above the ground. They were half way up the wall which appeared to be made from large brightly coloured irregular shapes. Dotted across it were what Dai took to be windows and balconies but these details did not remain fixed. As he looked windows appeared and disappeared, balconies flexed and stretched.

The flying-car came to rest against a section of the wall and began to merge into it. After a moment an aperture opened allowing Dai and the others to step out into a large empty room.

Dai looked around at the empty space. A new hole appeared in the living room wall, their possessions had arrived.

"Well my love," Neko said. "Welcome to your new home?"

Chapter 26 – Final preparations

David sat in a three thousand dollar leather backed chair in Bob's sumptuous New York office. Behind Bob's desk the picture window held a glorious view of New York city, filled with skyscrapers whose glassy windows twinkled in the morning blue sky.

"David, it's good of you to get here on such short notice," Bob said, from the chair opposite as he put his cup of tea down on the glass table that sat between them.

"I take it you've heard about the aliens leaving?"

"Yes, of course, it's been a traumatic time for Softly and I, but she will be staying here on Earth," David said, recalling the discussions that followed the announcement about the alien's departure.

"That's good, I'm pleased to hear it. It's been a trying time for everyone. Well, as you can imagine this is going to cause quite a few problems for Harding Industries, indeed the entire planet," Bob said.

"I see," David replied.

"We're OK on the shield and force-field craft supply side. The field-generators allow us to continue producing shields and field-craft, effectively forever. Artefacts will become rarewhich will put up the prices, but consumables, like kaolite, we have limited supplies of those, and they're a core sale for our distributors.

"Now I've got some ideas about manufacturing alien items here on Earth using alien designs and the remaining workforce, so I think that gap can be plugged to a degree, but we can't offer kaolate or any of the other foods and spices because we simply can't grow them here, we've no seeds for a start.

"Anyway the thing is I want to reassure all our employees, that this won't affect us in the long run, Harding Industries will still have a core business with or without Sashoo."

"Well that's great, we're still in business," David said.

"Yes, yes absolutely. I'm thinking about sponsoring a world tour of alien artists who've decided to remain here, I think that'll show everyone that things aren't going to change that much." Bob assured him.

The desk intercom came to life and a female voice said, "The Lowai Agent is here to see you Bob."

"Send him straight in," Bob said.

"Should I go?" David asked.

"No. I want you to stay and see this," Bob insisted. "I don't know what these people think they're playing at flying off like this, and I intend to get some answers."

The polished wood, double doors at the end of the room opened and six Vespida and a Cherubim entered the room. The Vespida took position along the wall as the elderly Cherubim hobbled towards Bob and David.

"Agent Gnarlec. a pleasure to see you," Bob said, standing up and taking a step towards the shrunken figure in the dark blue robe. The Cherubim stopped a foot or so away from Bob.

"Minister Harding," Gnarlec replied, using Bob's World Council title as Minister of Alien Affairs. "I'm here in my capacity as Agent of the Lowai and primary representative of the Astrosphere here on Earth," Gnarlec squeeked gravely. "I am to inform you of the imminent departure of Sashoo and to formally declare all business between Earth and Sashoo now at an end." The Cherubim held out a document. "These are the terms and conditions of the cessation."

Bob took the document. "And what about those of your citizens that are currently in our custody?" Bob asked. "What about the cost of containing the Vespida we have? Three are known murderers."

Gnarlec shrugged. "The Lowai have never had, nor have they ever sought to have jurisdiction on

Earth. We are unable and indeed unwilling to interfere in local law enforcement. Console yourself with the knowledge that the Vespida cannot breed without a queen and you have no queen here on the planet."

"Are you certain about that?" Bob asked sharply.

"Positive. The Vespida here will die long before their sentences are lived out. Their life spans are a mere ten years, and they don't use longevity drugs. As to the Langonai and Cherubim who have broken local laws, that is between them and the local authorities, we are not prepared to negotiate the return of criminals," the Cherubim stated flatly.

"So that's it then? You're just going to drop us in it? What about a field generator tool so we can develop our own field technology?" Bob insisted.

"That is also not possible as you well know Minister Harding. We don't have any such thing available to give you. You're familiar with the terms of cessation, this is notification that we are leaving, that those who stay are in the jurisdiction of this planet and all debts and outstanding matters are concluded. You do not have to agree, it is a statement of our intent."

Occasionally the Agent's speech was punctuated by the wasp-like buzz of a Vespidian guard easing its posture. David thought Bob looked like he wanted to hit the Cherubim whom he towered over, but the Vespidian guard was an unsettling deterrent to any such act with their shiny black carapaces, insectoid faces and the sinister sharp prong of their stings. They might only be thigh high, but they scared David, who sat as motionless as possible during the encounter.

"We can offer you nothing more today than we were able to offer you when we arrived fifty years ago," Agent Gnarlec said. "You shouldn't forget we've made you a very rich and powerful man Minister Harding." Gnarlec made a noise that David thought might have been a laugh.

"As I said Minister, our business is concluded. In one hour Sashoo departs for the Astrosphere at which time all business is ended. Now if you'll excuse me I've further matters to attend to before we depart." Gnarlec bowed, spun round and hobbled officiously out of Bob's office. The black Vespida, wings humming, formed a guard around the old Cherubim.

"See that?" Bob asked David.

"They're leaving us with their mess, their criminals, and no field tools. No compensation, nothing." He sat heavily in the leather chair.

"Perhaps they'll be back one day," David said. "They don't owe you money do they?" He added.

"No, It's all sorted out, I've known about this for weeks, but I have to put on a show, can't let them think that we're taking this easily. They came, they interfered, and they should pay."

"Um. I see. When you put it like that it does seem a bit shoddy of them," David agreed.

* * *

A vast number of bubble shaped field-craft had assembled around the inner edge of Sashoo. From their vantage point in a bubble-craft Dai Neko and Keneko had a good view from the island. Below them the sunshine blue Caribbean sea was dotted with thousand and thousands of field-craft which had gathered south of Jamaica, for the final farewell.

Dai could just about make out some of the larger banners that were being flown from the field-craft below. 'Come back soon', 'Good luck', 'bon voyage', 'find Elvis', 'good riddance', 'we love you all', 'may the force be with you'. Every sentiment you could think of seemed to have a banner.

Everyone waited in the hot Caribbean sunshine. More field-craft drifted along joining the mass of well wishers. After half an hour or so a large ornate golden carriage came floating over the horizon and moved slowly towards the island. As it approached the surface of the island, the island shield projected a firework display, splashing colour across its entire surface. From their seats inside the shield Dai and Neko watched the fireworks soar over their heads.

The golden carriage drifted slowly through the shield entrance and landed on the grass at the front of the island. Sashoo began to lift and as it did so it the petals of ten million pink roses fell from the island and floated gently down over the assembled field-craft gathered below, like pink snow on a deep blue sea.

As Sashoo rose the field-craft became colourful pinpricks. Dai could still see the vast pink carpet of petals lying on the blue water. Tthe island rose up through the atmosphere and Dai saw the entirety of Earth become a massive blue ball, flecked with white clouds, the Caribbean laid out below like a map with a new island, an island of rose petals.

Some of the bubble-craft began drifting away, taking their passengers back to their accommodation. Dai and Neko remained, watching the Earth shrink slowly behind them. Much of Sashoo's shield was darkened to protect the interior from direct sunlight, but the area facing Earth remained clear, giving the fifteen thousand humans on Sashoo their last view of home.

After several hours of Earth watching Neko was growing tired and said. "We can get a final look tomorrow before the Astrosphere departs, and we'll still be able to see Earth for several days after that. Lets go to our new home and have something to eat."

For Dai this was the experience of a lifetime and he didn't want to miss a moment of it. He could have stayed for days filling his senses with the magnificent view, the feeling of beginning a great adventure, of setting out to explore the universe, but he agreed to go back for something to eat, intending to come straight back out to watch the view again.

Their bubble-craft deposited them in the living room of the apartment. Neko traced a square on a wall with her finger and a display panel appeared in the area she'd defined. She flipped through the lists of alien words written in the galactic language which were displayed on the screen and touching a word caused the controls to be replaced by an image of Earth, as seen from Sashoo.

"You don't need to miss a moment of it dear, this is a live feed," Neko said, as she drew a second panel on the left hand wall of their room. This time, when she'd finished selecting from the options, the wall itself began to change. It shimmered and filled out into the shape of a kitchen complete with work tops and a cooking range.

Taking fruit and vegetables from a chilled cupboard in the corner she passed her hand over a section of the work top and several knives materialised. She spent a few minutes chopping and peeling, then gesturing like a magician over another section of the work top, she materialised several pans which she filled with the prepared food.

Further hand waving and the pans to heated up,

soon the smell of a delicious meal began to fill the room.

"I must learn how to do that," Dai said.

"Well you're going to need to improve your understanding of the galactic language," Neko said, passing him a glass of wine.

"Yes," Koneko said. "You can barely summon the bathroom, we don't want you peeing in the plant pots," Koneko and Neko giggled while Dai put on his best hurt look.

"It's not my fault, I didn't know how to summon the bathroom," They laughed. "At least I can now read the galactic for toilet," Dai defended himself.

Neko dismissed the cooking area and brought the food over to a table she'd summoned in the middle of the large room.

"I think a forest setting would be nice tonight," Neko said, as they sat at the table.

Sitting on her perch Koneko leant forward and summoned a panel on the table top. She began fiddling with a series of controls and functions. After a minute or so she sat back with satisfaction as the entire room shimmered. Slowly trees formed in the room, one at each corner of the table whose branches twined above the diners heads. Yet more trees materialised in the large room and on three walls they were surrounded by forest, but on the fourth wall, the image of Earth grew to fill the entire space. So they sat and ate their supper in a forest lit by Earth light, a big blue beautiful orb shinning through the trees.

"This is exquisite," Dai remarked, as candles grew from of the table. Koneko sat back with a satisfied smile on her lips. "I will sing for you both now," She declared and in a high pitched tone, like the tiniest of sopranos, her voice lifted in a soft and strangely lilting alien song.

* * *

The following evening a full moon was predicted. David and Softly sat on the roof terrace of their home built in the mountains behind Santiago in Cape Verde off the west coast of Africa. Commissioned by David and Softly, the five storey house was only accessible by air and it offered them a remote hideout from the rest of the world. Secured behind a house-shield visitors needed to be expected, if they hoped to be granted a landing.

The house keeper had just served them a light supper of cold meats and bread and they were half way through a good bottle of French Burgundy when the double moons rose. Tonight the Astrospherical moon was its usual swirling mass of glowing iridescence, as it had been for the last fifty years.

"You don't feel too sad seeing it leave?" David asked. "Don't you secretly wish you were going with it?"

"I've had enough of Sashoo." Softly said slowly. "I'm not keen on long intergalactic voyages. Life can get very tedious, it doesn't have the life and vibrancy that being here does. Everything on Sashoo is a game invented to pass the time away. That's the problem of survival without struggle, there are no risks to take, no obstacles to overcome, no real causes to fight for.

"Sure a little bit of me wishes I was going too, who wouldn't? But I'm happy here with you and a planet under my feet. There are those who must continue searching, and those like me, who have found their way home."

"My, my, we are being philosophical tonight," David said lightly.

"It's the poignancy of the moment I think," Softly said. "It makes me a little melancholy. There are friends I shan't see again and they will go places I will never see."

David picked up the bottle of wine from the marble table and topped up their glasses.

"You know I think I can see the Astrosphere beginning to move," David said.

They watched the twin moons for a while.

"I'm not sure," Softly said checking her watch. "I think its a little early still, I think another hour yet."

"We'll need another bottle of wine before then," David remarked and picking up the phone from the table he rang the housekeeper to ask for another bottle. "The Burgundy again?" Softly nodded.

"It will be strange when it's gone," Softly mused. "I'm so used to seeing those two up there, it will be quite like loosing an old friend."

"Talking of loosing friends." David said in a conspiratorial tone. "Bob wasn't too happy about it either. He seemed very angry with the Lowai Agent."

"I think you want to watch Bob," Softly advised. "He's not always up front with you, I think there's a little bit of using, going on."

"We're friends from way back," David insisted. "From before the Astrosphere came."

"I know dear, but even then..." she let the thought trail off, David was very loyal to Bob.

"You'll miss Fortune?" David said.

"I will and I wont. I saw her a few days ago you know. I went to say my goodbyes and I think the emotion of leaving or something must have affected her because she let a few things slip. When I first met Fortune she was wild and careless. I thought she was a fun person to be with and it was all so very romantic .

"It didn't click with me when we were aboard the Astrosphere, but now I think she may have been fleeing the authorities. She said something about the Lowai. They're inviting her to join their clan and she said their like gypsies, or pirates even. Apparently the ownership of the Astrosphere is under dispute and the so called owners, the Lowai, are hiding it here.

"And another thing I didn't realise was we have come through a wormhole, that star of yours, its a lot further away than it seems, it over five hundred million light years away, you're seeing it through the wormhole, your discovery was the hole opening. When we came through it to this remote extremity of the galaxy the wormhole wasn't even fully formed."

"What are you saying?" David asked in astonishment.

"OK think of the wild west frontiers of America in the eighteen thirties, the height of the cowboy era. As civilised society took hold in the East of the continent those afraid of the law spread west eventually reaching California, where they robbed the towns and villages. We're like those cowboys and Earth is like a Californian town. It's like the Astrosphereians have ridden into town and robbed the Earth of its natural resources, and now they're riding off into the sunset."

"That's why Bob's so angry with them," David

said.

Softly laughed. "I doubt it, he's helped them fill up their holds with gold, platinum, marble and diamonds and other riches. Now they're going to ride on in search of the next town to rob. I think Bob cottoned to them early on. Even before we arrived we made a total mess of our approach, sending the entire planet into panic, then when we did arrive, we arrived partying. Don't get me wrong, most of us were having a good time, we thought this was all just part of the cruise we were on. But my relationship with Fortune has led me to discover some of the darker truths behind our arrival.

"There was never any intention of making this a permanent state of affairs. They always intended moving on, and you know why?"

David was confused, Astrosphereian pirates, gold and treasure, cowboys. What was Softly saying here? Looking to the night sky he was sure the Astrosphere now seemed a sliver smaller than it had been earlier.

"The stargate is now completed. It has fully formed and that means others will be coming now. Some are very interested in meeting the occupants of the Astrosphere. The Inter-galactic Marshals are about to ride into town."

Softly paused, then raised her glass in a toast. "Here's to old friends soonest forgot," she saluted the moon and its artificial partner, and drank deeply from her glass.

Chapter 27 – New world order

The Astrosphere had been gone almost a year when Bing received a call from her old boss at the Pentagon, General Solomon. Bing had resigned her commission soon after the Astrosphere departed.

"Ms. Saunders," his familiar voice sounded a little older in her ear. "You'll appreciate I'm making this request via official channels. You're our leading expert on Alien approach behaviour and I'd consider it a personal favour if you'd proceed to Cape Canaveral to see the data we're currently receiving."

"I think I can do that. Has it been cleared through Bob's office?" she asked.

"Yes, we've his agreement, he's prepared to lend you to us for this."

Two hours later her field-craft was cleared for approach to the Cape Canaveral facility and ten minutes after that she was back in the monitoring suite which she had become so used to during the crisis fifty years earlier. The room was the same but the equipment was all new.

The display graphic showed lines of red and green, the star in blue, a new object and the position of Earth all drawn in.

"We're assuming this is something

approximating the size of the Astrosphere," A technician told her. "And we're predicting it'll take about the same amount of time to get here."

"There's not a lot we can do now except monitor the situation. I guess we can assume a six week lead."

"I guess so Ma'am," She arranged to have daily reports sent to her desk, then went to look up her old NASA contact Danny Brooks.

"Still not made Director yet?" she asked him as they shared lunch in one of Canaveral's canteens.

Danny ran a hand through his dark curly hair. "No I'm afraid not, the Director is still sitting tight and because of the longevity drug, the old bastard is going to be sitting at the top for another fifty years." They laughed at this.

"But seriously." Danny continued. "We've been doing some interesting things with force-field craft. They're not really suitable for deep space travel, we've no control over solar light penetration for instance. They do hold a constant temperature however, but without protective clothing you'd burn up in the sunlight. We've dumped all our shuttle and rocket programs of course, and concentrated on portable habitats, ones we can put inside field-craft. We're also getting pretty close to a solution. In fact, I think we may be able to begin colonising Mars within the next five years. We believe we can use existing limited area shields to create liveable habitats, the main issues are oxygen and food production." Danny explained enthusiastically.

"And the work that we've been doing on the moon has given us a great deal of information helping us plan for Mars. But you probably want to hear about our advancements in telemetry. We've been able to use field-craft to send several, large telescopes, deep into the solar system and we should have data from these which will give us a far more detailed picture of the approaching object than we had last time."

"Excellent," Bing said. "I want to know the moment you know anything Danny."

"Sure."

"Oh and Danny, good luck with the Mars project," she added.

The next stop on her schedule was a visit to Bob, currently near Minsk in Belarus, where the World Government headquarters were being established. At Canaveral she summoned a fast high altitude jet like field-craft from the strap on her wrist. Set like small round jewels on a simple black leather band, each jewel embossed with a stylised image of the craft type it offered. Once on board she gained clearance through the Cape Canaveral shield, the jet-craft shot through the air while Bing sat back and enjoyed the high speed ride.

field-craft had never been known to have an

accident. The tendril energy collecting filaments allowed the craft to detect objects around them in advance. Her jet-craft dove into the mass of traffic near Minsk carrying her onwards.

From her vantage point she could see construction of the new World Government Buildings, much of which was being done by Harding Construction. At the edge of the site nearest Minsk one building already stood tall and complete, its steel and glass façade gleaming in the weak northern sunlight. Her jet headed for the Harding Building.

Bing landed on the roof in the semi enclosed bay that proudly formed the pinnacle of the Harding Building, then she descended by lift to the sky lobby, a recent feature of high-rise buildings that had become popular, to have both a sky and ground lobby.

Unusually she was kept waiting. After twenty minutes in reception she was informed that Bob was no longer in the building but she might catch him on the construction site which spread out across the valley in front of the Harding Building. Bing took a field-craft from the roof down to the brown mud churned fields below, to a vast plate of concrete cut through with tree-lined pedestrian boulevards. On the concrete plate long thin fingers of reinforced concrete and iron rose like the branches of a tree in a cubist painting.

The site shield forced her to land at the edge of

the construction site and she entered on foot along one of the wide leafy boulevards. A security point guarded the entrance. Her Harding Industries I.D was enough to get her through the gates and where a security guard summoned an official site field-craft which whisked her across the ground towards Bob's last known location.

She set down some fifty metres from a small huddle of people standing outside a construction office which stood in what was to become the impressive World Government plaza which would be the centre piece of the entire site. On one side stood the World Parliament Building, its exterior completed, six vast pillars each ten meters in diameter rose the entire height of the eighty floor front, then reached above it by a further forty meters where the six pillars were topped off by a single long plinth. Along the plinth stood the flags of the Nations of the World, towards the middle the six continental zones were represented and in the centre the World Flag, modelled on the old League of Nations and United Nations flags, against a pale blue background over three hundred white stars each representing a country of the world, arraigned in three rings, representing the third planet from the sun, a single circle at the top of the outer ring represented earth and in the centre, a single star representing the sun. The three rings were held between two curving olive branches.

A second building intended to house the World Senate was nearing completion on the south side of the plaza, while the east and north sides were huge platforms of concrete piled with construction materials and plant machinery.

Bing walked towards the group by the site office. She could hear Bob's voice as she drew close and joined the edge of the group. Bob saw her and nodded while he continued to speak.

"I don't care how much more it's going to cost, we've five weeks to get this place looking impressive. I don't give a shit if nothing works, we've to look like we've got it together. We can get the south side building finished, and the plaza paved. I want all this construction material out of here. Just turf the east and west sides for now, and pave or turf everything else that looks a mess."

The group of construction engineers launched a barrage of questions and objections.

"Double, triple the manpower if you need to, just get the two existing buildings up and running and paper over the rest, we'll be back later in the year to finish the job properly." Bob turned and taking Bing by the elbow smartly walked her away.

"I take it you've come straight from Canaveral?" Bob asked, as he summoned a site vehicle and leapt in.

"Yes. They're saying six weeks till the new sphere arrives, they don't know yet exactly how long, or how large the sphere is yet, so those are just predictions, but they assure me we will know exactly what and when in a matter of hours," she reported.

"Yes. I have the same intel. OK I need to know the moment the details are confirmed." They landed at the shield entrance and walked through the security barricade. Bob summoned one of his favourites craft, a sleek blue flattened egg shaped one.

"You know this could work out rather well for me," Bob said as the blue egg carried them towards the Harding Building and Bob's office within. "With the presidential elections only three weeks away and being a front runner, I think I can swing a victory here."

"So you're serious about becoming the first World President?" Bing asked.

"Absolutely. I've got strong support behind me from most of the big players, the Americans, the Chinese the British of course. My people are out now, canvassing presidents. The people need a leader who can deal with what's coming. I'm the obvious choice, my companies employ a quarter of the world's work force, companies that are listed, that are owned by the shareholding peoples of the world. They may not love me, but they respect me, I make them a profit and who else is seriously in the running?"

Bing thought he was probably right. The

impending arrival of something new from deep space had again put the world on edge. This time there was none of the despair and anger, the riots and opportunism that there'd been fifty years earlier. This time there was pensive apprehension.

"Look, I'm going on to a meeting with the Heads of Nations. Why don't you tag along for a while, you can keep me updated on the 'new arrivals' situation?" Bob said. Bing agreed. Twenty minutes later they were landing at a secret location in the Black Forest, Germany.

The blue egg floated down between dark green fir trees to a turfed clearing. Set under the trees surrounding the clearing were the low wooden buildings of the meeting complex. Through the trees Bing could see the light blue uniforms of UN peace keepers who were providing security to the delegates. She and Bob entered a modest wood and glass building that served as a reception area, and this was where Bob left Bing to make arrangements for her communications requirements.

The meeting of the Heads of Nations was already well on its way by the time Bing was provided with a translation booth to use as an office. An secretary led her through the complex of glass corridors which ran across the forest floor to the main auditorium, a large dome covered amphitheatre sunk into the earth. From the booth Bing had a side on view of the main stage and a good view of the delegates. Bing fussed with the translation booth terminal and internet cables. She hooked up her laptop and connected to her private files and email.

The Continental President of Africa was addressing the delegates on matters of International Funding. The African President came to the end of his speech and gave way to the Continental President of Asia who continued on similar themes as his African counterpart. While he was speaking the electronic roster of speakers that hung at the back of the stage changed and Bob Harding's name was slotted in after the Asian President. He was the next speaker. Bing was impressed at the influence Bob wielded, with power like that no wonder he felt the presidency was in his grasp.

The Asian President finished his points and gave way on the podium. There was a moment or two of movement, polite side-stepping and paper shuffling and a few excused themselves, but most delegates stayed where they were; intent on hearing what Bob had to say.

He strode purposefully to the podium, looking every inch presidential material in a charcoal grey suit and light blue tie.

"Assembly of National Delegates, if I may first thank you all for giving me this opportunity to address you, and to thank you for the excellent work you're all doing to make this dream of ours, this dream of a united world, more than just a possibility, more than just a probability, but a reality. For this I thank you.

"I have come here today to talk to you about what lies ahead in the days to come as we face what approaches. I know many of you will be thinking, that in the past many mistakes were made which led to unnecessary loss of life and economic crisis. When we were last encountered by an space travelling species we were not ready, we were not prepared, we knew not what was to come. Not this time."

"This time we have the experience of the past, let us learn from it. We have the sound structures of the present, let's build on them. We have knowledge that allows us to see what's to come, let us use this.

"Let there be no mistake in understanding, what's coming is not a rock of ice, no rogue meteor, we have been there before. Make no mistake in knowing that this is an alien craft and we will have to deal with it. We cannot make the error of presenting anything other than a united front, a singular cohesive Governmental structure.

"The chaos of our first encounter was the result of the chaos we ourselves were in at the time, unprepared, incapable, unwilling to present an established unified protocol for negotiation with space travelling nations.

"Today we are so much closer to our goal of unity. Now we stand at the forefront of history, it is to us that future generations will look for inspiration and guidance, it is our duty to lay the best foundations we can for those who are to come.

"If we are to face this new challenge from a position of strength, one where we can get the best results for our people, where we can emerge from this knowing that everything that had to be done, was done, then we're going to need strength within and we are going to need strong leadership.

"I believe I'm the man for the job, and my time is now. I know many of you are already behind me in this and I want to assure you I will secure for us just such a position of strength in the negotiations to come. This time we will do it properly. And to those of you who have yet to decide, I ask you to give me a fair chance.

"But I can not do this alone. I need you to continue in your efforts to bring the nations of the world together, to unite us in a brotherhood of man, never before have the words 'together we stand, divided we fall', had more relevance, more meaning than they do today. We must make this parliament a living reality and we must do it now."

As Bob continued his rallying speech an email appeared in Bing's inbox. After reading it she contacted the communications centre and gained the permission she needed to send a message to the teleprompter in front of Bob on the podium console.

"If you would excuse me just one moment," Bob said, to the gathered delegates as he read Bing's message. "I've some important information coming in on the nature of the approaching craft." He paused, staring intently at the teleprompter while the entire auditorium waited.

"I've just received details confirming the approach of aliens," Bob said. "We can expect an alien flotilla to arrive here on Earth in one thousand two hundred and four hours time. In Just over seven weeks."

The room exploded with excited voices as delegates began shouting questions and talking amongst themselves. Bob signalled for calm and waited while they composed themselves again. When the room had quietened enough he said. "I'm sure that, like me, you have plenty of questions, and I'm sure that soon they will be answered. We have seven weeks to prepare ourselves, seven weeks to organise ourselves so we can speak with a single voice, to act with unity. We can not afford to fail. I will not fail you."

He turned and thanked the officials near the podium and left the stage as the delegates broke out into excited talk.

"Tough audience?" Bing asked, as she caught up with him in the reception area.

"Did you think so? I thought I had them eating out of my hand. Thanks for that last touch by the way, I think it might well be the deal maker. They're not going anywhere without me, it's me or chaos. What's your choice Bing?" Bob smiled at her.

"Perhaps if I don't answer that right now?" she smiled back.

"That's typically you, won't back the horse till after it's won."

"Being right guaranteed every time." Bing responded.

"But too late to lay a bet."

"OK, sure, Bob, if I was able to vote on this, which I'm not, you'd get my vote OK?" Bing offered.

"That's my girl," Bob grinned back. "Look, do you want to get something to eat, I know this fabulous little restaurant in Hong Kong where I can get us a table and we're guaranteed privacy."

Bing hesitated. "It might be the last chance you get, once I'm World President you'll have to wade through security just to smile at me."

"I can see you'd benefit from a meal with me, it might at least stop your head from swelling any further," Bing joked.

"Great, you agree," Bob summoned the blue egg

and offered his hand to help her in.

It was a swift forty five minute ride over Southern Asia to the restaurant in Hong Kong.

"You know what I think Bob?" Bing asked, as they sat opposite each other in the sleek snug cabin, relaxing on the plush dark, leather looking, seats which seemed to mould to the body. The polished wood, dark leather and soft carpet like interior of the blue egg had a relaxing executive atmosphere to it, one that smelt of expensive perfume and large glasses of whisky.

"What do you think?" Bob asked.

"I think you know more than your telling," Bing replied.

"What gives you that idea?" He responded.

"When you read my message, you didn't look at all surprised," Bing pointed out.

"I just hid it well."

"I don't think you were surprised at all. There are some things you're not telling us; like you knew there was an alien flotilla on it's way."

Bob laughed. "I was never able to get anything passed you was I Bing? I had my suspicions about the flotilla, and I have my suspicions about a few other things as well, but first, the Presidency."

The blue egg began to pass over the snow covered tops of the Himalayan mountains through large white clouds and on towards the south china seas.

Chapter 28 – New arrivals

Entering the vast reception room David saw a group of twenty or so people standing around chatting quietly. He began the long walk from the door he'd come in by, across the vast sea of light blue carpet, and round the fifty metre relief of the world that marked the centre of the room. The globe stood on the floor below the reception room with the top part, the North Pole and Greenland poking through, and the giant model of the Earth turned as the Earth itself, turned.

The enormous inhuman proportions of the reception room of the World Government Building made David feel small, childlike even as he walked across the sea of carpet. After what seemed an age he finally made it to an island of fellow dignitaries, all of whom he knew by reputation, most of whom he'd met briefly at some time, and non of whom he really knew at all.

He smiled at the group in general finding himself next to a large fat woman whom he thought might be the World Treasury Minister. Though she looked like an opera singer in a long dark blue dress with a strange feathery collar. On one breast she wore an enormous medallion of jewels set in silver and on the right breast she wore a row of medals. Despite appearing to be an opera singer, David knew, the World Treasury Minister possessed a formidably sharp mind and an equally dull line in conversation which David found reassuring. You want someone competent and dull when it comes to the important things in life like health and money. With money in particular, you don't want it in the hands of those with too much imagination and in this respect, she seemed highly qualified.

David also noticed several more World Ministers in the group, and as a token presence of other professions, a leading sports figure, an artist, a writer and a couple of business people. Four members of the group were Langonai and there was one solitary Cherubim amongst them.

Several technicians in black jumpsuits came into the room and went to the back where they began setting up equipment. Suddenly a large section of the back wall lit up as a huge display was turned on. All heads turned to look as flickering images magnetically drew their eye. A momentary glimpse of a news channel, a day time chat show flicked by, then the image they'd all become familiar with over the last few days.

The news feed came from a stationary telescope fifty thousand miles above the Earth's surface. Dark space formed the background with its black cloak of glittering stars. In the centre of the image, side lit by a sun that couldn't be seen, were three large objects. The nearest object was a shiny black sphere with red lightening streaming across it's surface. Behind the black sphere and to it's left, came a long silver lozenge and to its right, a round edged cuboid with colours that swirled and danced across it's shiny surface.

The P.A. system crackled into life and a serious young male voice said. "Alien convoy has respected authorised zone parameters and entered orbit at three hundred and fifty thousand miles. Planetary representatives are proceeding." Even as the voice spoke three tiny craft could be seen leaving the planet sized ships. As they watched the tiny dots grow, David recalled the measures Bob had insisted on so we Earthians, for we are no longer only humans, would arrive at just this situation.

Fourteen days earlier Bob Harding had been inaugurated as World President, along with the new World Senators and the Representatives of Nations. It had become a week-long celebration. World peace and unity achieved at last, in name, if not in fact. There were still plenty of loose ends, rogue states, states still petitioning for recognition as nations and the usual handful of bush-fire disputes, which in modern times were primarily contained behind limited area shields.

One of the first things the new President had done was to authorise a single broadcast to the approaching vessels.

"Incoming craft you have entered territory belonging to the Solar System of Earth, please identify yourselves. You are not permitted to land on any planet within our jurisdiction, please approach to a distance of three hundred thousand miles, a beacon marker has been provided." First in English, then repeated in Galactic.

The message had been broadcast directly at the leading ship and this ploy seemed to have worked. The flotilla, which had seemed to be perusing some kind of survey of planets, had changed course as it reached Jupiter, and headed straight across the solar system towards Earth.

"Ten minutes to arrival." The serious voice on the tannoy announced. There was a flurry of preening, tie straightening, make-up checking and hair tidying from the assembled dignitaries. David considered his dark blue suit, he wasn't sure it did him justice, he preferred something lighter, but Softly had persuaded him he'd look dignified in dark blue so he'd worn it to please her.

On the display the incoming craft loomed large as they passed in front of the satellite telescope. The broadcast was picked up next by a telescope closer to Earth. As the craft came even closer the point of view changed to a shot taken from the roof of the World Parliament. Clear pale blue sky and a scattering of soft sunlit clouds filled the screen. It took a further minute or so before the craft became distinct.

In colours corresponding to their mother-ships the three ornate alien vessels descended from the sky. The black and red craft shaped like a great sea going vessel without mast or sail. It presented a high bow with a dragon-like beast figurehead, it's wings furled back to form the tip of the bow. The silver vessel, like its mother-ship, was a flat silver lozenge shape, embossed with an angular pattern covering its entire surface. The third craft, a simple sphere, had a ring around its middle which gave it a saturnine appearance. The three vessels, each one easily the size of an ocean liner, began decelerating as they made their final approach and landed in the marked zones on the World Parliament building roof.

The familiar ramps formed at the front of the vessels and alien figures began descending to the roof top. At the same time the World President and his cortège came out to meet them, forming a loose line. The Alien representatives did likewise and began moving down the line towards the roof entrance. In the room below the Earth dignitaries began to line up in anticipation. David found himself near the far end.

Tall double doors at the end of the room burst open and the world's newest friends entered. David immediately recognised the Langonai and Cherubim aliens, but there was also a third kind he'd never seen before. Large quadrupeds, bigger than a horse, but smaller than an elephant with short brown coats of hair. They walked as if on their knuckles using their front limbs like a gorilla and their rear limbs like a horse. Their horse like heads rose from broad shoulders on surprisingly slender necks. Though similar to a horse's head there were several notable differences, the nose was sharper and the eyes more forward and predatory than a horse's, with an elliptic iris like a cat or goats eye. The ears at the sides of the head were barely visible, just two small whirls of pink flesh with small holes at the centre.

These aliens wore jackets that were tied kimono-style round their girths, while long flared sleeves hung to the floor, revealing only the knuckle-like front foot. Their rear ends were clothed in a kind of skirt that trailed along the floor as they walked. David wasn't sure but he thought the skirts might also hide a short tail.

One of the aliens approached David, and as it lumbered up to him it raised one if its front limbs, uncurled the fist it walked on and offered David a massive hand to shake. He was a bit concerned that this beast would crush his fingers but he offered his hand anyway in the spirit of inter-speceial friendship.

The hand while covered in short close hair down the outer wrist and back of the hand, had hard scaly black skin on the backs of the fingers, so when they were curled up in a fist they provided a hoof like sole to the hand. In stark contrast the skin on the palm was pinky grey and felt as soft as his own.

Soon the preliminary 'meet and greet' had been performed like a mad wedding breakfast at which all the guests were more than a little odd, and the two main groups, the Earthians and the Aliens were standing roughly opposite each other, the apex of the world sculpture turning sedately between them.

The Alien group was further divided into three. On either end the groups had little to distinguish each other, who was in which group and how they knew was a mystery. But the centre group stood out by virtue of their black and red uniforms. David also noticed the horse like Aliens were only represented in the right hand group.

Bob Harding approached the podium which stood to the south of the world sculpture. The massive display screen changed, the images of the human and alien dignitaries were replaced with a close up of the World President.

"Representatives of the Governments of the Galaxy we welcome you to Earth in peace and with the open hand of friendship," he said. There was a smattering of applause from both sides of the room.

"This is an historic moment for our peoples" he continued. "Today we have entered into a new era. Today our world has expanded from being this solar system, to the entire galaxy. We are no longer alone out here in space.

"But we are as infants, coming from darkness into the bright light. As infants we are dependant on the wise advice and guidance that you, representatives of the galaxy, have to offer us.

"Like infants we need tendering and nurturing if we are to successfully join the galactic brotherhood.

"This is also a time in which we must make our most important decision yet. For with these Representatives comes the responsibility of choice. Therefore we will not rush into the bright light of day but take our first feeble steps with caution. We look for guidance but we will keep our own counsel.

"You present us with an opportunity to join you, one of you. The Assembly Of Planets, The Imperium of Carknage and the Inter-planarity Trade Congress. We will listen to your advice and wisdom over the coming days and months and from this we will come to know which of the paths you offer is the way for the Federated Solar System of Earth.

"Please freely enjoy the hospitality we extend you, as we do our hand of friendship moving into this glorious new era." Heartfelt applause rose from around the room. When this quietened Bob continued.

"I now invite the Assembly of Planets' Ambassador to Earth, the Honourable Minister Dewtak Sharlin, to address the people of Earth." Bob welcomed a tall humanoid in a flowing green robe to the podium.

The Ambassador spoke in a sweet lilting tone. "People of Earth the Assembly of Planets welcomes you and invites your leaders to consider allowing the Assembly to represent Earth in the Federal Galactic Parliament. Which ever route you should ultimately choose we would hope always to be able to extend the hand of friendship and trade." Polite applause followed this and Bob introduced the next representative.

"The Imperial Oligarch, His Royal Highness Kazara Jahad, Attendant to the Supreme Imperial Being, Third Class." Bob introduced a short, immensly fat humanoid dressed in the Imperial uniform of black jacket and trousers with red piping. He wore a tall silver helmet with red and black plumes on it and carried a ceremonial sword on a large gold sash. The right jacket breast was covered in military decorations. He strode purposefully towards the podium his long whiskers twitching beneath deep green cats eyes while the long ginger tail that protruded from the seat of his pants swung gracefully behind him.

"I am authorised by the Imperium to invite Earth to join the Glorious Imperium of Carknage as a class nine planet, so designating you with a permit to travel space and allowing trade within the Imperium. You will have access to level four technology and will provide military support to the Imperium concomitant with your population level. Level four will give you access to planetary field generators and field tools as well as standard Galactic medicines. Consider us carefully, the Imperium does not make such offers lightly, usually the route to membership is through conquest." His Royal Highness Kazara Jahad, third class saluted the audience and marched off.

"Director Phplepophopolosi of the Inter-planetary Trade Congress," Bob introduced the third representative.

One of the large gorilla horse-like aliens walked carefully over to the podium. When it spoke it's voice was a deep rumble as if coming from the throat of a lion sat by a thundering waterfall.

"We too welcome Earth and would hope our offer of representation at the Federal Galactic Parliament would provide you with an equal and fair voice in the Parliament. The freedom to trade with any planet that Parliament or the Inter-planetary Congress does not hold sanctions against. Ours is a Federation of free trade in goods and knowledge, planetary independence and low Federal taxation."

Bob turned to the microphone and thanked the representatives then announced that press interviews would be taking place throughout the rest of the day. The giant display screen went blank for a moment before showing the New World Government logo.

The delegates began to mix with each other. Those with related interests and briefs began to match up to discuss science, economy and politics.

David milled about watching delegates earnestly discuss important topics, while not finding anyone to join himself. He was thinking about slipping quietly away when Bob caught him by the elbow and led him to a discrete door set in the wall on one side of the screen. The door led into wide white a service corridor behind the reception room.

"Come and have a cup of tea with me, I need a bit of sanity after that," Bob said. "It's a brave new world we're facing now, lot of challenges, we need to get the best deal for Earth." He directed David into an expensively appointed meeting room.

"You seem to have them where you want them at the moment," David remarked.

"It's all very friendly at the moment. I don't think the Imperium are going to be too pleased when we turn down their offer."

"Will we?" David asked.

"I doubt we'll be joining the Imperium, no its a three horse race, the Assembly, the Congress or we go it alone in the big bad galaxy, but I doubt we'll be doing that, it would leave us in competition or at war with powerful well established factions. The Lowai haven't left us in a very good shape, shit we don't even have a ship capable of reaching the wormhole yet, the field-craft we have are barely good enough to get us to

Mars, and we've no chance of mining the moons of Jupiter's without better equipment."

"So what's happened to the Lowai?" David asked, as Bob poured them tea.

"Well it's difficult to say. These guys raced over here the moment the wormhole was fully formed, and I understand they've sent exploratory forces in other directions, their main aim to try and lay claim to any useful planets. In a funny way the Lowai have given us a helping hand, first our new neighbours didn't know about the Lowai being here, so we were prepared for their arrival, they didn't expect that, secondly, it was the Astrospere's appearance that led us to become united ready for this moment, without unity and without shield technology, partial though it is, we might well be facing a fractured Earth, threatened with invasion and unable to agree amongst ourselves.

The Lowai appear to have upset the Imperium and are on their wanted list for trade infractions, the Assembly has an issue of contract of ownership with the Lowai, a dispute over ownership of the Astrosphere, so they're keen to drag someone into court to clear that up, nevertheless, the last we saw of the Astrosphere was it heading off out the other side of the solar system," Bob relaxed a moment and sipped thoughtfully at his tea.

"Well lots to do, I've got a world to run," Bob joked, draining his cup. "Wish me luck, oh and see you at the Grand Banquet tonight." With that, the President of the World swept out of the meeting room and disappeared up the corridor.

David thought a moment about returning to the delegation but decided he'd far rather get home and see Softly. He hoped she'd finally settled on an outfit for the evening. Then tomorrow they'd have a quiet night at home and maybe he'd get out his old Harding T-45 and take a good long look at the stars.